Also by David Stuart Davies

Forests of the Night

Without Conscience

A JOHNNY HAWKE NOVEL

David Stuart Davies

THOMAS DUNNE BOOKS
ST. MARTIN'S MINOTAUR
NEW YORK

THOMAS DUNNE BOOKS.
An imprint of St. Martin's Press.

WITHOUT CONSCIENCE. Copyright © 2008 by David Stuart Davies. All rights reserved. Printed in the United States of America. For information, address St. Martin's Press, 175 Fifth Avenue, New York, N.Y. 10010.

www.thomasdunnebooks.com
www.minotaurbooks.com

Library of Congress Cataloging-in-Publication Data

Davies, David Stuart, 1946–
   Without conscience : a Johnny Hawke novel / David Stuart Davies.
— 1st U.S. ed.
      p. cm.
   "First published in Great Britain as: Without conscience: A Johnny One Eye novel by Robert Hale Limited, 2008"—T.p. verso.
   ISBN-13: 978-0-312-38210-0
   ISBN-10: 0-312-38210-3
   1. Hawke, Johnny (Fictitious character)—Fiction. 2. Private investigators—England—London—Fiction. 3. London (England)—History—Bombardment, 1940–1945—Fiction. 4. World War, 1939–1945—England—London—Fiction. I. Title.
   PR6104.A857W58 2008
   823'.92—dc22

                                                              2008029372

First published in Great Britain as
Without Conscience: A Johnny One Eye Novel
by Robert Hale Limited

First U.S. Edition: December 2008

10 9 8 7 6 5 4 3 2 1

To old chums Howard Higton &
Matthew Booth & Laurie Stead
Thank you for the years of friendship

PROLOGUE

Dusk was falling as Harryboy Jenkins swaggered towards the barrack gates, clutching a brown paper parcel to his chest. His eyes shone brightly and a cocky smile played about his thick lips. With an assertive toss of the head, he presented his evening pass to the sergeant on duty.

'Off into the village, are you, Jenkins?' the sergeant remarked with ill-concealed contempt, returning the pass. He disliked Jenkins intensely. He was a born troublemaker who lacked both the self-discipline and application to make a good soldier. No amount of training and square bashing would turn this creep into one of the team. There was something about Jenkins' smarmy, pugnacious mug that made the sergeant want to punch it and punch it hard. The lad exuded a kind of mad, bomb-proof insolence as though he was challenging the world to wipe the grin off his face. One day, the sergeant thought, someone would and he hoped that he'd be there to witness the event. He would delight in seeing the shock and incredulity in those arrogant blue eyes as some clever bastard yanked the rug from under Harryboy Jenkins' feet.

'That's my business, ain't it, Sergeant?' Jenkins touched his snub nose with his forefinger and smirked defiantly.

'Maybe, but it'll be my business if you're not back here by eleven, or that we hear you've been causing trouble again.'

'Can I go now … Sergeant?' he asked with a thinly disguised sneer.

The sergeant did not rise to the bait. He could wait. He'd get his revenge sooner or later. With a dismissive nod of the head, he let Harryboy through the barrier.

'Cockney scum,' the sergeant muttered to himself, as he watched the soldier disappear into the growing October gloom.

*

The village of Smarden was nearly two miles from the barracks and the only way for a soldier to get there was to walk or, if he was lucky, hitch a lift. Jenkins was determined to get lucky. It was a cold night and already the moisture on the foliage was beginning to stiffen and whiten with the first signs of October frost. Jenkins pulled his army greatcoat tighter around him as he approached the crossroads. Here was his best place for thumbing a lift. Who would refuse a soldier on such a night as this, eh? He grinned to himself.

By the time he had made his way down to the road leading to Smarden, it was dark and a cunning moon drifted behind the clouds allowing only scant illumination. While Harryboy waited in anticipation of a passing motor car, he lit a cigarette and contemplated his future. His grin broadened. Life was about to get so much better.

He didn't have to wait long for a potential lift. He had just skittered the stub of the cigarette into the bushes when he heard the sound of a car engine in the distance. Stepping smartly into the road, he awaited its arrival. Around the far bend appeared a black Wolseley, its faint dipped headlights like two ghostly eyes penetrating the darkness.

Jenkins shone a pocket torch on to his face with one hand while he waved the vehicle down with the other.

The car glided to a halt some six feet from him. The driver, a grey-haired middle-aged man, wound the window down and stuck his head out.

'What's the trouble, soldier?'

'I just need a lift into the village, sir,' said Jenkins, in his most oleaginous fashion.

'Into Smarden? Is that all? Of course, hop in.'

'That's very kind of you, sir,' said Jenkins, his eyes twinkling as he pulled open the passenger door.

'You stationed at the barracks, young fellow?' the man said as he set the car in motion once more.

'That's right, sir,' replied Jenkins, glancing over at the driver, whose face was dimly illuminated by the lights on the dashboard. He saw that he was wearing a dog collar.

'You a vicar?' Jenkins asked automatically.

The man nodded and smiled. 'Yes, yes I am. The Reverend Simon Mellor. I've just been to a conference of local clergy in Canterbury.

We've been trying to work out more practical ways of how we can help the war effort. We want to feel we're doing our bit as well as you lads in uniform. I'm the vicar in Tenterden, that's about five miles beyond Smarden.'

'Yeah, I know it.'

The vicar smiled indulgently. 'I can tell from your accent that this isn't your neck of the woods. A London lad I should guess.'

'That's right, sir. I was born and bred in Pimlico.'

The vicar smiled to himself. 'I thought so.'

Harryboy Jenkins also smiled. But for a different reason. The poor sod of a vicar had no idea what he had let himself in for giving this particular soldier a lift. Harryboy snuggled back in the leather seat, enjoying the comfort and warmth of the car. He was going to be the master of ceremonies in this show and it was almost time for him to take control. It would only take the car a few more minutes to reach the village and things needed to be sorted out before then. Surreptitiously, he slipped his hand into the inside pocket of his great-coat and retrieved the revolver. It felt good to hold the gun in his hand once more. It gave him a sense of power and he liked that. Turning in his seat, he pressed the barrel into the neck of his companion.

'What the ...!' exclaimed the vicar with shock, the car suddenly veering wildly across the road.

'Keep steady, Vic. There's no need to get alarmed ... yet.'

While his heart pounded violently within his chest, The Reverend Simon Mellor quickly brought the car under control and then tried desperately to do the same with his own shaken emotions.

Jenkins leaned in closer to him, so close that the clergyman Mellor could smell the cheap cologne he was wearing. 'Now, this is a gun that's sticking in your neck, Vic, and it's loaded, so I suggest you do everythin' I say. OK?'

'What on earth do you want? I have no money.'

'I'm not in the mood for answering questions, so shut your trap and be a good little reverend and just obey orders. OK?'

The vicar turned briefly to look at the face of his passenger for the first time. The expression of contempt he saw there made him shudder. There was something manic in the eyes, and the tight, arrogant smirk suggested that the man felt no fear and was devoid of a conscience.

'Now then, Rev, I want you to pull over by this bank of trees just ahead.'

'What are you going to do?'

Jenkins prodded the gun harder against his neck. 'Questions, Rev. What did I tell you about questions? Just do as you're told and fucking shut up.'

Simon Mellor did as he was told. The car shuddered to a halt.

'There's a good boy. Now get out.'

For a moment the vicar hesitated, but on seeing the fierce cold hatred in the soldier's face he knew that it was futile to resist or ask why.

'Step over by the trees, Rev, old chap. That's the way. Don't look so worried. A good boy like you with lots of praying behind yer has nothing to worry about.'

The vicar had moved across the damp, overgrown verge and was now standing in the shelter of two large oak trees, their branches still laden with autumn leaves.

What now? he wondered.

The answer came swiftly.

Still grinning, Harryboy Jenkins stretched out his arm and fired two shots into the chest of the Reverend Simon Mellor.

The vicar opened his mouth in shock but made no sound as he fell like a stringless marionette to the ground.

Jenkins gave a whoop of joy. That had been good.

Really good.

After checking that his victim was indeed dead, he rifled his pockets for cash – not much of it – a ration book and some petrol coupons. He also stripped him of his blue overcoat. There was a little blood on the collar but that would come off with some water. Then he covered the body with dead leaves.

'Rest in peace, Rev, old chap,' he cried with a chuckle, as he scattered a last handful of leaves over the white vacant face.

Five minutes later Harryboy Jenkins was driving the car into the village of Smarden. He had dispensed with his army uniform and changed into his nice two piece, double breasted pin-striped number which he had brought with him in the brown paper parcel. He didn't stop in Smarden but took the London road out of the village. That's where he was headed: the city. Now that he had severed his army shackles, he intended to enjoy the war in London and no one was going to stop him.

ONE

She didn't even knock. She just strolled into my office as though it were her own living-room. Mrs Sandra Riley. Her features were bleached white with powder and a fierce red gash of lipstick gave the impression that someone had cut her face open. Along with her intimidating manner, she was in possession of a glance like an acetylene lamp. The fur of some dead creature loitered around her shoulders. She fancied herself did Mrs Sandra Riley all right. Her whole demeanour announced to the world that she believed that she was irresistible. She was mistaken. I could resist her. Women like that terrify me. But that's my problem. Her problem was of a different kind.

'I believe my husband is being unfaithful to me.'

He wouldn't dare.

Over several cigarettes she told me her sad story. It was delivered in a dramatic Joan Crawford fashion, peppered with sighs and emotional pauses but the eyes remained dry and the make-up firmly in place. It was quite a performance. Apparently hubby Walter was playing away from home with some trashy *femme fatale* in the city. Or that's what Mrs Riley suspected. She wanted me to obtain proof of Walter's lapse so that she could instigate divorce proceedings. During her recital she demonstrated no real feelings of being hurt or distressed at the thought of her husband's infidelity; she just wanted 'to nail the bastard'. I got the impression that she saw a rosy future for herself as an attractive divorcee, wrapped in furs and dripping in diamonds, enjoying a very pleasant lifestyle financed by most of Walter's money.

Being a private detective in London during the war is like riding a dysfunctional big dipper with more lows than highs. Sometimes I do have challenging and financially rewarding cases which take me up to the heights, but more often than not I am zooming downwards to the deepest depths where the mundane and generally grubby investigations just about keep me above the breadline. This was going to be one of those cases.

The war seemed to have relaxed and loosened many people's morals. It was a case of snatch some happiness, warmth, love, today, however illicit, for God knows if there'll be a tomorrow. As a result, I spend a fair bit of my time checking up on errant husbands or wives, exposing their desperate attempts to bring a little love and joy into their insecure lives. It certainly wasn't what I expected or desired when I set up Hawke Investigations at the end of 1939. I had been invalided out of the army because a rifle exploded in my face during army training, causing me to lose an eye. As a young but fragile Cyclops I was offered only a safe desk job by my old employers, the police, so I decided to set up as a private detective and enjoy the adventure and high drama of the profession as portrayed in the thousand films featuring the breed that I'd been watching since I was in short trousers.

If I couldn't fight the Hun in some foreign field, I could at least make some meaningful contribution on the home front. Well, that had been the plan.

And so here I was about to peek through another bedroom keyhole.

Sure enough, some days later after my encounter with Sandra Riley I found myself sitting in the foyer of a cheap hotel off the Strand waiting for the arrival of her husband Walter's illicit lady friend.

According to his wife, Walter was employed at the War Office. He regularly worked late on Tuesdays and Thursdays, not getting home until past midnight. It was on these evenings that Mrs R thought that he was seeing his new paramour. He came home 'smelling of alcohol and perfume' and on one occasion she had found an ear-ring in his jacket pocket.

The following Thursday I tailed Walter. Contrary to his story, he left the office building early, just after four, carrying with him a suitcase and a rather guilty look. It seemed as though my lady client's suspicions were correct. He ate a meal in a small café in Piccadilly on his own and then repaired to the aforementioned seedy hotel.

Apparently he had already had a room booked there in the name of W. Riley.

With the aid of a shilling, I obtained the room number from the desk clerk, an ancient fellow whom I guessed from his weary expression and mechanical manner was used to such enquiries. It was that kind of hotel: it smelt of damp and casual sin. The guests drifted surreptitiously through the foyer like guilty shadows.

After a decent interval – the only thing decent in the whole establishment – I made my way up the narrow ill-lit staircase to the room and listened at the door. It was most probable that the girl had already been waiting for Walter. However, there was no sound at all from within. Crouching down, I applied my ear to the keyhole. Still nothing. Not a squeak of a bed spring, not a rattle of a bed head, not a suppressed moan – nothing. Don't tell me that I'd missed all the action and they'd fallen asleep.

I waited a while longer but I still heard nothing through the door. There was only one course of action to me. I sighed and knocked discreetly. There was no response. I was beginning to think I had the wrong room. I knocked again, much less discreetly this time. More like a hammer blow. Loud enough at least to prompt a head to poke out into the corridor two doors down. It flashed me a guilty look and then vanished as quickly as it had appeared.

At last I got a response from Walter's room. I heard a muffled female voice say, 'Just a minute.'

Eventually the door opened, and, boy, was I in for a surprise.

Standing before me was a heavily made up blonde, rather plump in proportion, ineffectually squeezed into a black evening gown. She fluttered her sooty eyelashes inexpertly at me.

'Yes, what is it?' she said, in a rather throaty manner, not quite achieving the more desirable higher register.

For a moment I was lost for words and then I couldn't help it: I had to smile. 'Oh, Walter,' I said, 'what have you been up to?'

Half an hour later I was sitting opposite Wilma Riley – as Walter preferred to be called when wearing his feminine attire – in a drinks club known as The Loophole. The place was full of gentlemen of a similar persuasion to Walter/Wilma, some decidedly and convincingly glamorous, some comically less so. Somehow stubble and face powder don't mix. And there is a way of crossing your legs that ladies have that doesn't involve creating a draught. As one of the few men wearing trousers in the place, I felt strangely uncomfortable.

'I've always had a liking for women's clothes,' Wilma was saying, fingering her glass of gin and tonic nervously. 'When I was a kid, I'd go upstairs when my mother was out and try on her things. At first it was just for the novelty … and then it became a sort of compulsion. I can't really explain it: it just makes me feel … good, makes me feel safe. And when my marriage to Sandra started to hit the rocks, I sought solace in dressing up properly. Make-up, high-heeled shoes – the lot. And so Wilma was born. I actually went out and bought clothes for her. It was the best fun I'd had in years.' He gave me a wan smile. 'Then I found out about this place and realized that I wasn't alone. There were others like me. Others who get a thrill out of slipping on a pair of silk stockings and a brassiere.'

I held up my hand. 'Whoa. More information than I need,' I said, as gently as I could, pushing the unbidden image of paunchy Walter in his female undies from my mind. I didn't pretend to understand this strange obsession, but I certainly didn't want to be presented with graphic details to further my education. I'm a little queasy that way. However, I did sympathize with Riley's plight. We all have innate drives which we are helpless to subdue.

'I'm not a homosexual, you know,' my companion announced suddenly. 'I still feel normal passions towards women. This' – he indicated his wig and evening dress – 'is simply a kind of escape – a screen for me to hide behind. I'm in a rotten marriage with a bully for a wife and so twice a week I come here and mingle with my own kind for a few hours. Is that wrong?'

'Well, I suppose there are far worse things you could be doing. It's not for me to pass moral judgement.'

'But you don't approve.'

I shrugged. 'It's not that. I just have a little trouble comprehending. I suppose we all have our own individual forms of escape. With me it's jazz, booze and fags.'

'Are you going to tell Sandra?'

'She is my client …'

'And my behaviour would certainly give her grounds for divorce. She'd have great fun taking me to the cleaners, emptying my bank account … not to mention the scandal. It … it would ruin me.'

An image of the hard-faced Sandra Riley, with those vicious lips and gorgon eyes flashed before me. I could easily picture her playing the distraught wife in the witness box, dabbing the imaginary tears away with a lace handkerchief: a cunning performance full of gestures and sobs. A starring role, in fact.

'Well,' I said reflectively, 'she did ask me to find out if you were seeing another woman, not if you were changing into one. I suppose I wouldn't be lying if I told her that adultery has never been committed nor even contemplated.'

Riley smiled for the first time since I'd met him. He looked rather odd and somewhat pathetic in that obvious blonde wig and heavy make-up, clownish rather than alluring. He didn't make a convincing woman.

'As long as you don't tell her that the other woman in my life … is me.' Now he chuckled. It was a robust manly chuckle. His false chest rose and fell in a disconcerting fashion.

I smiled back indulgently. Walter/Wilma might have escaped the plotting of Sandra this time, but my instinct told me that she was not a lady to give up easily. 'I reckon you've got to stop this routine or find a way to divorce Sandra on your own terms. If you don't, she'll nail you in time. Another investigator may not be quite as sympathetic as me.'

'I expect you are right. People like me are easy prey to blackmail, I know.' The smile faded and the face sagged. 'I really have to get my house in order. I'm glad I met you. You've made me realize that I cannot go on living this lie. Whatever the consequences, I have to start being me.'

I nodded. 'I reckon you'll be happier in the end.' I wondered why I didn't fully believe him. Walter came over as rather a sad character, but somehow I felt I wasn't seeing the full picture. I was sure there was an element of steel in his nature that he was doing his best to disguise.

My companion gave a wry grin. 'You have been very kind. I must pay you for your trouble.'

I shook my head. 'No need. Sandra has paid my expenses. She hired me. I have come up with the answers to her enquiry; they may not be the ones she wants to hear but I still get paid.'

'OK. I suppose it still comes out of my wallet anyway.'

We both laughed.

'Let me get you another drink at least. Indulge yourself in one of your escapes, eh?' said Wilma as she rose unsteadily to her feet and then tottered in her high heels to the bar.

I stayed another half an hour in the club chatting amiably to my new, strange girlfriend and then suddenly I felt the need for some fresh air and the sad, stale taint of normality. As I rose to leave, so did Wilma. 'I'm not in the mood for socializing tonight,' she said, brushing back her blonde curls and looking nervously over her shoulder as though she expected someone to be standing there. 'After what's happened, I think I'd better get home. I've a lot of sorting out to do.'

Just as we were leaving, a figure emerged from the smoky gloom and led Wilma aside. It was a tall elegant creature in a long evening gown. I presumed it was a man, but he made a very convincing woman. The face was expertly made-up to emphasize the narrow features, high cheekbones and a pair of lustrous eyes. Had I not been in this particular establishment, I would have been taken in completely. Even with this knowledge, as I stared at her, I felt my libido stirring. Steady, Johnny, I told myself. This place is messing with your brain.

The two of them slipped immediately into a heated discussion. They were too far away for me to hear what they were talking about, but the expression on the beautiful stranger's face told me that she was incandescent with rage. At one point she grabbed hold of Wilma's shoulders and shook her. Wilma pulled away, issued some kind of warning with a wagging finger and then joined me on the stairs.

I raised my eyebrows in silent query.

'Just another jealous bitch,' was all Wilma said.

As we emerged on to the pavement together, the October breeze had stiffened. I buttoned my raincoat but to little avail as the creeping cold still penetrated the thin material, chilling me to the marrow.

Wilma held out her hand. 'I can't thank you enough.'

'The best of luck,' I said sincerely, thinking that he certainly would need it with Sandra. I watched him walk back in the direction of the hotel, looking as though he was stepping on hot coals. Size ten male feet are really not suitable for high heels. They must have been killing him, I thought, as I lit up a cigarette. I was just about to head homewards when I saw a black Wolseley screech to a halt by the kerb just in front of Riley. The side street was quiet with no other pedestrians about. The driver jumped out of the car and ran towards Riley who had stopped in his tracks, frozen with surprise.

I felt the hairs on the back of my head begin to prickle. Something was not right here. The driver was not asking for directions, or a light, or the time of day. His demeanour was threatening. Sensing danger, I started to walk briskly towards the two characters. I saw the man tug at Riley's handbag, trying to snatch it from him. Voices were raised, but Riley clung on to the bag. Then his assailant pulled back and drew a gun from his overcoat pocket. There was a sharp crack and Riley staggered backwards, uttering a strangled, guttural croak, before crashing down onto the pavement. The gunman scooped up the bag and within seconds was back in the car and speeding away down the street. By the time I got there, the Wolseley was already disappearing into the darkness of the night.

I knelt down by Riley. He had been shot in the chest and blood was seeping through the thin material of his dress.

'Walter, it's me Johnny Hawke,' I said cradling his head.

He turned his face in my direction, his eyes already misting over with the opaque veil of death.

'That was no way to treat a lady,' he said softly, and then his head fell to one side, his eyes remaining open in a glassy stare. All Walter and Wilma's troubles were now over.

TWO

'He's coming now!'

Tom Bates's unpleasant chubby features creased into a vicious grin and his eyes bulged with dark pleasure. His companion, Brian Harker, a thin weedy boy with an unusually large Adam's apple, emitted a nervous giggle at the news. They had been waiting in the bushes at the back of the school for almost fifteen minutes for their victim and had almost given up hope. 'He must have gone home another way,' Brian had suggested only a minute earlier. Tom Bates did not want to admit that Brian was right – after all he was boss and had planned the ambush – but he had begun to share the same doubts as his confederate until the door had opened and a narrow rectangle of light had revealed Peter Blake as he emerged from the school building into the gloom.

He had been kept behind to do 500 lines by Miss Forbush for not paying attention in class. Miss Forbush, a thin bird-like woman in her late sixties, dragged unwillingly out of retirement because of the teacher shortage, had taken an instant dislike to Peter when he was shoehorned into her already overcrowded class mid-term. She had learned that he was a runaway with rather a seedy past who had been evacuated from London. Peter had become her victim. She took delight on picking on the quiet boy with the pale features and enigmatic eyes. And the class had taken her lead in this, victimizing him in the play-ground and isolating him in lessons. None more so than Tom Bates, whose size and belligerent nature ensured he always got his own way. Most children were afraid of him and were deferential in his company or avoided him altogether. To Bates, Peter was the ideal victim: the easy target for the punch in the back, the tripping up along the corridor, the ink stain in the exercise book, the ripped jacket pocket.

Though thoroughly miserable, Peter bore this torment with fortitude. He didn't complain or retaliate for he knew this would only bring him further misery. It seemed to him that Miss Forbush turned a blind eye to all his torment as though she approved of it. One thing that kept Peter going was the thought of the Christmas holidays when he hoped he could visit London again and see Johnny. Johnny Hawke – the only person who seemed to understand him.

The boys waiting for him in the darkness thrilled with excitement as Peter approached the bush in which they were hiding. As he did so, they jumped out onto the path emitting vicious shrieks. Because Peter had been deep in thought he was not as shocked or frightened by this sudden confrontation as they had hoped. He simply stopped in his tracks and gazed at them with a puzzled expression.

'Where you going, cockneyboy?' challenged Bates, puffing out his chest and taking a step forward. He towered over the wiry Peter.

'I'm going home.'

'Home? Hear that Bri. The cockney bastard's going back to London.'

'Good riddance I say,' squeaked Brian from the shadows.

Peter attempted to pass them but Bates blocked his way.

'No so fast, cockneyboy,' Bates drawled, mimicking the cowboy films he'd seen at the pictures. And then he pushed Peter hard in the chest.

Peter's pulse began to race. He had been slow to realize that he was in danger, but now he knew all too clearly that these two lads meant him harm. They had caught him alone and in the dark. Suddenly he felt very frightened. What were they going to do to him?

'Let me go,' he cried, with as much confidence as he could muster, his mouth suddenly becoming very dry.

Bates replied by smashing Peter in the face with his fist. He was blinded for a moment and then with a stifled cry, he fell backward onto the wet path, jarring his elbow on the hard surface. As he sprawled out on the ground, his school cap flying off, he felt the gush of warm blood from his nose.

Now that their victim was down on the floor, Brian Harker felt brave enough to step forward. With a tight smirk, he kicked Peter hard in the shins. 'We don't like your type round here, cockneyboy. Bugger off to where you come from.'

Peter struggled to get up, but Bates jumped astride his body, his heavy bulk pinning him down. 'It's no good wriggling, I've got you,' he grinned and spat in Peter's face. 'No point in rushing off, is there? You've got no mam or dad to go to have you, orphan bastard!'

These words incensed Peter and uttering a wild inarticulate cry he thrust his body upwards in a desperate effort to dislodge Bates, but the boy was well built and determined. He remained put.

Bates stared down at his prisoner with maniacal hatred. For one frantic moment, Peter wondered if they were going to kill him. Why were they like this? What had he done to them for them to hate him so much?

'Please, let me go,' he said quietly, with as much dignity as he could muster.

Bates replied by hitting him hard in the face again. 'Shut up, orphan bastard, or you'll get more.' Turning his head to his confederate he hissed, 'Get the shit.'

Like an obedient robot, Brian Harker retreated to the bushes, returning moments later with a small rusty bucket.

At the sight of it Tom Bates giggled obscenely. 'We've bought you a going away present, cockneyboy,' he grinned, pushing his face into Peter's.

'Poo, this stuff don't half stink,' observed Brian Harker, wrinkling up his whole face in disgust.

'That's the whole idea, stupid,' Bates crowed, jumping up. 'Real cow muck. Great stuff.'

With a swift movement, he jumped up and stood well back, allowing his confederate a clear field. 'OK, let him have it.'

Before Peter knew what was happening, Brian Harker had thrown the entire contents of the bucket over him as he lay prone on the ground. It splashed in his face and smothered his raincoat and ran down the sides of his legs. He gagged at the smell of it and droplets fell into his mouth. He retched, his stomach heaving and he was sick.

His tormentors were delighted with this bonus as vomit sprayed their victim's already contaminated clothes and they burst into fits of uncontrollable laugher. Tom Bates in particular was highly amused. He raised his fat face to the moon and barked with hilarity like a mad dog.

Tears of humiliation and misery ran down Peter's face as he struggled to his feet. Then in a sudden burst of anger he picked up the empty bucket and hurled it at the two bullies but his aim was wide and it landed harmlessly somewhere in the bushes.

'Get back to where you belong, you cockney bastard orphan ... or there'll be more shit for you,' bellowed Tom Bates, as he turned on his heel and strode away, triumphant.

'Yeah,' agreed Brian Harker before joining his pal. Within seconds they had been swallowed up by the darkness leaving Peter standing covered in cow dung and vomit and shivering in pain and self-disgust.

Peter attempted to wash his coat in the stream not far from the farm where he was billeted hoping to cleanse it of its foul coating, but the excrement seemed impervious to icy water. After a time, with tears streaming down his face, he let the garment go, allowing it to be caught by the current and carried to God knows where. It was ruined anyway. He could never contemplate ever wearing the cursed thing again. It would only remind him of his humiliation. After swilling his face and hands in the stream, he sat shivering on a tree stump staring at the moon.

God, how he hated it here. Devon was nowhere. Mr and Mrs Booth were all right, he supposed, well, she was, but he never felt as though he was really wanted. He was an imposition. There were other evacuee children in the village, but they were mainly from Exeter and so they fitted in. They had the same accent and most of them had parents. He was the odd one out. A London boy with no one to call his own. He began to cry properly this time. Great huge sobs shook his young frame. What on earth was he to do?

'Where the heck have you been, boy?' Arthur Booth dropped his paper and rose from the armchair by the fire. 'Do you know what time it is?'

Peter shook his head slightly. He felt incapable of speech.

'And look at the state of you. What on earth have you been doing? And where's your coat?'

As the interrogation grew, Peter became more incapable of speech. He curled up within himself, his mind in a foetal position, hoping all this would go away.

'Come on, answer me, boy. You've got a tongue in your head.'

Rose Booth bustled in from the kitchen, wiping her hands on her paisley apron. At the sight of the bedraggled Peter she gave out a sharp cry. 'Heaven's above, what's happened to you, Peter? You look as though you've been dragged through a hedge backwards.' She knelt down by him so that her face was on a level with his and took his hand in hers. This gesture of kindness was too much for his fragile heart and he burst into tears. She hugged him tight. 'What is it?' she said softly in his ear. 'What is it?'

'Never mind hugging the boy. Ask him where his bloody coat is. It cost me good money that did.'

'Oh, shut up Arthur. Can't you see the boy's upset.'

Arthur Booth grunted, snatched up his newspaper and resumed his seat by the fire. 'Upset. I'll give him upset. He's nothing but a bloody nuisance.'

'You take no notice, Peter. Come on upstairs. Let's get you out of your damp clothes and into the bath and then we'll see about getting you some supper.'

Later that night, Peter lay awake in his little bedroom staring at the ceiling, wishing he were dead. He thought he'd been miserable living with his uncaring mother but this life was much worse: trapped with strangers in an alien world, far away from the streets of London which he knew and loved and being targeted by bullies. He knew the incident with the cow muck was only the beginning of a serious campaign of torment. Up to now Bates and his crony had been comparatively subtle in their attacks on him, the sly punch, the casual dig in the ribs, knocking his packed lunch on the ground professing that it was an accident. He could cope with these, but now there was no subterfuge, no pretence. The hatred was out in the open. As his stomach knotted in pain, he realized that this would give licence for others to join in. And he knew he couldn't tell anyone. That would only make things worse. Miss Forbush wouldn't care; Mr Booth would only tell him to stick up for himself before returning to reading his paper, and while Mrs Booth would be sympathetic, she could do nothing to stop it. Complaining to the school would do no good.

While he was having supper that night, Mrs Booth had tried to find out where he had been after school, why he was so late home and what had happened to his coat. He knew it was pointless telling her the truth. He had made up some tale of trying a new way home from school through the woods and he'd fallen in a stream. Then when he'd taken his coat off to try and shake it dry, it had dropped in the stream and had been carried away by the current before he could snatch it back. He could see from Mrs Booth's eyes that she didn't believe him but she didn't question him further. She knew that it was safer not to.

As he emerged from the bathroom before going to bed he heard the Booths arguing downstairs. Snatched phrases came to his ears. It was clear that Mrs Booth was trying to placate her angry husband while he maintained that 'the boy was nothing but trouble' and 'a bloody nuisance'. So here he was again; alone in the dark – unloved and unwanted. He shivered at the awful realization of his situation.

Above him he heard the drone of a lone aircraft. The sound temporarily diverted his thoughts from his own troubles. He wondered if it were a Nazi plane on its way to bomb London. He hoped not. He thought of Johnny in his little flat. The image of his strange one-eyed friend and the scruffy little room where he stayed the night Johnny found him sleeping in a doorway made him tingle. An idea crept into his mind that made him sit up in bed. Suddenly, he knew what he had to do. He'd done it before when he'd been very unhappy. He would run away. He would leave this terrible inhospitable place and make his way to London. He would go to Johnny; he was sure that he would make everything all right.

With a wide grin, Peter snuggled down under the covers willing sleep to come and carry him away, for tomorrow he would make his escape.

THREE

I slept badly that night, my slumbers punctuated by dreams about giant heels invading London. They clomped heavily down the Strand on their way to Trafalgar Square. These visions were interrupted from time to time by the face of Walter Riley, heavily made-up as his alter ego Wilma, floating towards me in the darkness, his red lipsticked mouth agape in a silent scream. Eventually I woke around six o'clock, bathed in sweat, knowing that it was pointless trying to get back to sleep.

I made myself a cup of tea and sat hunched over the gas fire smoking my first cigarette of the day, waiting for the dawn light to force its way around the crimped edges of my blackout curtains. I was surprised how depressed I felt. I had only known Walter Riley a few hours and yet I felt terribly sad about his death – his murder. I smiled wryly at my use of the word 'known'. Of course I hadn't known the man, but I had become party to his secret, a secret that he had only shared with a few. Even his wife did not know of his hidden passion. He had struck me as a decent chap and there were already too many decent chaps losing their lives in this bloody war. To become the victim of a fatal handbag snatch seemed unnecessarily cruel. God had a lot to answer for.

After covering Riley's body with my coat, I had called the police from a nearby telephone box and waited for them to arrive. I gave a statement to an Inspector Barraclough, a middle-aged stoical copper of the old school, who, from his appearance, looked as though he'd long passed the age of retirement – but then no one retires now there's a war on. I had never encountered him before, but he approached the situation in a calm, business-like manner. He hadn't raised an eyebrow when he discovered the corpse was a man dressed up as a woman.

'Takes all sorts, I suppose,' he said, lifting Riley's wig away from his head. 'We've had a spate of handbag snatches in the last month. It's been like a craze that's caught on. It started slowly and now it seems every little slimy spiv is having a crack at it. It's the blackout. It makes it so easy for 'em.' He tipped his hat back and sniffed. 'Still, this is the first time someone's been killed in the process. That puts it in a different league.'

Unfortunately, I couldn't give any useful details about the appearance of the killer. I had been too far away and it had been too dark for me to see him clearly. I just knew that he was of a stocky build and about average height – like half of the men in London.

'Can you keep the unusual nature of the victim's attire out of the press report?' I asked with some delicacy and went on to explain my connection with the dead man. I wanted Riley to retain some dignity at the end of his life.

Barraclough nodded. 'There's nothing to be gained by titillating the readers with the poor bastard's private quirks. Obviously his wife will have to be informed.'

I grimaced at the thought. How would hard-hearted Sandra react? I believed I could guess. 'I'll leave that little task to the official police, if you don't mind,' I said, affecting a shy smile.

I treated myself to another cup of tea and a slice of toast before I set about my morning ablutions. It was just after eight o'clock when I was ready to face the day. I wandered into my office and checked the appointment book. As I suspected, the page was blank. Another day of crosswords and thumb-twiddling lay ahead while I waited to see if the doorbell or the telephone would ring, heralding a client with a nice juicy, lucrative case. Not a likely prospect but one had to live in hope.

As things turned out, I did not have to wait long for the thick metal clatter of my doorbell. It was not, however, the precursor of a client or a case; it just announced the arrival of my old mate Detective Inspector David Llewellyn of Scotland Yard. He didn't even wait for me to answer the door. He just barged in, flung his hat on my desk and sat in the chair opposite me.

'I hear you've been keeping company with strange lady friends,' he said, unable to keep the merriment out of his voice.

'News travels fast at the Yard.'

'News like that has got bloody roller skates on.'

'Mr Riley was a client.'

'Oh, *Mr* Riley was it? I heard different.' David smirked one of his annoying smirks.

'I suppose you have a reason to call on me so bright and early, Inspector,' I said wearily, ignoring his levity.

'Well, if you could rustle up a cup of char that would be a start. Unless, of course, you're busy ...' he said pointedly, running his finger in the dust on my desk.

'You'll have to do with black coffee. I'm out of milk.'

He pulled a face. 'I suppose so ...'

I went through to the kitchen and made the coffee. On my return, David had slipped off his overcoat and was smoking a cigarette. I plonked the mug down by his elbow.

'That's great, man. You don't have a digestive biscuit or a fig roll to go with it do you?'

'The sign outside says Hawke Investigations not the Cosy Café.'

'Touchy this morning, aren't we?'

'Much as I'm pleased to see your wrinkled Welsh face, I presume you have a reason for this visit.'

David sipped his coffee and gave a sharp intake of breath. 'Boy, that's hot,' he said. 'Purpose, yes. It's about your lady friend, Mr Walter Riley. As it's really no longer a case of handbag snatching but one of murder, it's landed on my desk.'

'Good for you.'

'I just thought I'd pop round and have a chat with you. I've read your statement but I wondered if you could talk me through the business again. I want to try and determine whether this was a casual killing or a premeditated murder.'

'Well, there was nothing casual about the killing, but for my money Mr Riley just happened to be in the wrong place at the wrong time—'

'And in the wrong frock, eh? Tell me about it.'

I did as David requested, giving him a full blown detailed account from the capital letter to the full stop. When I'd finished, he remained silent for a few moments, stroking his chin.

'Poor bugger,' he said at last. His demeanour was now more sober and the wry amusement regarding Riley's murder had evaporated.

'Exactly.'

'And you really can't give me any more detail about the bastard who did this?'

I shook my head. 'I wish I could. It happened so quickly and it was dark.'

'What about the car? Number plate?'

'It was a Wolseley. Number plate, no.'

'Oh Johnny. And you call yourself a detective.'

'There's no need to rub it in. I feel bad enough about it already.'

David ruffled his thinning blond hair. 'I'm only joshing, boyo. You know me.'

'Yeah.'

There was an awkward silence and then suddenly David gave a deep sigh and galvanized himself into action. He took a final swig of his coffee before grabbing his coat and hat and heading for the door. 'Well, I'd better get back to the Yard and start banging my head against a brick wall. A random killing with no clues. Where the hell does one start? Man, I hate days like these.'

'Let me know if I can help in any way. I'd really like to be a party to nailing the vermin who did this.'

'I'll keep you informed. Perhaps we can have a pint in the Guardsman one lunchtime later in the week. In the meantime if you remember anything else about the shooting that might help ...'

I nodded.

'Thanks for the coffee. Get some biscuits in next time, eh?'

With a friendly wave, he was gone. I sipped my coffee and felt glum. It wasn't only David who hated days like these.

FOUR

Mrs Booth observed that Peter was much more cheerful the following morning. It wasn't anything he said – indeed he said little – but it was in his brisk and easy manner as he attacked his breakfast. His eyes were brighter and the soulful disposition that had held him in an emotional strait jacket the previous evening seemed to have vanished overnight. She was glad about this and determined not to question him any further about his lateness and the loss of his coat. She guessed something unpleasant had happened to him and no doubt it would take a team of wild horses to drag the truth out of him. He wasn't a bad lad and she was quite fond of him despite the fact that although he'd been staying with them for some months now she had not been able to get close to him. Their relationship still bordered on the polite and the formal. There was an invisible barrier around Peter. He allowed you to get only so near. It was as though, she thought, he was afraid of trusting anyone for fear of getting hurt.

Ever since losing her own son to diphtheria many years ago, Rose Booth had given up the idea of having children – a child about the house again. The idea was too painful. The ghost of her own little boy, Robert, still haunted the place. She caught sight and sometimes the smell of him from time to time and her heart ached.

It was because of this that she had resisted the idea of taking on an evacuee when the war started and the youngsters came down to Devon in their droves, but when her sister had asked her to look after Peter, she reconsidered the situation. Perhaps having a boy in her home would be good, not just for her but for Arthur as well. He had not been keen and had also resisted but she had talked him round. Reluctantly he agreed. Arthur had never lost the anger he felt over the death of their son and having Peter in the house opened the wound further. He kept away from the boy and was surly with him purely because he saw the slight pale London lad as someone who was trying to take the place of his Robert.

At first Rose Booth was enthusiastic and optimistic, but Peter's quiet withdrawn ways had merely reawakened painful memories and reminded her that she was much older now and past the mothering stage. She was discomforted by his presence and she felt guilty that she couldn't be more for the boy than a glorified landlady.

As Peter cleared his plate, she felt the urge to ruffle his hair in an affectionate gesture, but she resisted it. It just didn't seem right to her and she knew the lad would stiffen and feel awkward at such an open show of emotion.

Breakfast over, Peter went upstairs ostensibly to clean his teeth and have a wee before setting off for school. However, after his ablutions, he stole into his bedroom and from under the bed he retrieved the small suitcase that he had packed in the middle of the night. It contained some of his clothes and a few of his favourite comics. Opening the bedroom window, he leaned out and carefully dropped the suitcase so that it landed safely in the branches of a bush below him. It was just the sort of trick that his hero Tiger Blake would perform when he was making one of his many escapes.

Returning down stairs with his little school satchel, he discovered Mrs Booth in the hall. She held out a rather shabby and worn little raincoat. It was the one that Peter had arrived in.

'I'm afraid you're going to have to wear this for the time being,' she said, trying to affect a smile. 'It'll be a while before we're in a position to get you a new one.'

Peter felt a deep pang of guilt. 'That's OK,' said Peter, returning the half smile sheepishly. He was sorry to be deceiving Mrs Booth. He knew she was a good woman. Kind and caring. He was also aware that it was as much his fault that he wasn't happy here.

She helped him on with the coat and then unexpectedly gave him a hug. 'You be a good boy at school today, eh,' she said planting a kiss on his cheek. She had never done that before and Peter felt a lump forming in his throat. It was as if she knew he was leaving for good. Momentarily incapable of speech, he nodded and headed for the door. Just before closing it he turned and smiled at her.

'Bye,' he said.

Once outside, Peter raced to the side of the house, retrieved his suitcase from the straggly bush, replacing it with his satchel. He wouldn't be needing that now.

Then he set off at a brisk pace down the lane that would lead him to the bus stop. He was taking his first step for London.

And Freedom.

And Johnny.

FIVE

'Like a fag?'

Rachel Howells looked up from the contemplation of her empty tea cup. Standing over her was a young man with a cheeky grin, a pug nose and piercing blue eyes. His hat was pushed to the back of his head so that his Brylcreemed quiff escaped over his forehead like a set of greasy clockwork springs. In his hand was an open packet of Senior Service. She eyed it cautiously.

'Go on,' he said cheerily, holding the cigarettes under her nose. 'Take one. They won't bite. And neither will I.'

'Ta.'

'S'all right. My pleasure.' He pulled a chair up to her table and slipping a lighter from his pocket lit her cigarette. 'Looks like you could do with another cup of tea an' all.'

She said nothing but gazed at the young man shyly from under hooded eyes and gave a winsome smile.

'Hang on,' he said, jumping up and heading for the counter. He returned a few minutes later with two cups of tea.

'There you go, girl. Get that down you.' He grinned as he placed the tea by her elbow.

'That's kind,' she said quietly, stubbing out the half-smoked cigarette. 'Why are you doing this? You don't know me.'

'Nah', he said, leaning forward and winking at her. 'But I'd like to. When I sees a pretty girl all alone in a milk bar staring into space, I reckon she's in need of a friend. And I think, well, maybe I could be that friend.'

Harryboy lounged back in his chair eyeing the girl up with all the confidence in the world. She was quite tall with mousy brown hair and a diffident manner which marked her out as an easy target. She was a bit on the plump side but quite a looker. Good figure with nice breasts swelling beneath her tight woollen frock. He didn't half fancy prising those juicy thighs apart for a bit of the other. He'd been watching her for a while. As soon as he had spotted the battered brown suitcase stowed beneath her chair he reckoned this was a naïve piece of skirt up from the country somewhere needing a little bit of help and human succour. And he reckoned he was just the man for the job.

'Harryboy Jenkins is the name. What's yours?'

'I'm Rachel. Rachel Howells.'

'Nice name. Nice accent. You're not from London, are you?'

She shook her head. 'I've never been here before. I just arrived.'

'Where you from, Rachel Howells? Edinburgh, eh?'

She laughed at his joke and gave him a gentle slap on the arm. 'Course not, you idiot,' she grinned. 'I'm from Wales. A town called Mumbles.'

'Blimey, that sounds a rum place.'

'It's a dull place.' The smile faded. She hadn't wanted to be reminded of home just now. A few lonely hours in London had dented her confidence and she had just begun to wonder if she had done the right thing in leaving.

'So you've come up to the metrops to see a bit of life, 'ave yer?'

She lowered her head. 'You could say that.'

'Yeah, well, that's why I'm here too. Life's too short not to have fun, ain't it? Especially with this war on. Never know when the bleedin' Nazis'll be knocking at your door ready to cart you off to one of them concentration camps. So I says, have a laugh while you can. That's my motto. What d'you say?'

She gazed at him with a kind of simple admiration. He oozed confidence and self-assurance and she liked that. 'I reckon you're right.'

' 'Course I am. Only a fool has regrets. You takes your chances while you can. So, now you're here in London, might as well enjoy it, eh?'

Rachel grinned and nodded. She felt her spirits reviving.

'That's the ticket. Well, if you've nothing on today I reckon we could have a good time together. You and me. Y'know, see a few sights. Have a bite to eat. My treat. What d'you say?'

'Oh, I don't know.' Her voice was hesitant but Harryboy could see that her eyes told a different story.

'Come on, gel. As I say, you only live once. I'm a harmless bloke. You'll be safe with me. Honest.' A sudden thought struck him and he pulled out his wallet and spread it open on the table. It was bulging with notes. 'See there, Rachel Howells, I've more than enough money for both of us.'

Her eyes widened with surprise as she gazed at the contents of the wallet. She had never seen such a large amount of cash before. 'Is that yours?'

'Well, it's not bleeding Churchill's, is it? 'Course it's mine,' he added proudly, stowing the wallet back in his jacket. 'I'm not just a pretty face, yer know.'

'Not backward in coming forward either are you, Harryboy?'

'I fancy coming forward with you,' He leaned closer as though he was going to kiss her, but he stroked her cheek gently instead. 'So, my gel, what d'you say?'

'OK, then.' She smiled shyly. 'But I hope you don't think I'm a cheap pick-up.'

Harryboy pulled a long face, adopting a hurt expression. 'Do I look like the kind of bloke who goes in for cheap pick-ups? I ask you.'

Her smile broadened. 'No, I suppose not.'

'Right then. Drink up and I'll show you some of the sights of London.'

Rachel Howells did as she was told.

The pattern had been set.

As it turned out, Harryboy never quite showed Rachel the sights of the wounded city. He had never intended to. He was more interested in getting the girl back to his hotel room for a bit of how's your father which he managed to do quite easily without raising a sweat.

This gullible country mouse was no match for him. Two hours later little Rachel Howells was spread on her back on the bed in his hotel room, stark naked while Harryboy laboured over her, thrusting himself deep into her plump willing body. Now he *was* raising a sweat.

He was more than happy. She might be a little naïve piece from the valleys, but when it came to sex, she knew all the right moves. Eventually, he reached his climax and slumped beside his new conquest on the bed.

After a while, Rachel sat up. 'I need the bathroom,' she said quietly.

Harryboy laughed. 'Be my guest. It's a free country – for the time being anyway. Then perhaps we can have another little love session, eh?' He chuckled to himself.

'Er … where can I…?'

'If you wan' a pee, the lav's down the corridor. I don't advise you nip down like that. You'll get yourself arrested. Either that or a job at the Windmill.' He chuckled again at his own joke. 'See if there's a pot under the bed.'

'I can't – not in front of you.'

'Cor blimey, now's not the time to get precious. Not after what we've just been doing. I'm not curious, if that's what you think. Just get on with it, woman.'

His voice had taken on a darker, intimidating tone that unnerved Rachel. Reluctantly she extracted a metal bowl from under the bed. It was dusty and chipped. She turned her nose up at it.

'Got all the mod cons 'ere,' grinned Harryboy, leering over the side of the bed at her.

'You turn your back while I've finished. This is private.'

With a laugh, he did what she asked.

When she was finished and the pot stowed away out of view, she moved around to her side of the bed, her libido rising once more at the sight of her new friend lying naked on the bed, his penis not yet limp. He wasn't a very tall chap but he was well put together with a good chest and some firm muscles and he certainly knew how to make love. Much more than Will did. The thought of that name, her old boyfriend from back home, made her flinch. She had told herself that she must forget it – now that she had a new life away from all that. She hadn't realized how difficult it was going to be. Here was his name just popping into her mind without any warning, like a ghost coming to haunt her. It wasn't going to be that easy to sever the ties with her past. It was waiting in the dark corners of her conscience ready to reach out and spoil her present pleasures. Suddenly, at the thought of this, she felt sick and unsteady on her legs. Her stomach lurched and she staggered backwards unsteadily, knocking into the chair by the dressing table. Harryboy's jacket, which had been hanging there, slid to the ground. She waited a moment for her head to clear and then she bent down to retrieve the jacket. As she did so something dark and heavy fell out. It landed on the floor with a dull thud as it hit the thin carpet.

It was a gun. A black, shiny pistol.

Without thinking, she picked it up.

Harryboy was off the bed in a flash and by her side. 'Give that to me,' he snapped. 'Hand it over, quick.' His voice was high-pitched, angry and threatening. Gone were the smiles and the cheery demeanour. Here was a demon.

'I'm sorry ... I didn't mean to ...' she stammered, unsure what she felt or meant to say.

'Give me the fucking gun!' he bellowed, his face glowing with anger.

With a trembling hand she passed the pistol to him. Without a word, he slipped it back into his inside jacket pocket and then with the back of his hand he hit her hard, sending her spinning across the room. She crashed to the floor, banging her head on the door. So sudden and so violent had been the blow that it had squeezed all the breath out of Rachel and she lay there in shock gasping for air, unable to speak, moan or scream.

'If I ever catch you touching my gun again, I'll kill you. D'you understand? I will kill you.' He walked over to her and knelt down, grabbing her hair from behind until he was able to pull her head back-wards. He pushed his face close to hers so that all she could see were his cold, cruel blue eyes. 'I said, do you understand?' he growled in a fierce whisper, his spittle showering her face in a fine spray.

'Yes, Harryboy, I understand. I'm sorry.'

Without a word, he released her and she slumped back, her body limp with fear.

'Right, get back on that bed. We have some unfinished business to perform.'

Slowly, she picked herself up and climbed back on the bed, surrep-titiously wiping the tears away with her arm.

He came to her and kissed her nipples gently while he cupped each breast in turn. 'Lovely tits,' he murmured to himself rather than to her. It was as though the incident with the gun had never happened. Then he ran his hand down her belly until he reached the thicket of pubic hair. Here he began to arouse Rachel once more.

Remarkably her body responded to his sensitive touch, her body gently rising and falling with the pleasure his fingers were generating, while her mind struggled with these sensations. How could she give herself to this man who had treated her so cruelly? She wanted to pull herself away. She wanted him to stop touching her, touching her in that way. But part of her didn't want to; part of her was too frightened to try.

It wasn't very long before he entered her again and, as she surrended her body to the passion, she tried hard to forget the monster who had nearly knocked her senseless. But she couldn't. She was reminded of it vividly each time his face came close to hers as he pumped rhythmically towards his climax.

S I X

I suppose I am a stranger to personal grief and bereavement. As an orphan, not having known my parents, I have never lost anyone who was very close and so I don't really know how I will react when one day this happens to me. However, in my line of business, I've seen many times how grief affects others. From strange forms of self-denial to almost total collapse, there is a broad spectrum of emotion to tap into for those experiencing the loss. Somewhere in there is the angry and selfishly arrogant response. How dare God allow this to happen to me? How dare He make such a mess of my life? What's going to happen to *me* now? This is specially tailored for the egocentric individual to whom the death of their nearest and dearest is an inconvenience rather than a tragedy. I thought Mrs Sandra Riley would slot very neatly into this category, but as things turned out, it wasn't as simple as that.

It was late afternoon when she came calling. I really hadn't expected to see her again. She had paid my fee up front on our first meeting and now that her husband had been killed in rather embarrassing circumstances, I thought she would want to let the matter lie. What remained was a job for the police. There was no point stirring up the embers with me.

But, not for the first time, I was wrong.

The October day was already darkening and I had just drawn the blinds and turned on the lamps in my office when she arrived. She entered like a ship in full sail. There it was again, that heavily made-up face with a scarlet gash for a mouth and those arctic eyes staring at me with a mixture of anger and haughty disdain.

'I fully expected to hear from you today, Mr Hawke,' she said imperiously.

'Would you like to take a seat, Mrs Riley?' My response was civil but cool.

She looked at the shabby padded chair before my desk as though something unpleasant had just died on it, but she took it all the same. 'Well?' she said expectantly, settling her capacious handbag on her lap as though it was some kind of leathery pet dog.

'Please accept my condolences on the loss of your husband. I am sure the police will have explained the unfortunate circumstances of his death.'

'The sordid details, you mean. Indeed. Apparently my husband was some sort of freak who achieved a kind of sexual thrill by dressing up as a woman.'

'It was a foible of his,' I said easily, lighting a cigarette. I was determined not to be intimidated by this heavily powdered gorgon. 'At least you have the comfort of knowing that there was no other woman in the case. Your husband was not being unfaithful to you.'

'Not in the usual way. I wish to God he had been seeing some tart. At least that would have been normal. How can I face people when this news gets out?'

'It is not likely to. The police have kept those details from the press. I believe your husband's secret is safe.'

'My husband's shame you mean.'

'I'm sorry things ended so unhappily,' I said evenly, hoping to bring the conversation and indeed her visit to a close, but Sandra Riley showed no signs of leaving. She hadn't done with me yet.

After a pause, she said, 'I know the police version of what happened last night but I want to hear your account. What my husband said to you and … and how he was killed. In detail. You owe it to me.'

I supposed I did.

Simply, but without leaving anything out which I thought rele-vant, I told her the story: my visit to the hotel and later the conversation I'd had with her husband at The Loophole. And then how he had been killed by the handbag snatcher. As I talked, to my surprise, I saw that great white mask slowly crumble and the eyes mist with tears. This formidable ice maiden was melting. She was genuinely moved. This was indeed a turn up for the book.

When I finished, I waited for her to say something but she remained silent, her mouth moving slowly, lips quivering, as she attempted to control her emotions. To cover the awkwardness of the moment, I offered her a cigarette. She waved her hand at me in refusal and unclasping her bag withdrew a handkerchief and dabbed her eyes.

'If only he'd told me. If only he had confided in me ...'

'That would have been very difficult.'

She nodded, a faint smile touching her lips. 'For Walter, yes. He hadn't much backbone. But I loved him, you know. In my own way.'

I wondered which way that was and hoped I never experienced it.

'I was quite prepared to divorce him if he had been seeing another woman ... but I didn't expect all this. To be killed by a common thug.' She leaned forward, her tear-stained face harsh in the direct beam of my desk lamp. 'It offends me,' she said. 'It makes me sick to my stomach.'

'I am sure the police—'

I got no further. She threw her head back and gave a harsh theatrical laugh. Joan Crawford was making a return. 'The police,' she repeated with a sneer, as though she was referring to something she had stepped in. 'Don't tell me that you were going to say that the police will get their man – the man who killed my husband?' She gave another mirthless laugh. 'It's just another handbag snatch to them, one with a little complication of a dead body. London is seething with crime: gangsters, petty thugs, looters, con artists, Nazi sympathizers. How are the police going to catch the anonymous bastard who murdered Walter – the weirdo in the dress and wig? I can see the case being filed away already as yet another unsolved crime of the blackout.'

I sat quietly while she expelled this anger. Sadly, what she was saying had the ring of truth to it. Unless her husband's killer made a habit of shooting women for their handbag, Walter Riley would be just another statistic on the growing list of unsolved murders.

Suddenly, Sandra Riley clunked open her capacious handbag once more. This time she extracted a long brown envelope and plopped it on my desk.

'That's yours,' she said tartly. 'Fifty pounds in fivers.'

'What for?' I said quietly.

'For services you are about to render. Mr Hawke, I want you to find my husband's killer.'

I stared in surprise at the envelope for some moments as though it was going to speak to me and explain the workings of Mrs Riley's mind. Here was a woman who, twenty-four hours earlier, was all set to crucify her husband in a divorce court for his adulterous behaviour and now she was the tearful widow begging me – all right, bribing me with money – to find Walter's murderer.

And tearful widow she was. In my line of work I've seen quite a few performances in my office of varying effectiveness, men and women who have come to me with emotional tales of pain and anguish. Nine times out of ten they are contrived and theatrical in nature and usually transparent, however polished.

This was no performance.

Sandra Riley was a woman in turmoil. I think I had misjudged her. Here was a wife who had believed that her husband was having sex and other intimacies with another woman and had steeled herself for the uncovering of this sordid, illicit affair. She had stiffened her sinews and boarded up her heart, even to the extent of fooling herself that she didn't care for the swine. But the shocking unexpected blow of losing her Walter in a brutal killing had brought home to her how much she really had cared for the man. It seemed that now, despite learning the hurtful truth about Walter's sexual peccadillo, Mrs Riley was a woman swamped by grief and was fighting it the only way she knew how – by getting her own back.

By getting even.

'I'm not sure I'm going to be able to do that,' I said softly, fully aware of the finding a black cat in a dark cellar challenge that this investigation would present to me.

'Why not? You're a detective, aren't you? Or are you only capable of spying into people's bedrooms?'

It hurts when the nail is walloped on the head. She had a point: I was a detective. And murder was the worst of crimes. I looked across at her, her features having regained something of their resilience, despite the tear-smudged mascara around the eyes. She seemed to have more faith in my abilities than I had. This pricked my conscience. Curse my ever dutiful conscience. I knew in my heart of hearts, that prompted by Sandra Riley's request, I could not just let the matter rest where it was.

'Very well,' I said with a sigh. 'I'll try my best.'

She gave me a tight smile and pushed the brown envelope further in my direction.

'Tell me about your husband's job. You said he held a menial post at the War Office ...'

Sandra Riley nodded. 'That wasn't quite honest. I was feeling angry and very betrayed when I said that. Actually he is ... *was* on the secretarial staff to Brigadier General Anstruther, Commander in Chief of the Home Forces. Walter had been there since the outbreak of the war. My brother Edward had managed to get him the job.'

'Your brother works at the War Office, too.'

'Yes.'

'What sort of work was your husband involved with at the War Office?'

She shook her head. 'I don't really know. I never asked, but if I had, he wouldn't have been allowed to say anyway. He was a journalist on a local paper before the war but because of his defective eyesight he was graded B1, fit for office duties only. He so wanted to do something to help the war effort and so Edward pulled a few strings and got him into Whitehall.'

A cold shiver ran down my spine. The irony. The cruel coincidence. Graded B1 for defective eyesight. My own fate. Well, in the sense that having only one eye clearly marked me out as someone with 'defective eyesight'.

'Did he form any friendships at work?' I asked, quickly derailing this particular train of unsettling thought and getting back to the matter in hand.

'None that I was aware of ... but then I didn't know he dressed up as a woman, so you could say that I knew very little about my husband.'

'I'd like to speak to your brother at the War Office. I need to find out more about Walter's life and duties there. Can you arrange that?'

She nodded. 'His name is Captain Michael Eddowes. I'll let him know to expect you to call on him at the War Office; although I'm not sure he'll know any more than me.'

She snapped her handbag and rose from her chair, her imperious manner fully reclaimed. 'I expect you to keep me informed of any progress you make. Don't disappoint me, Mr Hawke. Don't disappoint me.'

After she had gone, leaving behind the strong smell of her own perfume which lingered in the air like a threat, I sat for some time staring blankly into space. I wasn't happy. I didn't know why, but I felt for the first time that with this investigation, I had really bitten off more than I could chew.

I had just decided to spend a little relaxing, amnesia time at The Velvet Cage where, with the help of some jazz and alcohol, I hoped to soften the edges of ragged reality when the phone rang calling a temporary halt to my plans.

'Johnny. This is Susan McAndrew. Nurse McAndrew.'

It only took a few seconds for me to reach into my memory bank and withdraw the relevant information. Oh, Nurse McAndrew. Susan. The lady who had looked after the little boy Peter in hospital during the Pamela Palfrey case. I'd had more than a little soft spot for Nurse McAndrew – and it wasn't just because of the uniform – but she was a dedicated professional with little time for gentlemen admirers. Well, I may be a scruffy private detective but I still think of myself as a gentleman. A kind of knight in rather shabby armour. In another time, another place, in peacetime maybe, there would have been time to woo Nurse McAndrew. Maybe.

It was Susan who had arranged for Peter to be evacuated to her sister's farm in Devon, away from the bombs and the terrors of London.

'How nice to hear from you,' I said, with as much assimilated Hollywood charm as I could muster.

'It's Peter,' she said sharply. The tone and urgency of her voice robbing me of any delusion that she was ringing me for pleasurable purposes.

At the mention of the lad's name, I stiffened. What now? I thought. It must be bad news.

'What about Peter?' I asked, hesitantly fearing the worst.

'He's run away.'

I don't know why I chuckled, but I did.

'You think it's funny.' Suddenly the nurse had turned stern.

'Not funny, no, just a relief. I thought you were going to tell me something far worse.'

There was a brief silence at the end of the line. 'Oh, I see. I'm sorry. I don't want to sound overdramatic, but this is serious. My sister is beside herself with worry.'

'Of course. What's happened? Give me the facts …'

'There aren't many facts. It seems that he never really settled down there and then there was some trouble at the school.'

'What sort of trouble?'

'Apparently, he was being bullied.'

I felt a pang in my stomach. The orphan boy bullied. I'd been there. I'd suffered the hurt and humiliation too, but I'd never had the courage to run away.

'The poor sod,' I murmured, my mind filled with an image of Peter when I'd first encountered him in that dark doorway, curled up, hiding from the night and all the cruelties of the world.

'I'm ringing because we think that he's headed back to London. Rose, my sister, thinks he'll come looking for you.'

'Me?'

'Of course, you. You're his hero. He missed you. He said very little to my sister, but he was always happy talking about you. You never did get down to visit him, did you?'

Another pang. This time of guilt. I had intended to go and see the lad, but it never happened. Things had cropped up and ... well, I made excuses I suppose. Created reasons for not traipsing all the way down to Devon to see a ten-year-old boy I hardly knew. Well, that's what I told myself.

But I did know him.

He was me.

I should have gone and now I felt angry and disappointed with myself.

I kept my reply simple. 'No,' I said.

'Well, now it's likely that he's coming to see you. He was spotted on a coach travelling to Exeter and no doubt he'll have tried to get a train to London from there.'

'The police have been informed then?'

'Of course. Look Johnny, I'm just ringing to warn you. If he does turn up on your doorstep please let me know. Rose is out of her mind with worry. She blames herself ...'

'I understand. I'll be in touch if ... he ...' I found my throat getting very dry. 'And please let me know if you hear any news.'

'I will. OK then. Goodbye Johnny,' she said, in a flat matter-of-fact voice. I could tell that she was disappointed in me too.

I had hardly time to say my 'Goodbye' before she had put down the phone. The resulting click and buzz resonated accusingly in my ears.

SEVEN

'I'm hungry,' Rachel said, as she slipped out of bed and started to dress.

Harryboy grunted and stretched lazily, before reaching out for the packet of cigarettes and matches on the bedside table. 'Yeah, well, I reckon you've earned some grub,' he said, lighting up. 'What say you and I slip out for a meal in some decent gaff, spoil ourselves a bit.'

'That would be nice.'

'Yeah, it would, cos then we gotta get to work.'

The smile on Rachel's face faded. 'Work? What d'you mean?'

'We need to increase our stash, baby. Hotel rooms and fancy meals don't come cheap.'

Rachel was frowning now. A fearful notion had just struck her. 'I'm not going on the game, if that's what you had in mind. You can knock me about all you want, but I'm not up for that.'

'Do I look like a pimp?' Harryboy snapped, before blowing out a cloud of smoke that drifted past his face, obscuring his features.

'What then? What d'you mean, work?'

Harryboy grinned. It was an unsettling grin which turned his already unpleasant countenance into something resembling a lascivious gargoyle. 'Patience, my sweet. Let's eat first and talk about that later.'

Rachel gave a reluctant nod and turned away so that he could not see the worried look on her face. What in Heaven's name had she got herself into? Never had she been as reckless, her behaviour as outrageous and unfettered as she had been with Harryboy. She didn't know what had possessed her. It was just that being in his company seemed to have intoxicated her with a strange feeling of release. She had sloughed off the shell of the old, dull, respectable Rachel, the girl who had only had one man in her life and only made love under the covers with the lights out. The chains of Welsh Methodist respectability had melted away and it was exciting. At least it had been exciting, daring even, in the heights of the physical passion … but now … now she was not so sure.

Like a drunkard who had had a raucous time the night before, with the bleak dawn she felt differently. She felt ashamed and frightened. She was adrift on a vast dark sea with only one man for company – a man who had threatened to kill her.

For a brief moment she wished she were back in Mumbles with boring Will. He wasn't very exciting in bed, or anywhere else for that matter, but at least he had never hit her. She glanced back at Harryboy, who was still smiling as he watched the smoke from his cigarette spiral towards the ceiling. Although she found him attractive in a dangerous kind of way – he was probably the most exciting man she had ever met – now a little rat of fear gnawed at her innards. She knew, even at this early stage of their relationship, that there was no escape. She was the fly and she was well and truly caught in his treacherous web. Unless she was pliant to his demands, he would devour her. Despair settled like a dark dust on Rachel Howells' heart.

Later that evening they were finishing the best meal that Rachel had eaten for ages – possibly the best meal ever, she thought. Harryboy had taken her to a swanky restaurant, the kind of establishment she had never dreamed of being able to visit. It was the sort of place where crinkly white notes had more currency than food coupons. She began to realize that it wasn't just the poor who exploited the black market. The restaurant was cocooned in a fake gentility. Both waiters and customers behaved in a blinkered artificial way which belied the reality of the war that had ravaged much of the city that lay just beyond its pampered portals.

Harryboy had been at his most relaxed that evening and she had felt bold enough to ask him to tell her about himself.

'What d'yer want to know? I'm very good in the sack! 'Course y'know that already.' He laughed at his own wit.

Rachel blushed.

'I'm a London boy. Brought up in Pimlico. Number seven, Waterloo Street. Brought up by my mum. Dad dropped dead a year after I was born. He was gassed in the last war and never got over it.

That's why you'll never get me fighting. All those bastards sitting in offices in Whitehall drinking tea and sticking flags in maps while our lot are getting blown to smithereens. I'm not offering myself up for cannon fodder, I can tell you. Suppose I was a bit of a tearaway when I was a lad. Still am, eh? I was always the outlaw, the baddie when we were playing as kids. I was tough, see. And I had my hideout. When the goodies were after me, I always went to my hideout and no one would dare come and get me.'

He chuckled at the memory.

'I get easily bored,' he continued, easy for the moment, talking about himself. 'Can't stand rules and regulations. That stuff is for little toads with thick glasses and celluloid collars.'

'Do you have any brothers or sisters?'

Harryboy's smile faded and his relaxed features stiffened. He hadn't thought of his brother in a long while. He deliberately blanked him from his mind, but on occasions, he managed to slip past the shield. Rachel's indirect reference to him was one of those occasions. Suddenly, he saw his face and could hear his voice and Harryboy was back in that railway yard. He heard the clanking and groaning of the shunting train. He smelled the smoke and oil of the locomotive. And he heard the scream again.

'Yeah, I got a brother,' he said gruffly, shaking off the memory as he might shake off an opponent. 'What is this? The third degree?'

'I was just interested.'

'Look, darling, there's no need for a history lesson about Harryboy Jenkins. What you see is what you get. OK?'

She knew that he was effectively drawing the shutters on his past, so Rachel just nodded.

At this moment the waiter arrived with their dessert course. This timely interruption helped to restore the relaxed mood once more. Harryboy, like a greedy schoolboy, devoured the pudding with glee.

'Great stuff,' he said, allowing his spoon to clang noisily into the empty dish.

Rachel gazed across at her companion. Harryboy certainly knew how to live. He seemed at ease in these surroundings. He had even given the waiter a large tip just to demonstrate his extravagance. Harryboy grinned at her, rubbing his tummy in a pantomime display of pleasure and then sat back in his chair cradling a brandy glass. 'Now that's what I call a tasty bit of grub. You enjoy that, angel?'

Rachel nodded. 'It was lovely.'

'Good girl.' The gargoyle grin returned. 'You stick with me and I'll see you all right.'

Although he hadn't mentioned it yet, Rachel knew that there would be a price to pay for such an allegiance and she felt sure it was a price that she wouldn't care to pay.

For a moment Harryboy stared reflectively at the brandy in the glass as he swirled the liquid around, as though hypnotized by its circular motion. She ventured to break the spell to ask him again about the 'work' he had mentioned, but she thought better of it. He didn't like questions.

Suddenly, he downed the brandy in one gulp, the fiery liquid causing him to choke a little.

'That's good stuff. I'd have another if we weren't doing the business tonight.'

Rachel leaned forward across the table. 'What exactly do you mean?'

Harryboy clutched her hands and lifted them to his lips and kissed them. 'You're my girl now, ain't you?'

There was something unnerving, threatening almost in this assertion which chilled Rachel. She knew there was only one response that would be acceptable. She lowered her lids and nodded gently. 'I guess so,' she said.

' 'Course you are. We're good together, you and I. We're a team.'

She nodded, half delighted, half terrified.

'Well, my dear, if we are going to continue enjoying ourselves in the current manner, we need to get our hands on some more dough. I'm running a bit low on funds. The old wallet ain't as full as it was this mornin' what with the hotel and this nice meal. Got to make sure we have enough to continue living life as we like it, don't we? So, we need some more cash. And as far as I know there are only two ways of obtaining cash: get a job or take it. Now which method do you think appeals to me?'

It was a question that did not require a reply.

He released the hold on her hands and lit a cigarette. She waited for him to continue.

'There's an off-licence on the Old Kent Road. Stays open late. Little gold mine, I reckon. Just run by an old Jewish geezer. We're going to do the place tonight. It'll be a pushover.'

Rachel's stomach squirmed violently; she felt all the food she had just consumed rise up into her gullet so that she could taste it at the back of her throat. For one horrible moment she thought she was going to be sick.

'You mean ... rob it?'

Casually, Harryboy blew a cloud of smoke over his shoulder. 'That's the idea, darling,' he said.

'I can't ...' was all she managed to say.

Harryboy smiled, but the eyes remained glacial. 'Oh, yes you can, angel. Yes you can. And what's more, you will. That's if you still want to have a pretty face in the morning.'

It was just after nine o'clock that evening when they drove slowly down the Old Kent Road past the off-licence. 'That's the place. Looks pretty quiet now,' Harryboy said. He pulled the car into a side street less than a hundred yards away from the shop and turned off the engine.

'Right, baby, as I explained, all I need is for you to be my lookout. I'll do all the hard work. Me and my little friend.' He pulled the gun from his jacket.

Rachel's blood ran cold at the sight of the weapon. 'You're not going to use that, are you?'

'Nah. Not unless I have to. This is just a frightener. You'd be surprised how persuasive you can be with one of these in your hand.' For a joke he pressed the muzzle of the gun to her forehead.

She pulled away sharply. 'Don't ... For God's sake ...'

He giggled. Harryboy loved his little games.

'Right. C'mon, let's do the business.'

In a trance-like state, Rachel followed Harryboy down the side street into the Old Kent Road towards the little off-licence. It was a cool dry night. A couple of pedestrians hurried past them, blurred shadows in the gloom.

'Right. Wait outside. Keep watch. If anyone comes, delay them comin' in.'

'How?'

'Ask 'em for a light or something. Use yer head. If you spot a copper, come in and let me know. I shouldn't be long.'

Pulling the collar of his coat up and tugging his hat down over his eyes, he went inside the shop.

Rachel found herself alone and terrified on the pavement. She had wanted excitement and drama in her life when she left Mumbles to come to London, but she hadn't expected this. To become involved in a crime. What would she be? An accessory to a robbery. And an armed robbery at that. In such a short time her life was spiralling out of control. She wanted to cry. She wanted to run away. But she knew she mustn't and indeed she knew that she wasn't capable of doing either.

She gazed at the door of the off-licence and wondered what was going on inside. What drama was being played out beyond that shabby entrance? She prayed that Harryboy didn't use the gun. He was so reckless, so hot headed; she knew in her heart that he wouldn't think twice about shooting someone.

The whole situation seemed so unreal. If only she could shut her eyes and in the darkness squeeze out this threatening reality, expunge it and wake up somewhere else. But she was too sensible to try. Her fear told her that this was her new reality.

Suddenly she heard footsteps approaching, clip-clopping in a regular beat along the pavement and her heart gave a jump. They were the steady, even footsteps of a man. She peered into the darkness as the footsteps grew nearer. Emerging from the gloom was a tall figure with a familiar silhouette.

It was a policeman.

For a brief moment Rachel thought she would faint on the spot. She felt all the breath leave her body. She knew she should warn Harryboy, but her feet were glued to the pavement. Before she could do anything, the policeman approached her.

'Evening miss,' he said, in a kindly fashion, touching his helmet in a gentle salute. 'Is everything all right?'

'Yes ... yes. Yes. I'm fine. I'm ... just waiting for a friend.'

The policeman nodded and smiled. 'As long as everything's all right ...'

'Yes, yes,' she nodded, her voice breathless and strained.

He seemed not to notice her unease. 'Good night, then.'

He was a young fellow with a neat moustache and a kindly face. He saluted her once more before moving on.

'Good night,' she said faintly, her voice almost giving up.

Thankfully, the policeman was soon swallowed up by the dark. For a brief while she could hear his footsteps and then even they faded away. She returned her gaze to the door of the off-licence. What on earth was going on in there? Why was Harryboy taking so much time?

She glanced up and down the pavement. No one was coming either way. On impulse she pushed open the door and stepped inside.

The interior was dimly lighted and smelt of alcohol and dampness. Harryboy was on the other side of the counter scooping money out of an ancient till. For a moment he froze and then pulled out the gun.

'What the fuck are you doing in here?'

'I was worried.'

'So you should be,' he said with a snarl slamming the till shut. 'There's bugger all in the till. I reckon there's less than ten quid.'

'Where's the man ... the shopkeeper?'

'Down here.' Harryboy glanced at his feet.

Rachel leaned over the counter and saw the inert form of a little grey-haired man. His gold-rimmed glasses were broken and blood was streaming from a wound on his forehead.

'He's not dead, is he?' she cried.

'Nah. He should be by rights. He was an awkward devil. I had to clout him with the butt of my gun to make him see sense.'

Harryboy gave the unconscious man a hearty kick.

'Come on, let's scarper,' he snarled. 'There's no point in hanging around here. What a waste of time.'

With great agility, he skipped over the counter and dragged Rachel out into the cold night air.

'We'll have to choose our target with more care next time. It's not worth all the effort for ten bleedin' quid,' he was saying as they walked briskly down the road away from the off-licence.

As they turned into the side road, they saw a figure standing by the car examining the number plate with his torch.

It was the policeman Rachel had seen earlier.

At the sound of their approach, he looked up and spotted them.

Again, he saluted. 'Hello, miss,' he said, evenly. 'I see you met your friend.' He nodded at Harryboy. 'Is this your car, sir?'

For a moment Harryboy seemed lost for words. Cogs in his mind whirred, considering the various options for his response.

'I've borrowed it from a pal,' he said at length. 'Nothing wrong, I trust, officer?'

The policeman did not reply, but shone his torch onto the number plate. 'This is a stolen vehicle, sir. And I have reason to believe it was involved in a crime some days ago. A murder, actually.'

Harryboy gave a strangled laugh. 'That's bloody ridiculous. There must be some mistake.' He retained the grin as he approached the policeman.

'Well, I'm sure we can sort it out at the police station, sir. I'm afraid I'm going to ask you to—'

The bullet caught him straight between the eyes. For a moment his spare six foot frame froze, just hanging suspended in the darkness and then dark froth gurgled from his mouth. With a short subdued groan, he fell neatly to the ground.

Rachel let out a scream. Harryboy smacked her across the face. 'Shut yer mouth, yer silly cow, and get into the car.'

'You've killed him. You've killed him,' she whimpered, as he flung open the passenger door and attempted to force her inside.

'Of course I've killed him. What else could I do? Get me down the police station and I'd never see the light of day again. Now get in!'

Rachel collapsed inside the car, her chest heaving with sobs.

Harryboy jumped in the driving seat and revved up the engine before turning the car round and then lurching off at speed. 'I gotta dump this motor now. It's too hot. That's another job for tomorrow,' he said matter-of-factly, as he turned into the Old Kent Road.

Rachel closed her eyes, her forehead resting against the cold glass of the side window, her world collapsing around her. In the darkness, she could see the dead face of the young policeman with the dark red, bloody third eye staring back at her accusingly.

Peter's attempt to reach London proved more difficult than he imagined it would be.

He had used most of his pocket money to pay for the bus fare to Exeter and so his plan was to sneak on to a train to London and hide from the ticket collector in the lavatory. At Exeter station, he checked on the train times. He was in luck: the next London train was in thirty minutes. He bought a cup of tea and a small packet of rich tea biscuits in the buffet bar and then sat at a little table nervously, not daring to look around him in case someone asked him what he was doing there, why he wasn't at school and why he had treated Mr and Mrs Booth so badly by running away. At last the tannoy announced that the passenger train for Euston was ready for boarding and would depart from Platform 3 in ten minutes. He gulped down the last of his tea and bought a platform ticket before making his way towards Platform 3. His heart sank as he saw that there were two men in railway uniforms checking the tickets before passengers were allowed down on to the platform.

He had to think fast. He really didn't want to miss this train. He wasn't sure how long it would be before Mrs Booth realized that he had done a bunk and got the police looking out for him. The thought of being dragged back to the village and having to go to that school again filled him with dread.

He must catch this train.

But how?

What would the great comic book hero Tiger Blake do in this situation? Well, he would probably just shoot his way onto the train and make the driver take him to London at gun point, but, really, if he had to go under cover and not be discovered, he'd have to do something more subtle.

A minute later with a rough strategy sketched out in his head, Peter approached the two railway men. The older of the two, a ruddy faced, bewhiskered fellow whose nose bore witness to his fondness for alcohol looked down at him with a smile.

'Don't tell me you're travelling on your own, sonny?' he said with a smile.

Peter shook his head. 'With my mum and dad,' he said quietly but with some confidence.

The man looked over Peter's shoulder as though he expected these phantom parents to be close at hand.

'Where are they then?'

Peter shifted awkwardly. 'They went ahead of me. I've just been to get something to eat.' He held up the packet of rich tea biscuits as evidence. 'They're in Coach C,' he added hurriedly.

'Are they now,' said the railway man, the smile fading. 'And where's your ticket then?'

'They've got it.'

'Have they now?'

The other ticket inspector, a thin wiry fellow with a bald head, gave a sneering laugh and turned away with a bored expression on his face.

'Yes,' said Peter. 'Please let me through. They'll be expecting me.'

The ruddy-faced inspector shook his head. 'Can't do that sonny. I'd lose my job if I let you through without a ticket.'

'But my mum and dad are waiting,' he said, his face crumpling with despair.

The inspector laughed. 'Here Bert, we got a proper Donald Wolfit here. Tears an' all.'

Bert just grinned in a bored fashion.

The inspector bent down until his rubicund face was on a level with Peter's. 'Look, my lad, I wasn't born yesterday. I know your parents are not on the train. And you know your parents are not on the train. You're not the first one to try and pull this little trick for a free train ride.'

'But it's true,' cried Peter, his heart sinking as he realized his plan was not going to work.

The smile on the man's face had faded altogether now. 'Why don't you run along, sonny, before I fetch a policeman to you?'

Peter gritted his teeth with frustration. He couldn't let this old fool get the better of him. And he had to catch that train.

'Look,' he said suddenly with great excitement, his arm shooting out directing the attention of both men down the platform. 'There's my dad now.'

As both men gazed down into the gloom of the platform, Peter slipped past them, heading, as fast as his legs would carry him, towards the train. It took a few seconds before the two porters realized what had happened. With a cry of, 'Hey, stop. Stop that boy!' the red-faced porter hared off in pursuit, while Bert, the wiry, bald-headed fellow, leaned indolently on the barrier and chuckled. It was no skin off his nose, he thought. If the little blighter wanted a free train ride, let him have it. It was hardly a capital offence. Let old Dennis blow a gasket trying to catch the kid. Much good it would do him. He fumbled in his pocket for his packet of cigarettes. Might as well have a smoke while he waited.

Meanwhile red-faced Dennis, whose visage was even more rubicund now with his exertions, was catching up on the boy, as he dodged in and out of the unsuspecting passengers. Peter cast a glance back and saw to his horror the inspector close behind him. He put on an extra spurt to reach the end carriage and clamber aboard.

'Bugger!' snarled Dennis, aware that it would be far more difficult to catch the little bastard now he was actually on the train. Why had this to happen on his shift? With a weary sigh he hauled himself up the steps and into the carriage. The corridor was empty apart from a young soldier who was leaning out of the window, his hand casually holding a cigarette as though he was watching the smoke rise gently towards the station roof.

'You seen a boy in a raincoat come down here?' Dennis asked brusquely, disturbing the young man's reverie

'Went down there,' he said casually, nodding his head towards the next carriage.

Mopping his brow, Dennis squeezed past him and carried on to the next carriage. He now realized he had a monumental task. The corridor was heaving with passengers. By the door a large man in a smart three-piece tweed suit was having great difficulty hauling a trunk on board. On seeing Dennis his eyes lit up. 'Just the fellow!' he cried, in what Dennis thought of as a posh accent. 'Help me get this brute stowed away, old chap.'

'I'm sorry, sir, I can't just now. You see I'm—'

The posh man was having none of it. 'You're a bloody porter, aren't you?' he snapped, his face suddenly clouding with anger.

'No, sir, I'm a ticket—'

'Then do some bloody portering,' the man cried, ignoring Dennis's attempt to explain his rank.

'Did you see a young boy go past here?'

The posh man gazed at Dennis as though he were mad. 'I saw a bloody large trunk that I can't move on my own. That's what I saw. Now get hold of that strap and stop prevaricating.'

With a sigh of resignation, Dennis bent down and grabbed hold of the strap ready to haul the trunk into one of the compartments. He knew that there was no chance of catching the boy now. There were ten other carriages; he could be hiding in any one of them. And the train was due to leave in about five minutes. He hated to admit it, but the little blighter had got the better of him.

As he helped to manoeuvre the trunk into the compartment, he felt a sudden twinge in his back. Oh, no, he thought. The old trouble. He stood up awkwardly, biting his lip to avoid crying out with pain. That would serve him right, chasing after young lads. He needed to take a page out of Bert's book. He noticed that he'd done bugger all. He'd probably be back at the barrier, all calm, cool and collected, having a smoke with a big dopey grin on his face.

'Thanks for your help, old boy,' said the posh man in the smart tweed suit, after the trunk was safely stowed. He held out a three-penny bit. 'That's for your trouble.'

Dennis looked down at the coin disdainfully. He was about to say something derogatory, but, as he straightened himself up, he suffered another spasm of pain which effectively silenced him.

In the first carriage the young soldier took a final drag on his cigarette before letting it fall out of the window to land on the edge of the platform. Strangely the sight of it satisfied him and he stared at the tab end for a moment still glowing with life. Then he moved into the adjacent compartment which was empty apart from his greatcoat which was piled in the corner opposite the window.

Closing the door to the apartment, the soldier addressed the coat, a smile playing about his lips. 'I think we've managed to lose your friend, but I reckon you'd better stay there until the train sets off.'

The coat moved slightly, but Peter knew better than to show his face until he heard the guard's whistle.

NINE

The night Harryboy shot and killed the policeman, he had sex with Rachel again. It was hard, fast and brutal. There was no sense of tenderness, affection or consideration on his part. It certainly could not be regarded as love-making. He was just satisfying some dark feral appetite. It was as though he was on some drug-induced high, a state stimulated by his killing of the young policeman. The murder and the power that it suggested to Harryboy's mind inflamed his libido. To complete his own twisted image of himself as master of the world, this fevered bout of sexual self gratification was the sealing dominant act.

Rachel lay there in the dark, terrified and traumatized, fighting back her tears, as he pounded into her. Tonight she learned that she was not a person to him at all, just a convenient object. His passion – if one could call it that – was purely an exercise in self-pleasure. It could have been anyone or anything that lay beneath him, as long as he was in control and he reached his climax.

He did so with a hoarse cry of triumph, sweat rolling down his face, eyes aflame in manic euphoria. Once his fury and passion were spent, he rolled over without a word and within minutes was grunting in a dreamless, contented sleep.

Rachel remained lying on her back, unable to move, tears now rolling down her cheeks, sick to her heart at the pain and indignity of her violation. The man was an animal and a murderer and, God help her, she was his. She was his to do with as he wanted. She brought her fist to her mouth to stifle the sob that was festering deep inside her. For the first time in her short life she wished that she was dead. What she would give to be in her own cramped little bed at her mum and dad's back to back in Wales. But now the milk had been spilt and no matter how many tears she shed, they were to no avail.

Sleep evaded her for several hours. She lay staring at the cracked ceiling, trying not to think of the man who lay at her side, breathing heavily in untroubled slumber. Eventually, tiredness overcame her, overcame her misery and fears, and she slipped into the dark refuge of sleep.

When she awoke, daylight was streaming into the room and the space beside her in the bed was empty. For one moment, one precious moment, as she dragged herself from protective slumbers, with her mind not fully functioning, Harryboy's absence brought her a sense of relief and almost joy. Had he really gone? Had he really left her? Was she really free? However, these half-formed drowsy thoughts lasted for a few seconds only until Harryboy's voice broke into her brief reverie.

'Mornin', sleepin' beauty. I wondered when you were going to join the land of the living.' He was over by the washstand stripped to the waist shaving, white lather masking the lower half of his face like a hoodlum Father Christmas. He gave her a wink and turned back to the shaving mirror.

That phrase of his, 'The land of the living' echoed in Rachel's mind and again she witnessed the shooting of the kind young policeman. The scene flashed before her like a movie: she heard the gunshot, she saw the open mouth frothing with blood and the neat crimson crater in the pale flesh of the forehead. She ached at the thought of it and tears moistened her eyes once more.

'C'mon, Rach. Rise and shine, we've a lotta work to do today and I reckon we'd better leave this dump and get ourselves some-where else to stay. Best to keep on the move. Never stay too long in one place, that's my motto. So get your face on and pack your bag. OK?'

He was businesslike and chirpy, showing no signs of concern, worry or remorse – no signs that he had actually killed a man the night before. The event had been wiped from his memory and it had certainly never reached his conscience. Rachel now believed that he didn't possess one.

'OK, Harryboy,' Rachel replied, in the manner of an obedient child who had just been told to eat up her greens or she'd be sent to bed early. Like a robot she got out of bed and slipped on her under-clothes.

'Good girl. First thing we do is grab ourselves a good breakfast and then we have a new gaff to find and then ...' – he rubbed his finger and thumb dramatically before his face – 'more moolah.'

With effort, she affected a smile and began to pack her bag.

Within the hour they had left the hotel. Harryboy had engineered it so that they slipped out down the fire escape to avoid paying the bill. 'Might as well save as much money as we can,' he grinned. 'Anyway, the place is a rat hole.' Having now abandoned the car because 'it was too hot', they wandered down Shaftsbury Avenue for a while until Harryboy spied another small hotel. 'This'll do for a few nights,' he said dragging Rachel through the swing door.

Later they went into Soho in search of breakfast. An emaciated autumn sun broke through the thin clouds from time to time dusting the wounded city in a pale, melancholy amber light. The sunshine, feeble though it was, seemed to emphasize the damage and decay that the bombing had brought to the streets. This depressed Rachel even more and once again she thought of the comparatively untainted contours of her home town, the fresh cool Welsh wind and the green undulating hills. Why had she entertained the idea that London, this dusty crumbling, noisy heap of smoke-stained buildings was glamorous and would offer her a more exciting and happier life? She had been so wrong.

By contrast, Harryboy, on his own patch, felt perfectly at home and at ease. He saw the rubble, the dust, the bomb-crippled buildings, but they meant nothing to him. They did not impinge for one moment on his feelings and did not affect his happiness in any way. In essence, they had nothing to do with him. In fact, to Harryboy, nothing had anything to do with him, but himself. He was the only one that mattered and always would be. That was the way you survived and he intended to survive come what may.

Eventually they found their way down Dean Street and discovered Benny's café.

'This'll do,' Harryboy sniffed, pushing Rachel through the door. They grabbed a table by the window. He ordered the 'Airman's Special' while Rachel just asked for toast and coffee. Benny in his usual friendly manner served them with a smile, trying to persuade 'the pretty young lady' to have something more substantial than toast. 'Warm bread alone will not set you up for the day, miss,' he cooed. Rachel was touched by his kindness but assured him that toast would be fine. Harryboy ignored the little café owner, retreating behind his newspaper.

When Benny left them, Harryboy folded the paper over and passed it to Rachel pointing out the late news column. There was the report of the shooting: *Constable Alan Reece, 29, was shot on Calder Street, just off the Old Kent Road at around ten o'clock last night. His body was discovered by a young couple, Peter Dawson and his girlfriend Avril Watts on their way home from the cinema. Reece leaves a widow and two children aged four and seven. The police are following up leads and hope to make an arrest in the next few days.*

'What does it mean … *the police are following up leads?*' she asked, a note of panic in her voice.

Harryboy leered at her. 'Ah, they always say that. They don't want the public to know they ain't got a clue. There are no leads and they certainly will be no arrest.' He chuckled. 'Don't wet yer knickers, angel. We're as safe as houses.'

A horrible thought suddenly struck Rachel. So horrible that her blood ran cold. What had the policeman said about the car being stolen … and involved in a murder? 'You've done this before, haven't you?' she said evenly. 'You've killed someone before.'

Her deadly seriousness seemed to amuse Harryboy and he grinned broadly. 'Might have,' he said at length, stroking his chin. 'Might have.' And then he winked at her. 'Practice makes perfect.' He chuckled like a gurgling drain.

Rachel felt a tightening across her chest and her mouth went dry. She couldn't speak and if she could she wouldn't have known what to say. Now she knew. She really knew. The man she was with was a callous, heartless killer who didn't think twice before snuffing out someone's life. How many people had he killed? Two, three, more? Oh, God, numbers didn't matter now.

Across the room behind the counter Benny was drying some plates, but he couldn't help watching the young woman sitting with the rather unpleasant pug-faced man. She was so pretty and yet she looked as though she had all the troubles of the world on her shoulders. The man didn't seem to care. He showed no concern for her. In fact he seemed to be grinning all the time. There was something harsh, even repulsive about his demeanour. Perhaps, thought Benny, he's the reason she's sad. When the man left the table to go to the lavatory, Benny went over to clear the table.

'You all right, my dear?' he said gently, as he placed the mugs and plates on his tray.

She seemed surprised that he had spoken to her at first and then she nodded vigorously. 'Sure,' she said in a quiet voice without much conviction.

'I hope so,' said Benny kindly, knowing it wasn't true. He felt sad that someone so young should be so unhappy.

Rachel forced a smile in an attempt to reassure the kind stranger, hoping that he would leave her to her own thoughts.

Benny gave a brief nod and went about his business.

Moments later, Harryboy returned. He slipped Rachel a ten shilling note. 'Here you are. Take yourself off to the pictures or something. I got a little business to attend to this afternoon. I'll see you back at the hotel about six. You be there!'

'What ... sort of business?'

He clicked his tongue and adjusted the brim of his hat. 'Nothing that you need worry your little head about, angel,' he said with a leer and then left.

Harryboy's departure did not lighten Rachel's spirits. She had thought of fleeing in the night, but it was hopeless. What were a few hours of false freedom? There was nothing she could do in this lonely, alien city to resolve her plight. She knew that she would obey orders and return to the hotel at the appointed hour. She feared what might happen if she did not. Harryboy would seek her out and then ... She shuddered to think of the consequences. She sighed deeply. It was pointless to struggle or plan. In her heart she knew that there was no escape.

TEN

Whoever had come up with the phrase 'looking for a needle in a haystack' got my vote. How on earth was I to find the killer of Walter Riley in a city of several million people? London was a very dense haystack indeed. To make matters worse, it was apparently a random killing, a snatch and grab affair. I had no clues, no leads and no suspects. Just what a private investigator loves! I should have returned the brown envelope with the fifty pounds in cash to Mrs Riley and told her to put her faith in the efficiency of the police force. But a mixture of guilt – at not being able to prevent Walter's death – and greed had prevented me. Now I was stuck with a seemingly impossible task. Yes, I could still return the money, I supposed, but I'd already made a few inroads into the stash. Well, a man's got to eat and drink and I'd been able to emerge from the shop with the three brass balls reunited with my thick winter overcoat. Once again I could walk the streets without hugging myself for warmth. Nevertheless, spending some of the money without actually doing any detective work only increased my sense of guilt.

As usual, when I was down a one way alley facing a brick wall, I called on the help of my old Scotland Yard buddy, Inspector David Llewellyn. I arranged to meet him for an early evening drink at his favourite watering hole, the Guardsman public house, a short truncheon's throw from the Yard. I'd explained my dilemma to him over the telephone. I hoped that his down to earth, common sense approach to life might help me to find the end of this mysterious tangled skein. I listened stoically to his barrage of sarcastic comments. There were the usual supposedly humorous taunts on the lines of 'call yourself a bloody detective' and 'has Mr Sherlock Holmes run out of steam at last?' It was a kind of routine we had, or to be more precise, he had. It amused him to abuse me in this fashion. I knew that after the banter he would do his best to help me, although he assured me that on this occasion his best was not likely to be very useful. After all two men looking for a needle in a haystack doesn't really improve the odds that much. This did little to lift my spirits.

I was just about to leave the office when Susan McAndrew called. She wanted to know if I'd had any news of Peter. I felt a pang of guilt as I told her I hadn't. It was not that I had forgotten about the boy or that I didn't care about him, but I had deliberately put the problem to the back – way back – of my mind. I had reasoned there was little I could do about the situation until I had more information. Well, that's what I'd tried to convince myself was the case. Perhaps it was because I couldn't face the reality of the situation. I'd been happy in the knowledge that Peter was away from the dangers of London, breathing in the fresh untainted air of Devon, living in a caring household and settled at last. Now I knew different and it pained me.

I assured Susan that if Peter attempted to get in touch with me, I'd let her know straight away. Even as I spoke the words, I wasn't sure that they were true. For all her kindness and concern, Nurse McAndrew represented officialdom. As soon as Peter was in her care again, the authorities would step in. It would either mean a return to Devon or – the nightmare loomed before me – the orphanage.

As I put down the receiver, I realized I was sweating. Even the thought of an orphanage churned me up inside. These places had been part of my life. I still bore the scars and I wouldn't wish one on my worst enemy, let alone little Peter.

I mopped my brow. God, did I need a drink.

It was already dark when I entered the pub to be met by a warm wall of smoke and noisy chatter. No matter what horrors the war threw at Londoners, they never failed to be cheerful in a pub. There was laughter, giggling women and somewhere a tinkling piano was thumping out a popular melody, creating the impression that all was right with the world. And to some extent after a few drinks in the cosy, fuggy atmosphere you could almost kid yourself that it was.

I wandered over to the corner of the long counter in the saloon bar, hitched myself up on a stool and ordered two pints. I knew

David wouldn't be long: he could smell a freshly pulled pint from a mile off.

I had just taken my first gulp of ale, hoping the alcohol would either raise my spirits or bring on a bout of amnesia, when I felt a firm hand on my shoulder.

'Nice coat. Coming up in the world, are we?'

It was David. I'd recognize those dark, lilting Welsh tones anywhere.

'It's just out of hock,' I said.

David hopped on the stool beside me and smiled. 'As I said, coming up in the world.' He glanced at the full pint standing on the counter and expanded his grin. 'Mine, I take it.'

'Yours. You take it.'

'Good man.' And without further comment he raised the glass and downed at least a third of it in one long swallow.

He was a broad-shouldered, thickset man, getting broader now that he'd hit his mid-thirties, with a thinning mop of curly blond hair and a broken nose, a trophy of some youthful rugby match. There was a lively intelligence in those pale-blue eyes that illuminated his rather craggy countenance.

'Did I need that,' he said, plonking the glass down. 'It's been a hell of a day.'

'You and me both.'

Suddenly David's features darkened and he looked decidedly glum. 'I reckon I might win this contest.'

'Oh,' I said, surprised at his sudden change of mood. 'What's happened?'

He took another deep swallow of beer before answering. 'It's always worse when you lose one of your own. One of our lads got shot last night. Alan Reece. Young chap with a wife and kiddies.'

'You certainly have won the contest,' I said quietly. 'How did it happen?'

'We're not sure. He was found late last night by a young courting couple just off the Old Kent Road. Shot through the head.'

Suddenly I felt more guilt heaped upon me. How could I be feeling sorry for myself?

We both lapsed into silence for a while. David finished off his pint and ordered another round from the crusty old barman. 'Still,' he said, slipping the damp change into his pocket, 'we have a pretty good idea who did it and it might be the villain you're after, too.'

'You're joking,' I said, although it was perfectly obvious he wasn't. 'You'd better put me in the picture.'

'About a week ago a young bruiser called Harry Jenkins, known to his intimates as Harryboy, went AWOL from an army camp in Kent. He took with him a revolver and enough ammo to kill a regiment. In his flight he stole a car, killing the owner, a local vicar, in the process. We reckon that Harryboy made his way up to London to lose himself here.'

David pulled a small snapshot from his pocket and passed it to me. 'That's the bastard. It's an old picture I'm afraid, but it's the best we've got,' he said, grimly.

The snap was blurred and grainy and the face that stared back at me was fairly indistinct, but what caught my attention were the man's eyes. They were dark, unemotional and cruel. One could easily believe that this was the face of a killer. I passed the photograph back.

'So you think he's here in London.'

'Let's face it: the city is full of bloody deserters. They're swarming about the place like rats in a sewer. Well, it turns out that the bullet that killed the car owner, the unfortunate vicar, matches exactly the one we took out of poor Alan Reece's head today. The same gun killed both men. Not only that but we found a car registration number in Reece's note book which—'

'—is the same as the stolen car.'

'Yes.'

'Was this car a Wolseley?'

David nodded.

'That was the make of the car used by Walter Riley's killer.'

'So you said. You are sure about that?'

'As sure as I can be. It was dark and I'm not the world's best car spotter.'

'Well, I've asked them at the Yard to check the bullet that killed your *lady* friend, Mr Walter Riley to see if it matches the other two. We'll find out tomorrow.'

I screwed my face up. 'It's a long shot. There are lots of black Wolseleys around.'

'Not driven by brutal killers, though.'

'You have a point. What do you know about this Harry Jenkins?'

David screwed up his face. 'Not much. Bit of a wrong 'un from the start it would seem. Truant at school. Tried to set fire to the gym. Drowned the neighbour's cat for a bet. Several minor offences as a teenager. The usual stuff. And then he joined up in '40.'

'And now he's on the loose.'

'And now he's on the loose ... with a gun.'

And after that we ran out of conversation. Two old friends, frustrated and tired by the evil in the world and unable to shrug off our innate conviction that it was part of our duty, our *raison d'être*, to do something about it.

David stared at the dregs of his second pint and sighed. 'You know, boyo, I don't fancy another. I think I've had enough stimulation for one day.' He slipped off the stool and patted me on the shoulder. He forced a grin. 'It is a very nice coat,' he said but the humour was not there in the voice. 'I'll be in touch when I get the report back on the bullet.'

'Thanks,' I said, realizing that that was the last concern on his mind. I knew he was thinking of Alan Reece's widow and children and the unfairness of life.

He left me to the cheery, noisy warmth of the saloon bar which somehow had lost its escapist charm. For some moments I sat in a brown study and then I downed the last of my beer and left. I contemplated moving on to The Velvet Cage but somehow tonight I wanted hearth and home, however humble they might be – and they were very humble. I knew I could muster a Spam and mustard sandwich and a glass of Scotch. That would do me before an early night and the blessed oblivion of sleep.

ELEVEN

Harryboy Jenkins liked to think that he did not have a sentimental bone in his body. He was too self-obsessed and too concerned with his own welfare for such a weakness. Nevertheless he did have one emotional itch that he needed to scratch. He would die rather than admit it to anyone, indeed he tried to deny it to himself, but in quiet moments the desire, the want, returned and taunted him. It was a need that had to be satisfied. He only admitted it, accepted it, by downgrading this feeling to the status of a whim, a slight fancy. That fitted in nicely with his view of life. He enjoyed indulging himself in this fashion. He told himself, for example, that it had been a whim that had prompted him to approach the young tart in the milk bar a couple of days before. He had seen her, was attracted to her and thought it would be fun to take her to bed and now here he was shacked up with the girl, allowing his sexual appetite full rein for the first time in months.

Now he was following another whim. Or so he tried to convince himself. But in reality it was something more serious, more deeply rooted than a fickle fancy.

After leaving Rachel in Benny's café, he had gone off to fulfil this need that was gnawing away inside him. He had lied to her about having some business to attend to. There was no business – just something he wanted to do. If he had been more of a man, he would have accepted that it was in fact something he *had* to do.

He walked to Charing Cross Road where he hailed a taxi which took him to Pimlico. As he neared his destination, Harryboy sat forward in the cab staring out of the window, gazing at the familiar dull buildings and streets of his childhood. They swept by him in a nostalgic panorama, those grey shabby edifices and dreary thoroughfares. But then there came a gradual change. Streets littered with rubble and the skeletal remains of houses stark against the blue sky. Casualties of the blitz! For a brief moment a pang of fear seized him but with a heavy shrug he blotted out the emotion.

As he had requested, the taxi driver dropped him outside the Malt Shovel pub, a great three storey monster occupying a corner site of Belgrave Road and Charlwood Street. It was like an island in an area of derelict and deserted houses, boarded-up ghosts that were decaying quietly. Some had suffered bomb damage, but mainly they had been abandoned by families who couldn't put up with their bellying walls and crumbling conditions any more.

'You'll have to wait a couple of hours before they open,' observed the cab driver nodding at the pub as he collected his fare.

Harryboy made no comment. He stood on the pavement and waited for the cab to depart. The street was eerily quiet. The only movement was a discarded newspaper that rippled and shifted its way along the gutter as the breeze caught its faded pages. Harryboy gazed at the dark, blank windows of the pub as the phantom noises of raucous drinkers and a badly played piano filled his ears. It was in the Malt Shovel that he'd had his first drink – an illicit pint, of course. He'd only been about thirteen. He remembered the moment with crystal clarity. He saw the dark ale slopping over the sides of the glass as it was handed to him. Handed to him by a fellow with black curly hair, a freckled face and a broad gap-toothed grin. Handed to him by his brother.

Harryboy felt his first ache. It was real and physical. His bowels stirred and he gasped for air.

His brother. Jack.

There he was: white collarless shirt, sleeves rolled up to the elbows, scruffy black trousers held up by a broad brown leather belt, his curly locks falling across his forehead. Leaning easily on the bar, he raised his pint in a toast to Harryboy, his smile almost splitting his face in two. 'The first of many, eh?' he'd said before taking a large gulp from his own glass so ferociously that dark drops of beer spattered down on to the front of his shirt leaving beige teardrop stains there.

Jack.

The sound of his brother's laughter echoed in Harryboy's ears. He snarled an obscenity under his breath. He didn't want to feel this.

This was not the man he was. This sort of stuff was for tarts. He gritted his teeth, fighting back the emotion that was welling up within him. Why the hell had he come here?

A gaunt old man walking a greyhound passed by and cast Harryboy a casual glance. He wasn't used to seeing someone so smartly dressed or fresh faced in his neck of the woods. He was about to say, 'Good morning', but the young man with the sour face turned away. The old man spat in the gutter and carried on walking.

Harryboy stood for a moment staring into space and then he moved off. Now he was here, in Pimlico, he might as well go and have a look. Then it would be over. Then he could let it lie. It would be a kind of exorcism. A five-minute walk brought him close. With each step he felt his heart constricting as though a hand was gently squeezing it. He had never experienced anything quite like this before and he hated it. It was a weakness. He was behaving like a bloody emotional schoolgirl. But, however much he hated himself, he could not stop and turn around. Something propelled him forward. He knew he had to go on. The compulsion was too great.

In keeping with his mood, the sky had clouded over, shadowing the area, blocking out the pale sunlight. It seemed as though he was walking in a monochrome landscape. He passed the large area of waste ground where he'd played as a kid. There were still the remnants of the old hut that he and his mates had used as a den and the stream of water running like a shiny silver finger across the scrubland, emanating from the large concrete drainage pipe, the gaping mouth of which emerged like an alien spaceship out of the dusty earth. The aperture was covered in wire meshing, but the kids knew how to get past that to make this watery cave part of their playground. In the echoey dark, down deep in the pipe was where he had his hideout when they had been playing cowboys. Harryboy had always been the baddie – by choice. He had hidden deep down in the manmade tunnel where none of the other lads dared venture.

Leaving the waste ground behind he came upon an enclave of narrow streets: terraces of red-brick houses cheek by jowl with other identical red-brick houses. Victorian hutches for the workers. The dry, warm hand increased its firm hold on his heart. At the end of Waterloo Street, he stopped and gazed down the dusty thoroughfare, across the cobblestones, and down past Aspinall's General Store, which was still there apparently untouched by time. It was here where he'd bought many a halfpenny liquorice and bags of gobstoppers. Then his eyes finally rested upon number seven. Number seven, Waterloo Street.

His home.

The home he hadn't seen for five years.

It looked much the same as it had done, but then so did all the other houses in the street. They had been frozen in time like in some fading sepia photograph. There was a large rug hanging over the washing line in the tiny front garden. The colours were dull and it looked threadbare in places, but he recognized it as the one that used to be in the parlour.

For over half an hour, he stood, staring as though mesmerized at the street, the house, the garden, the faded rug, the straggly privet hedge, the paint peeling off the front door. He felt strange, invisible even, as though he had entered some time machine and was visiting the past. No one could see him. He was an alien from the future.

In the distance he could hear the goods trains, like clanking ghosts on the morning air. Once more his stomach lurched as forbidden memories forced their way into his consciousness.

A little lad in baggy short trousers and a Fair Isle jumper emerged from one of the houses, ran across the cobbles and went into the shop. He came out a few minutes later carrying a couple of bulging brown paper bags and scooted back home. Doing an errand for his mother, thought Harryboy with a smirk, probably got whatever he bought on tick. That was the trick. Don't go yourself. Send your little boy to get sympathy from Fred Aspinall. The old softy couldn't refuse an urchin with a note requesting some food. That little boy could have been him.

Suddenly emboldened, Harryboy left his lookout point at the end of the street and walked slowly until he stood outside Aspinall's. You used to be able to buy anything here from a galvanized bucket to a box of matches and from the tatty eclectic window display it seemed you still could. Without further thought, Harryboy found himself entering the shop. A little metal bell tinkled above the door as he did so. Even the bell was the same.

A grey-haired man dressed in a brown smock was leaning over the counter reading a newspaper, his finger following the lines of print. 'Morning,' he said lazily, not glancing up from the sports pages. It was old Fred Aspinall himself, still here and not looking much different from the days when Harryboy scampered in wearing short trousers with a note from his mother. When the shopkeeper prised his gaze away from the paper and viewed his customer he seemed surprised. Not only was this an adult but a stranger, someone new to his premises. It was clear to Harryboy that old Aspinall didn't recognize him. He was very glad of that.

'What can I do for you, sir?' asked the shopkeeper in a faintly obsequious tone.

'Packet of Players and a box of matches,' said the young man without a smile.

'Certainly, sir.'

Aspinall ducked down below the counter and retrieved the cigarettes and took the matches from a shelf behind him. 'Anything else, sir?'

'Nah.'

Aspinall's friendly demeanour frosted a little. There was something unpleasant, rude even, in this young man's attitude. He was dismissive of his courteous and attentive service. Aspinall looked closely at the pugnacious face, the cold eyes and the thick lips that seemed to be set in a constant leer. There was something familiar about them, that and the arrogant stance of the fellow. He reached down the dark corridors of his memory but failed to come up with anything. He sighed. His memory, like every part of him, was not what it was.

'That'll be one shilling and tuppence.'

The man picked up his purchases and threw some coins on to the counter while he gazed around as though he was sizing up the premises for some purpose.

Suddenly Aspinall wanted this creature out of his shop. He certainly had no desire to cultivate his custom. The fellow gave off a very unsettling aura. Without a word he picked up the money, opened the till and extracted the correct change, placing it on the counter.

Harryboy was oblivious to Aspinall's change of attitude. He was just drinking in the sights and smell of the old shop, recapturing his childhood, that golden time before things turned nasty and life became an unfair battle. Suddenly he realized that the old shopkeeper was staring at him. Was he starting to remember? It had been a stupid risk to come in the shop in the first place. What if there had been another customer who *did* recognize him? It was time he was out of here. Snatching up his change, he turned on his heel and left.

As the door clanged shut, old Fred Aspinall gave a sigh of relief. He hoped he never saw the young man again. 'There was something quite unpleasant about him,' he muttered to himself, before returning to his newspaper.

Once outside Harryboy made his way back to his lookout post at the end of the street. He didn't want to get any nearer to his old home. He began to think that he should curtail this expedition now. He wasn't quite sure why he had succumbed to the urge to come out here in the first place. He hadn't given it much thought in the five years he'd been away. Maybe it was his way of making a kind of formal goodbye to his old self, an attempt to acknowledge that a chapter of his life was now well and truly closed. He was severing the link. His departure had been unsatisfactory – untidy – to say the least. He knew that he would never be able to meet his mother or brother again but being close to the old house, to *his* old house, helped him to put the final bold full stop to that particular paragraph of his biography.

He was just about to leave when he saw someone emerge from number seven Waterloo Street. It was a slight figure in a floral patterned wraparound apron, with wispy hair pulled back in a bun.

It was his mother.

Harryboy felt his throat constrict and his eyes prickle with tears. His mother.

She was carrying a cane carpet beater and she set about thrashing the faded rug on the line. A fine spray of dust exploded into the air, causing her to stand back momentarily and cover her mouth, before attacking the rug once more. Harryboy stared mesmerized by this little woman as she beat the decrepit rug with a determination that he remembered of old. He was too far away to see her face clearly, to see how time and hardship had treated her fair skin and gentle features but her shoulders were bowed now and there was a stiff awkwardness with her movements which suggested the onset of old age.

After a while she sat on the garden wall to catch her breath, staring at the old rug. Here was his chance. He could just walk up the street and greet her. 'Hello, Mum, it's me, Harryboy,' he could say. How would she react? Would she burst into tears and throw her arms around him or try to smack him across the face with the carpet beater? He'd never find out because he wasn't going to do it. That was not part of his plan and however tempting it was, he knew it was not an option. It would be madness. He wasn't the prodigal son. He was a deserter and a murderer on top of his other crimes to the family. Bad pennies remain unwelcome.

Harryboy had had enough. He'd done what he'd set out to do. More, in fact. Now it was time to get back to London and get on with his new life. Then as he made to go, he saw something that stopped him in his tracks, the fist squeezing his heart so tight that he could hardly breathe.

Turning into the street from across the road was a man in a wheelchair. Oblivious of Harryboy, he skimmed along the uneven pavement at a fast pace and although he held his head down, Harryboy had no difficulty in recognizing him. The prominent nose and the wild corkscrew hair were unmistakable.

It was Jack.

His brother.

On instinct, he almost called out his name, but the word didn't come. His throat had seized up.

On the faint cool breeze came the train sounds once more and there he was, his thirteen-year-old self again. Running, running as hard as he could, his chest aching with the exertion. His legs aching as his scuffed red sandals pounded the pavement.

Running.

Running away.

He'd been found out and he was trying to escape. He'd been caught red-handed.

Stealing.

He thought his chest would burst open but he couldn't stop. He mustn't be caught. He turned his head. Yes, there he was, still on his tail, still determined to catch him and make him pay.

He'd stolen from his mother's purse. He'd been doing it for weeks. But they'd laid a trap for him – his mother and his brother. They'd caught him in the act. There could be no excuses, no prevarications. They had seen him take the money. And so he did what he always did when faced with an unpleasant truth: he ran. He pushed his mother to the ground and raced through the door and down the street. But Jack was after him and Jack would show him no mercy when he caught up with him.

He scrambled up the wall of the railway sidings thinking that if he could get down the other side he might well lose Jack in among the many wagons stationed there in an apparently higgedly-piggedly fashion. His shoes slipped and slithered as he hauled himself up, his fingers bleeding as he scuffed them on the crumbling brickwork. As he reached the summit Jack bounded up and scaled the wall, it seemed, in one go. He sat astride the top facing Harryboy and grabbed hold of his jumper.

'Come on, lad,' he bellowed. 'You're coming home to face the music.'

Suddenly Harryboy exploded with anger. His frustration at being apprehended like this possessed him with a wild fury and he lashed out at his brother. With great ferocity he pushed him. Jack hadn't expected this. He wasn't prepared for the strength or the swiftness of the action. Immediately, he lost his balance and toppled over the wall.

As he landed, his legs sprawling across one of the railway tracks, he lost consciousness. Harryboy gazed in shock and horror – all anger now dissipated – as a little shunting engine juddered its way along the track, the driver oblivious of the obstacle on the line.

Harryboy's scream merged with the high-pitched whistle of the engine.

The wheelchair creaked and rumbled its way down the street until it reached the house. His mother had seen Jack and she came to the gate to greet him. She bent over the wheelchair and threw her arms around him and gave him a hug.

Harryboy shook as with a fever, his body drenched with sweat. His stomach churned violently and for a moment he thought he was going to be sick. He made the gagging sound of a strangled man. Why the hell had he come back here a voice screamed in his head? He cursed himself for being so stupid. Tears blurred his view of his mother pushing Jack up the path and down the side of the house. He retched and gasped for air, leaning on the wall for support. And then, suddenly, panic engulfed him and he turned and fled. Like he always did; he ran away. He ran wildly, desperately, in a frantic attempt not only to leave the area but also this part of his life. He wanted to amputate it, rip it out of his consciousness and consign it to some furnace where it would be consumed by the flames. It was the only thing that he had no control over. No bullying, no force or threats with a gun could eradicate the past and the damaging effect it had on his mind.

He ran along the pavement, across cobbled streets, his legs hardly obeying him as he tried to make his way back the way he came. More than once he stumbled, almost crashing down onto the ground. He could hardly see now, his eyesight bleary with tears. Soon, he found himself on the waste ground where he had roamed as a kid, the terrain shifting and undulating uneasily before him as though he was seasick. He felt like stopping, gaining his breath and calming himself down, but he knew must carry on. If he stopped, he might be trapped, hauled back into his old life. He might be made to face the consequences.

He must escape.

He carried on running, his feet catching against errant clumps of grass which still survived in this vast crater of dust, causing him to stagger forward in an unsteady fashion. He was now running blind and he had lost all sense of direction. He splashed his way across the little stream and then his foot caught upon a large jagged rock hidden by a fine layer of soil. A sharp electric pain shot through his foot and this time he did lose his balance completely. With a cry, he fell spread-eagled, face down in the dirt. He lay there, his mouth full of dry grit and his body rippling with sobs.

Above him the grey clouds parted and a small patch of pale blue sky appeared, but in the distance he thought he could still hear the faint sounds of the railway engines.

TWELVE

I suppose that London after dark has always been a strange place. When the sun goes down the city becomes a different animal. But with the war, the change is even greater. Gone are the bright flashing lights, the neon signs and the glare of theatres and restaurants. The blackout changed all that, cloaking the city in dingy blackness where everything is reduced to a dim silhouette or a vague shadow. Now when the daylight fades, the lively buzzing city retires and in its place there emerges an indistinct skulking creature, reluctant to reveal itself for fear of harm and exposure.

On leaving the Guardsman after my drink with David, I emerged into London's cool ebony night, the clouds above me hiding the stars and the moon. In this monochrome half-world I made my way home along the disguised streets. From time to time I would hear voices and sharp footsteps approaching me in the gloom and then suddenly their owners would magically appear before me as though someone had pulled back a curtain to reveal them. Oblivious of my presence, they would drift past like spooky apparitions and then just as magically be swallowed up by the all consuming night once more.

The malefactors of old London Town must be offering up their grateful thanks to Herr Hitler and his air force for creating the ideal conditions for their activities. The petty crook, the thief and the murderer have never had it so good. They can now become invisible to carry out their dirty deeds, with shadows always ready to hide them, like the bastard who killed Walter Riley. As these depressing thoughts percolated their way through my mind, what little intoxication I felt as I left the pub dissipated quickly and by the time I was approaching the building that housed Hawke Towers, I was cold sober and sorely in need of another drink. Well, I told myself, as I slowly mounted the stairs with a heavy heart, I have a bottle of Johnnie Walker stashed away in my office with enough whisky inside to provide at least one decent nightcap.

I had just put the key in the lock when a voice called to me from the shadows. 'Johnny.' This was followed by a sharp tug of my coat. I didn't need to turn around to identify the owner of the voice. I knew it instantly.

It was Peter.

Some ten minutes later, Peter was sitting on my shabby sofa in my shabby living quarters, situated just beyond my shabby office. He was still wearing his old raincoat while clutching a mug of hot tea in both hands. He looked pale and tired, but his eyes were bright and his expression was a lively mixture of relief and pleasure. We had spoken little so far. I had bustled him in, given him a quick hug and brewed up the tea. I had made no attempt to interrogate him about why he was here, how he had got here and what he expected me to do now that he was here. That could come later. At the moment I was just relieved that he was safe. And I was very pleased to see him.

'You hungry?' I asked, lighting up a cigarette, sitting on the arm of the chair opposite him.

Peter nodded. 'I've only had a packet of biscuits and the pork pie the soldier bought me since I got up this morning.'

'What soldier?'

'The one on the train. He hid me from the railway man, 'cos I hadn't got a ticket. He said that he used to get free rides on the train when he was a kid. I … I think he felt sorry for me. He looked after me until we got to Euston and then he gave me half a crown.'

I gazed down at the slight, rather pathetic figure sitting on my sofa and smiled. Who could not help but feel sorry for this little boy in the threadbare raincoat with the earnest expression?

In my inexpert way, I created a Spam sandwich and brewed up another cup of tea for my guest. He devoured the sandwich caveman fashion as though he had never eaten before. I watched him with silent pleasure.

With a final slurp he finished off his second mug of tea and grinned at me. 'That was good,' he said simply. 'Thank you.'

I ruffled his hair in what I hoped was an affectionate manner in order to soften what I was about to say. 'You've been a naughty boy.

The people who were caring for you, Mr and Mrs Booth, are very worried about you. So is Nurse McAndrew. How could you be so thoughtless, Peter? To do a bunk like this. You know the police have been told about your disappearance.'

Peter's mouth dropped open with alarm. 'The police,' he said, the words emerging as a hoarse whisper.

I couldn't help but laugh at his shocked expression. He relaxed immediately.

'Oh, you're kidding me.'

'No I am not,' I replied quickly, wiping the smile from my face. 'And you've put me in a hell of a pickle.'

Peter stared at his shoes. 'I'm sorry. But I couldn't stand it any longer. I just hated it down there. And they didn't like me. Mrs Booth was all right, I suppose, but Mr Booth ... well, he ignored me. I could tell he didn't really want me there. I could hear them arguing about me sometimes. I heard him call me a London guttersomething. And then there was Tom Bates. He bullied me at school and covered me in cow muck ...' He lifted his head and stared me directly in the face. 'I just want to stay with you, Johnny.'

His eyes watered briefly as this very personal admission released emotions that he had been keeping at bay for a long time. For a moment his frame shook with suppressed sobs but then with a determined shake of his body, a strong sniff and a little cough, he fought them off. I knew he didn't want to cry in front of me. Crying was only for cissies and Peter was no cissy.

'Can't I be your partner? I could help you catch crooks.'

'I wish you could,' I said flippantly, almost to myself. 'Just at the moment I need all the help I can get.'

Peter gave me a mock salute. 'I'm reporting for duty, sir.'

'No you are not,' I said, standing up, brusquely, attempting to sound authoritarian. 'You are reporting for bed. You need some sleep and I need to decide what the hell I'm going to do about you.'

'Please let me stay,' wailed Peter, jumping to his feet, his empty mug crashing to the floor.

'No more talk tonight, my lad. We'll sort things out in the morning. Now, out of those clothes, a quick wash and then bed. You take my bed. I'll doss down on the sofa for tonight.'

'You don't have to. I'll sleep on the sofa. I don't want to be a nuisance.'

'It's a bit late for that,' I said wearily and then softened the comment with a brief smile. 'Now are you going to do as you're told or am I going to have to come the heavy handed sergeant major with you?'

'I'll do as I'm told. Always with you, Johnny.'

Ten minutes later my little runaway was curled up in my bed. He had hardly had time to say goodnight before his eyes closed and his body relaxed as exhaustion overtook him and he drifted off into a deep sleep. I stood watching him for a while, a whirlpool of conflicting emotions sloshing around in my mind.

Eventually, I returned to the sitting room and poured myself the delayed whisky and slipped a Duke Ellington record on the gramophone. The meditative wailing saxes complemented my mood exactly. I sipped the whisky slowly, savouring each warm mouthful. Well, I mused, as Oliver Hardy would observe, here's another fine mess I've got myself into. Logic and common sense told me that I should ring up Susan McAndrew in the morning and inform her that Peter was with me. She could then contact the police and put the Booths' minds at rest. But then the poor blighter would be hauled away and either dumped back in Devon or carted off to some orphanage. I didn't want that. I'd had plenty of that myself and I couldn't be responsible for abandoning Peter to such a life.

Oliver Hardy was right. It was a fine mess and despite their soothing influences, Duke Ellington and Johnnie Walker were not going to help me solve it tonight. As I began to grow drowsy, one thing above all others was clear to me: I liked the idea of having Peter around.

THIRTEEN

It was late morning when Rachel managed to pull herself from the bed. Her body was stiff and her face throbbed. She had slept much easier than she had thought possible. It was only now as she dragged herself into full wakefulness that she became conscious of the pain and discomfort. The aches returned and she remembered why she felt so bad. Once more the steel grip of fear took hold of her. So strong was it that her body shook with remorse. If only she could turn the clock back. If only she hadn't been stupid enough to leave home in the first place; or at least not been blindingly naïve enough take up with Harryboy. He was still asleep, snoring like the filthy pig he was. If she had a knife, she'd stab it right through his heart now. There would be no hesitation. Her hands clenched at the thought of it, the thought of the knife tight in her hand slicing through his flesh, bursting through the walls of his heart and the blood, rich hot blood spurting out, staining his vest a wonderfully bright life-draining crimson. She'd stab him time and time again. If she had a knife.

Well, maybe she wouldn't, she admitted to herself, as reason reasserted itself. That's what she'd like to do, but if it came to it, she'd probably chicken out. Deep down, she didn't think that she really could kill anyone, no matter how much she hated them. And she really hated Harryboy. She never realized that it was possible to hate and despise someone with so much intensity.

And yet ... would she really kill him? She sneered at herself. Of course not. The truth was that she didn't have the guts. She didn't have it in her. It shocked her to realize how much he had tainted her mind that she now regarded this as a weakness.

Perhaps she ought to consider what she was going to do now, she told herself, rather than fantasize about sending Harryboy Jenkins to his grave. She sat on the edge of the bed, her body aching and tears streaming down her face, feeling very sorry for herself. Then in blinding flashes it all came back to her, the blows, the curses, the hurt.

After leaving the café in Soho she had done some window shopping and then gone to the pictures to see an old Fred Astaire picture. She had stayed in the cinema and watched the programme twice. It had been wonderful to escape into that improbable musical world where love and a happy ending were assured. Afterwards, she treated herself to some fish and chips and then returned to the hotel room to wait for Harryboy.

And she waited. And waited. When it got to nine o'clock she was seriously worried. She reckoned something must have happened to him. Or worse, that he had been picked up by the police. Arrested for murder. Her blood ran cold at the thought of it. If the police had nabbed Harryboy, it wouldn't be long before they came for her too. Her stomach started to tie itself into knots and she began pace up and down the dingy hotel room in worried frustration.

Then at ten o'clock, the door burst open and Harryboy staggered in. He looked terrible. His suit was crumpled and stained with mud and his face was flushed and bloated with alcohol. He was very drunk. After feeling a certain relief at his return, his return on his own without the police in tow, she demanded to know where he'd been and why he had left her waiting all this time. He told her to shut up. But she didn't. The tension that had built within her had given her some courage and now she couldn't help herself. She wanted an explanation.

'Come on, Harryboy, I have a right to know. I have a right to be treated decently,' she cried, grabbing him by the shoulders.

At that moment, something snapped inside of Harryboy. All the pent up anger, self pity and guilt that had been seething inside him since his visit to Pimlico boiled over. 'Shut up!' he roared, turning on her, his eyes bulging with fury. 'Shut up!' Then he hit her. He hit her with great force, the back of his hand smashing into her face, sending her spinning backwards against the wall. She cried out with pain and shock. However he wasn't going to leave it there. He rushed at her, his fingers grasping hold of her blouse, ripping it as he dragged her forward again. She was too terrified to scream as he punched her in the ribs.

Her face crumpled into an agonizing grimace and she doubled in pain, falling onto the bed clutching her stomach. Her vision blurred and the room began to sway. But Harryboy hadn't finished with her yet. He was on fire with alcohol-fuelled fury and it was all focused on this helpless young girl who'd had the temerity to question him. To raise her voice to him. No one spoke to Harryboy Jenkins that way. No one! He'd show her. He'd fucking show her. Now he had found a target for all his fear, guilt and anger which had dogged and haunted him all day. And in his fury, he found a certain perverted pleasure also.

Grabbing Rachel by the hair, he dragged her from the bed on to the floor, where she lay sobbing, curled up in a foetal position.

'Now will you shut up?' he snarled, kicking her hard, each word, a blow. 'Eh? Will – you – shut – up?'

'Yes,' she sobbed quietly. 'Please stop. Please don't—'

He spat at her. 'Shut up!' he bellowed. It had gone beyond his anger with Rachel and her nattering questions. He was using her along with the alcohol to exorcize his own feelings of weakness and guilt that had been brought on by his visit to his home in Waterloo Street. He kicked her again, a fixed rictus grin blighting his features.

She moaned and then lay very still.

Harryboy stared at her, a cruel satisfaction damping his inflamed temper. An arrogant smirk lighted upon his lips. That'll teach her. The bitch'll think twice before she messes with me again.

Rachel lay so still that for a moment he thought that she was dead. It didn't frighten him that he might have killed her. She had deserved it anyway. Unsteadily, he knelt down and turned her over. As she flopped on her back, he could see that she was still breathing. The stupid bitch had just blacked out.

He left her there on the floor and, staggering about the room in his drunkenness, he managed to get out of his clothes until he was just in his vest and underpants. Then he collapsed on the bed and within minutes he was diving deep into untroubled alcohol-induced dreams.

Gradually Rachel regained consciousness, her whole body aching and throbbing with pain. At first she couldn't move. It was as though she was locked in a vice which was gradually crushing her body. She lay there a long time, willing the ache to subside and her limbs to regain their movement. Eventually, she managed to pull herself into a sitting position with her back resting on the side of the bed. It was a long, painful process and she paused from time to time, biting her lip as the pain became too great to bear. Now her fingers gingerly explored the contours of her face. She could feel the swelling and the bruising and she began to weep once more. The tears flowed and her chest heaved with quiet sobs as a wave of desolation and utter despair drowned her.

Suddenly Harryboy shifted his position on the bed, grunting in his sleep as he did so. This frightened Rachel into silence. The last thing she wanted to do was wake the swine up. He might start attacking her all over again. With gritted teeth, she wiped her tears away, pulled herself to her feet and staggered over to the washbasin. She stood for some moments with her eyes closed, too scared to open them and see herself in the mirror. At length she summoned up enough courage to look at her reflection, to view what he'd done to her. What she saw made her moan softly as though her soul was being drawn from within her. The bruised and battered face which stared back at her from the mirror was barely recognizable as her own. It was the face of a stranger. The puffy eyes, the bloody nose, the bruised flesh, already darkening to a deep blue, transformed the pretty girl she had been into a walking monster from a horror film. She had become the Bride of Frankenstein.

She sniggered hysterically at this thought and swung round to look at Harryboy in the bed, his bestial mouth open in a pig-like snore, his cheeks rising and falling like little pink bellows. Well, she thought, if I am the bride, he certainly is the Frankenstein monster: an unnatural, heartless fiend. The tears came again and she turned away.

Slowly and carefully, she washed her face and then patted it dry. If anything, it looked worse. I'll need a mask for a week, she thought. Longer possibly. Like a drunken man trying to prove that he's sober, she made her way to the bed, her whole body racked with pain. She wanted to sleep. She wanted to escape from reality into the safe land of dreams. There she could escape to that fairy-tale world where Fred Astaire would whirl her round a shining dance floor and nobody would hurt her, ever again.

She gazed down at the bed with hunger. But she certainly wasn't going to get under the covers with that beast. Gingerly, she lay down on the edge of bed as far away from Harryboy as she could get without falling off, the pressure on her bruised ribs causing her to wince. Then she turned her back on the snoring creature beside her. With some effort she turned out the table lamp on her bedside table and plunged the room into darkness. The absence of light soothed her and somehow seemed to take some of the pain away.

But still in that Stygian void she could hear the buzz saw rasp of Harryboy's snoring. In time she got used to its regular grating rhythm and was able to remove it from the front of her consciousness. After lying there for some fifteen minutes, blessed relief came to her as she drifted off to sleep. So exhausted and traumatized was she that Rachel slept a deep and dreamless sleep.

Now she was awake and having to face the terrible reality of her plight. Again, with some effort, she forced herself to concentrate on the practicalities of the situation. She needed to wash and dress and try to make herself look as presentable as possible.

With stiff and awkward movements, ignoring the pain, she made her way to the sink and splashed her face with cold water and once again stared at herself in the mirror. Surprisingly some of the redness had disappeared but she had a swollen nose, a cut lip and a black eye. Slipping off the torn blouse she examined the unsightly bruises on her body.

With tears in her eyes, she smiled wryly at herself. She would live, she told herself.

Almost in slow motion, she washed herself, changed into some clean clothes and then set about camouflaging as much of the damage to her face as was possible with powder and paint. Twenty minutes later, with her hair combed differently so that it fell in Veronica Lake fashion across her blackened eye, she looked almost normal. From a distance, at least, she thought.

Rachel was just applying her lipstick when Harryboy stirred. Scratching his head, ruffling his greasy hair, he pulled himself up into a sitting position, his tongue roaming around his dry mouth in a futile attempt to lubricate it. He gazed at Rachel over by the wash-basin, the curve of her body arousing him.

'Morning, babe,' he called, grinning.

Rachel turned sharply to face him, her heart beating wildly with apprehension.

'You look good.' His grinned widened. 'Good enough to eat.' He patted the bed at his side. 'Come alonga here, baby. I fancy a little nibble.' He leered at her. 'You know what I mean.'

She knew what he meant.

'No,' she said, quicker, louder and with more passion than she had intended. She repeated the word more softly as she shook her head. 'No.'

Harryboy frowned. 'What do you mean? Come on here.'

'I can't,' she grinned nervously. 'It's … not possible. It's … it's my time of the month. You know.'

Harryboy screwed his face up into a snarl. 'You women,' he snapped.

'Sorry.'

'Yeah. So am I.' With a heavy sigh, he leapt off the bed. Rachel flinched, but he ignored her and headed for the wardrobe. 'Better get dressed then and grab some breakfast.'

It was as though last night had not happened. The hurt, the blows the indignity. They meant nothing to him. He had a kind of amnesia which erased all the ugliness of his behaviour from his mind. He was still treating her as he had done the day he met her. The fact that he had beaten her senseless and involved her in the murder of a policeman was of no consequence. He had forgotten these things, forgotten because they meant nothing to him. Now he was sober and clear-headed, he experienced no remorse or shame. There was no apology, no 'I'm sorry, babe', nothing. He didn't even seem aware that she was upset. It was at this moment that Rachel Howell's knew then that she would kill him. Her fear and conscience had evaporated. She knew now that it would only be like destroying a mad dog. She would bide her time, wait for the right moment so that there could be no mistake, no escape for the vile pig and then, God help her, she would kill him.

F O U R T E E N

The piercing ring of the telephone was my rude reveille the following morning. I jerked up automatically like one of Pavlov's salivating dogs at the shrill sound, cricking my neck in the process. In fact my whole body felt stiff and rusty. Sleeping scrunched up on a two-seater sofa had transformed me into Dorothy's tin man. With awkward creaky movements I reached for the receiver, realizing by the bright chinks of light at the edge of my blackout curtain that I had slept in rather late. I glanced at my watch. It was a quarter past nine.

'Hello,' I growled into the phone. I didn't feel up to giving the full, 'Good morning, Hawke Investigations, John Hawke speaking' routine.

'And hello to you. You sound as though you've got a mouthful of cotton wool.'

It was David.

With my brain not fully awake yet, I did not feel up to indulging in witty repartee. 'Good morning, David,' I replied simply.

'I thought you'd like to know – the ballistic report on the two bullets landed on my desk ten minutes ago. Disappointing news, I'm afraid.'

'They don't match.'

'You got it, boyo. The gun that shot PC Reece was not the same one that was used to kill your lady friend, Mr Riley. So it's most likely we are looking for two different fellers.'

'Ah well,' I said with a sigh. 'That would have been too easy.'

'Sorry, old boy. It certainly makes your job a lot harder. At least *we* have a name and a description. Anyway, give me a call if you think I can help. Best of luck, Sherlock.'

'Thanks.'

I sat down and lit a cigarette. Suddenly I felt very miserable and sorry for myself. I had effectively been shunted down the big snake and was back to square one: I had a murderer to find and I had no clues, no leads, no nothing. And in the next room I had a runaway boy whom I knew I would eventually have to disappoint hugely because, no matter how long I delayed it, in the end I would have to inform the authorities of his whereabouts. Peter couldn't live with me, however much he thought he wanted to. He needed a proper home and schooling, not dingy quarters with a not very successful private detective in the heart of dangerous London. For a fleeting moment, I wanted to get back on the sofa, curl up and pray for sleep to take me away from all my dilemmas. But I didn't. I gave myself a quick talking to, stubbed out my cigarette and set about my morning ablutions. I would feel better after a wash and shave, I told myself as I padded down the corridor to the little bathroom shared by all the inmates of Prior's Court.

Half an hour later, I had a smooth chin, tidy hair and was dressed in a clean shirt. However, while I did feel livelier and more alert, the little dark cloud of trouble still hovered over my head reminding me that my big problems remained in place.

I roused Peter who was reluctant to leave his dream world and introduced him to soap and a flannel and a comb. Eventually, looking reasonably presentable, the two male inhabitants of 7 Prior's Court set forth.

'Where are we going?' asked Peter with apprehension.

'First port of call is Benny's. I reckon we both could do with a hearty, well-prepared breakfast … but we'll have to settle for Benny's cooking instead.'

Peter laughed at my little joke and slipped his hand in mine.

One would have thought the king had condescended to visit Benny's little café on Dean Street the fuss he made of Peter. He hugged him, patted him on the head, kissed him on the forehead and outdid the Cheshire cat in grins. Peter took all this quietly with a shy smile.

'Right, you sit down, Peter, while Benny makes you top class breakfast,' mine host said with spry good humour. 'You look as though you could do with feeding up.' Gently, he guided the boy to a table in the far corner of the room. Then he pulled me to one side and the smile and light-hearted demeanour disappeared as quickly as it had arrived.

'What goes on here, Johnny? I thought the boy was in Devon. What's he doing back in town? Is he in trouble?'

I pulled a long face. 'He's run away.'

Benny slapped his forehead. 'Again! What for?'

I really didn't feel like going over all the details, partly because I didn't know them all myself, so I gave Benny the severely abridged version. 'He was unhappy.'

'I'm unhappy. You should see my profits for last week, but I don't run away.' His expression softened. 'This is bad news, Johnny. What are you going to do about the little mite?'

'I really don't know. If they take him back to Devon, he'll be just as miserable and go AWOL again.'

Benny nodded. 'And next time he might not run to someone who cares for him. It's a cruel world out there.'

'The other alternative is an orphanage ...'

Benny's eyes widened in surprise. 'You can't do that, Johnny. You of all people ...'

'I know. I know.' I shook my head miserably. 'I couldn't live with myself if that happened.'

Instinctively we glanced over at the table where Peter was sitting. He was gazing back at us, his brow furrowed with concern. He knew only too well that we were talking about him.

Benny switched on his smile again and gave a little wave. 'You go to him. Keep the little blighter amused while I fix your grub. We'll sort something out, eh?'

'I admire your optimism,' I said, before wending my way through the tables and joining Peter.

'I reckon you're ready for this feast,' I said, pulling up a chair, affecting a cheery grin. 'I could hear your tummy rumbling from over there.'

Peter also affected a matching cheery grin. We both knew we were acting, covering up the truth.

Suddenly I felt Peter's hand on mine. 'Please don't make me go back,' he whispered.

I should not have said it. I had no right to say it. I was mad to say it. But I said it. 'No, course not.' And I squeezed his hand in reassurance. The cloud over my head grew darker.

*

Benny did us proud. The food was good and there were extra portions for young Peter. We ate in contented silence, each of us concentrating on the moment and shelving thoughts of the future for another time. Later Benny came to clear the dishes and sat with us.

'You like a little job, Peter, my boy? I got a lot of dishes piled up in the kitchen; I could do with someone to give me a hand washing them up. How are you fixed? I pay good rates.'

Peter's eyes shone with excitement. 'You mean me?'

Benny looked around mysteriously as though searching for another candidate for the job before returning his gaze to Peter. 'Guess I do.'

'What do you say, Johnny?'

I nodded. 'It's OK with me.'

Without further debate, Benny took a joyful Peter off to the back room and set him on washing the dishes and then returned to the table.

'Thanks, Benny.'

'It'll keep him out of mischief. I'm happy to take him off your hands for the day if it'll give you a chance to sort things out.'

'I can't guarantee that, but I'll try. And I have a living to earn into the bargain.'

'Life is never easy, my friend.'

'Certainly isn't. It's bad enough when you have only yourself to think about.'

'How is business anyway?'

I was in no mood to start discussing the Riley case and its attendant complications so I responded with a non-committal shrug.

'You should have been in the café yesterday,' said Benny, his face suddenly becoming animated. 'I could have got you a case. There was a young couple in, sitting at that table over there. She was in such a state: sad face, black eye. It needed no detective to work out the fellow with her had been beating her up. She needed help, Johnny.'

'I'm a private investigator, Benny, not a wet nurse.'

Benny gave an exclamation of disgust.

I rose to leave. 'Thanks again for looking after Peter,' I said, happy to change the conversation.

Benny lifted a finger of warning. 'Be back here by closing time, eh?'

I nodded, planted my battered trilby firmly on my head and made my way out into the cool London street.

By the time I'd got back to my office, I had made one decision at least. I rang Charing Cross Hospital and asked to speak to Sister McAndrew. I was told that she was doing her ward round, so I said the matter was very urgent and left my number. Half an hour later she rang me back. By then I had rehearsed what I was going to say. I just hoped that I could make it sound believable.

'Hello Johnny, you have news.' She sounded breathless. Whether this was due to the rigours of hospital duties or her anticipation of news of Peter, I couldn't tell.

'Sort of.'

'Sort of? What do you mean?' Her tone was sharp and cool.

'I've heard from Peter. I got a call.'

'He rang you? Where is he?'

'I … I don't know. He just called to tell me that he was fine and I was not to worry. And Mr and Mrs Booth had no need to worry.'

'How can he be fine? He has no clothes, probably no money and nowhere to live. Was he ringing you from London?'

'I don't know.'

'You don't know!' The dam burst now and her anger cascaded unhindered. 'My God, man, you are supposed to be a detective. Couldn't you get any information out of him? What's he doing for food? What are his plans? Is he heading for London?'

I suppose I should have expected this rapid interrogation and been ready with realistic responses but I wasn't. In the process of trotting out my hastily conceived untruths, I had suddenly realized how shaky and feeble they were. I attempted to retaliate.

'Look, Susan, I didn't want to scare him off with too many questions. I needed to make him feel he can trust me, so he'll ring again. And then maybe come to see me. It's softly, softly catchee the young monkey. If I'd come down heavily with a barrage of questions, he would probably have hung up on me.'

That sounded good, I thought. There was a brief silence as she considered my argument and then she replied. Her voice was softer, conciliatory.

'Yes, I suppose you're right. I'm sorry I snapped at you.'

'Don't worry. In my job I'm used to it. Look, Peter assured me that he was fine. He sounded fine. I am certain he can look after himself. He's done it before. We just need to wait for the next call. We must be patient. In the meantime, have a word with your sister and put her mind at rest.'

'I'll try, but she blames herself for Peter running away. A phone call saying that he's all right will hardly ease her conscience.'

I couldn't argue with that.

'Well, do what you can. I'll be in touch.'

'Make sure you are. Bye, Johnny.'

The line went dead and I felt a sharp pang of conscience for deceiving her, but, I assured myself, it was necessary to buy a little time. Time was a small bonus, but it certainly didn't solve the Peter problem.

I lit a cigarette and tried to turn my mind to business matters. In particular, the Riley case. The deep mire that was the Riley case. Where did one start with this unpleasantly hot potato? After a few minutes of contemplation, the answer became obvious to me.

FIFTEEN

It was mid-morning by the time I reached Whitehall. Although in the heart of London, it was a quiet thoroughfare. I made my way to the War Office. It is a squat, ugly building with four improbable turrets, like a reject fairy-tale castle. I made my way up the broad sweep of steps and entered. I didn't get far. Passing through a pair of great double doors, I found myself in a high-ceilinged entrance hall with two sets of a large marble staircases leading up to the second floor. There were numerous armed soldiers on guard.

I was stopped at the desk in the entrance and asked for my documents. They were scrutinized thoroughly and returned to me by an authoritative looking plump fellow wearing Arthur Askey glasses.

'Now, Mr Hawke, what can I do for you?'

'I am here to see Captain Michael Eddowes. He works on the third floor.'

My plump friend grinned sarcastically. 'Do you have a security pass?'

I shook my head.

The eyes narrowed behind the round glasses and the grin broadened even more sarcastically. 'This is the War Office, Mr Hawke. And if it has passed your notice, there is a war on. Do you think we let any Tom, Dick or Herman wander around these premises?'

'You've seen my identification documents.'

'But not your security pass.'

'I don't have one.'

'And so you get no further than my desk. It's as simple as that.'

'Then would you contact Captain Michael Eddowes and inform him that I am here?'

'This is not a telephone exchange, Mr Hawke. Unless you have an appointment and a security pass, the answer is no. Now I suggest that you leave the premises or I shall be forced to ask those two strapping guards over there to escort you from the building.'

I gave a little cry of surprise and nodded my head vigorously. 'An appointment! Of course, how silly of me not to have mentioned an appointment. Yes, indeed, old Mike is expecting me. It's very important business.'

The gatekeeper did not seem fully convinced by my effusive outburst, but I could see by his rapid eye movement that I had sown the seeds of doubt in his mind.

'What was the name again?'

'Captain Michael Eddowes. If you'll just remind him that it's the matter concerning the Riley conundrum.'

With grumpy reluctance, my plump friend consulted a log book and then dialled a number on the internal telephone. It didn't take long for it to be answered. 'Captain Eddowes? This is Sergeant Broughton on reception. I have a John Hawke here who says he's got an appointment with you ... concerning the Riley conundrum.' As he said this he gave me a fierce glance. I responded with a broad, sweet smile.

After a moment Sergeant Broughton replaced the receiver. He did not seem best pleased. He gave an embarrassed cough before addressing me in a far more civil manner.

'Captain Eddowes will be down to see you shortly, Mr Hawke. If you don't mind waiting. Just take a seat over there.'

What a miraculous *volte-face*. It was *Mr* Hawke now and if I didn't *mind* waiting instead of being booted out of the building in the manner of a drunk who had stayed too long after closing time. I was gracious in victory. I just nodded casually and said, 'Thanks.' I took a seat as directed and waited.

A few moments later a tall figure in an elegant blue mohair overcoat flapping around him entered the building and swept by me as he made his way to the desk. He was a youngish man, with a sallow face and chiselled features. His dark hair swept back in a severe style glistened under the artificial lights.

'Good day, Sergeant Broughton,' he said cheerily, his voice rich with public school resonances.

At his appearance Broughton shot to his feet and stood to attention, his features colouring pink.

'Good day, Sir Robert,' he responded with some awe.

Without further intercourse, Sir Robert carried on his way up one of the staircases, taking three or four steps at a time.

When he had disappeared, Broughton relaxed and then turned to me, 'That was Sir Robert Gervais,' he announced in hushed and reverent tones. 'He's one of the most important persons who works here.'

Well, I thought, whatever else he does for the war effort, he certainly keeps you on your toes.

Captain Michael Eddowes was a tall, lithe man with prematurely grey hair and a youthful face, housing two lively blue eyes. We shook hands and he leaned forward conspiratorially. 'My sister told me to expect you. We'll go up to my office for a private chat.'

He moved over to the entrance desk. 'Broughton, can you give this chap a temporary security pass. He's my guest.'

In silent tight-lipped obedience Broughton did as he was asked. As he handed me the pass, I gave him a mock salute and winked.

Captain Eddowes led me up the two flights of stairs to the third floor of the War Office where there was another security check before I was allowed into the warren of corridors and offices to be found there.

Eventually I was ushered into room 443, Eddowes' tiny office which housed a desk, a filing cabinet, two chairs and little else. There was no window.

'Grab a pew and I'll see if I can rustle up some tea,' said Eddowes languidly and made the request via an intercom.

'My sister told me to expect you and confirmed that you are a bona-fide private detective. I also note that you were a policeman before the war and were invalided out of the army after losing the sight in you left eye.'

The fellow had done his homework. I nodded with a grim smile.

'One can't be too careful, Mr Hawke. We can't let any Tom, Dick or Herman wander around these premises, you know.'

It was the exact same phrase my old friend Broughton, the gate-keeper, had used. It must be the War Office mantra.

There was a discreet knock at the door and a uniformed sergeant entered with a tea tray and placed it on Eddowes' desk.

'Thank you, Chapman. That will be all.'

Without a word the soldier departed.

'Now then, Mr Hawke, how can I help you?' Eddowes asked, as he passed me a mug of tea.

'Tell me about Walter Riley. What job did he do here? Did he have any friends? Any enemies?'

'Do you really believe that he was murdered on purpose rather than being the unlucky victim of a somewhat nasty robbery?'

I nodded. 'Yes. Evidence is growing to indicate just that.'

'Really. What would be the motive?'

'That's what I'm trying to establish.'

'I see. Well, you probably know I was instrumental in getting Walter a job here as a favour to Sandra. His work wasn't very demanding but it required reliability and loyalty.'

'What did he do?'

Eddowes took a sip of tea and then stretched back in his chair. 'Here at the War Office we employ hundreds of individuals, all slaving away like little hamsters in their own individual cages, oblivious of what is going on in the next cage. That's the way we like it. It helps to strengthen our security. Most of the stuff is mundane and repetitive but nevertheless vital to the war effort. I can't really go into details about any of the tasks or individuals – even my own brother-in-law. All I can tell you is that Walter was mainly involved in dealing with army pay of members of the Royal Household Staff and the overseas requirements of a number of Fleet Street war correspondents. Not exciting work, but essential.'

'Nothing very hush hush then.'

'Good God, no. We keep all that stuff for the top brass.'

'Like yourself?'

He grinned. 'I am a mere captain, a very small cog in this vast machine, Mr Hawke. Certainly I am higher up the pecking order than Walter was, but I can assure you I am privy to none of the really important operations decided here.'

'If you wanted to find out things could you? Could Walter?'

Eddowes thought for a moment, absent-mindedly tugging at his chin. 'If I were totally unscrupulous, I suppose it's possible. But only because I was known within the building. A stranger wouldn't stand a cat in hell's chance. You, for instance – put one foot wrong, enter an area you were not supposed to and you'd soon find yourself down in the guard room with a rifle aimed at your heart.'

'And Walter?'

'Surely you're not suggesting—?'

'I'm just trying to establish some facts that's all.'

Eddowes performed the chin-tugging ceremony again. I could tell that he didn't like the kind of questions I was asking.

'I suppose if Walter had the determination he might have been able to sniff out some secret info but it just wasn't in his nature. He was fully screened before he put a foot over the threshold. Nothing is absolutely secure in wartime – but we're as near watertight here as we can be.'

'Did you know about Walter's penchant for dressing-up—?'

Eddowes gave me a sour face. 'I did not. If I had, he'd have been out of here in a flash.'

'Not that watertight then,' I mused.

'As to friends or enemies …' he continued, ignoring my little trenchant observation, 'I can't say for certain. Although we worked in the same building, he was on the second floor and I rarely saw him. From all accounts he seems to have been rather a solitary character. Keeping himself to himself. And with his particular predilections, I am not surprised. But, to be fair, that's the way of the job. We do not encourage fraternization.'

I was getting a little frustrated at the circumspect nature of this conversation and I realized that I would have to place a number of my cards on the table in order to scrape some advantages from the visit.

'If Walter was not killed in a robbery, then he was killed because he was a problem to someone. I'd like to find out what that problem was.'

'I've really no idea what you mean.'

'Maybe he knew something he shouldn't and so he had to be silenced.'

'That's rather melodramatic isn't it? What could he know?'

'Some kind of secret.'

Eddowes frowned and leaned forward over his desk. 'Such as? You surely don't mean some War Office secrets? Why that's preposterous,' he exclaimed, but his expression somehow denied the sense of his words.

'Preposterous, but not impossible, eh?'

'Well, no, I suppose not. But that would mean that Walter was a traitor. I can't accept that, I'm afraid. He was obviously a strange bod, stranger than I could have imagined, all that unpleasant dressing up bit, very distasteful, but he wasn't the sort to sell his own country down the river.'

'And so you have no notion why anyone would want to kill Walter Riley.'

'I'm afraid not.'

With these words Captain Eddowes rose from his chair to indicate that the interview was over. 'I'm sorry that I can't help you any further, but in all honesty I think you are barking up the wrong tree if you believe he was murdered because he knew something he shouldn't.'

'Thank you for your time.'

He flashed his standard smile, bland and indecipherable. 'I'll show you out.'

'That's OK. I'll find my own way.'

'Not without me, you won't,' Eddowes asserted, leading me to the door. 'You'd soon be cornered, or, worse still, shot down, if you, as a visitor, tried to move around this building unaccompanied.'

He led me into the corridor and back towards the staircase. As we passed the last office in the line, the door opened and a man with large horn-rimmed glasses popped his head around the door. 'Ah, Michael, the very man. Sir Robert wants to bring the three o'clock meeting forward an hour. He's got some function on this evening and he needs to get back to his flat. Can you do two o'clock in the Red Room?'

'That's fine by me,' replied Eddowes.

'Good show.' The man disappeared behind the door again as quickly as he appeared.

I grinned. 'He's like the White Rabbit. Who was that?' I asked casually.

'Oh that's Bernard. Bernard France. He's secretary to Sir Robert Gervais, one of the whizz-kids from the code-breaking section. Gervais has a first class brain. One of the unsung heroes of the war effort.'

Ah young Sir Robert, the fellow with the flapping mohair over-coat who keeps Sergeant Broughton on his toes. I nodded and smiled my appreciation for the information.

*

I grabbed a bite to eat in a little café, girding up my loins before my next port of call. The Loophole Club was virtually deserted. Well, it was the early afternoon and no doubt most of the exotic regular customers would be at work at this hour. They would have to hold down a decent job in order to afford the expensive gowns and make-up they wore in the evening; and heaven knows what a decent pair of nylons costs these days on the black market – if you can get hold of a pair. Personally, I'd not felt the need.

It was clear that like a vampire, the club only came alive at night. During the daylight hours, there was a ghostly air of funereal melancholy about the place. The room was still gloomy and dimly lighted but now it smelt of old fag ends, cheap perfume and stale alcohol. Somewhere a gramophone was playing some slow jazz tune which added to the dreary atmosphere. Despite the scarcity of clientele, which consisted of about four 'ladies' sitting around a table in the deep shadows at the far end of the room, I felt more uncomfortable than I had done on my visit with 'Wilma' Riley when the place had been crowded. Now I really was sticking out like a sore thumb; the only person in trousers in the place.

However, it seemed that I attracted little attention. The ladies gave me a casual glance without comment as I entered, their faces hovering like indistinct clown's masks in the artificial twilight, and then they turned away and returned to their hushed conversation. Relieved, I picked a stool at the bar and ordered a drink. The 'girl' who served me was broad-shouldered and stocky, wearing a tweed skirt and a tight-fitting cardigan, but she needed a shave.

It wasn't long before I had company on the stool beside me. My heart skipped something like a beat; certainly it behaved in an irregular fashion when I clocked the gorgeous individual smiling across at me. She had emerged from nowhere like a cunning spider waiting in the darkness for the unwary fly. And here I was at the centre of her transvestite web. This vision had all the sexual allure of Jean Harlow with some of the mysterious suppressed passion of Greta Garbo mixed in. She had flawless skin, seductive blue eyes and a delicious red-lipped mouth. All she had to say was 'Could I have a ginger ale, baby' in a husky voice and I'd be melting. Sadly, it took my brain a little time to catch up with my crotch. You fool, I eventually told myself, this isn't Jean Harlow or Greta Garbo. It isn't even a woman, Johnny. This was a gentleman in a frock!

But what a gentleman. I never knew they could be so ... convincing.

'I've not seen you in here before,' the vision said, the red lips parting into a gentle smile.

'This is only my second time,' I said shyly, as though I'd been caught doing something naughty behind the bicycle shed by the vicar.

'I'm Amanda. Care to buy me a drink?'

I nodded. What else could I do?

'My usual, Jocelyn,' Amanda called to the unshaven one.

'I'd better warn you, I'm not here seeking company,' I said. 'I just ... it's a matter of ... well, you see, I need ...' I felt my explanation spluttering and phuttering to a juddering, hesitant close like a car running out of petrol. I couldn't really tell Amanda I was a private detective making enquiries into the death of one of the customers – that was guaranteed to drive her away pronto – and yet I didn't want her to think I was in the club on the lookout for, how could I put it, an unconventional girlfriend.

It was clear from Amanda's expression that she had heard my kind of stuttering protestations before from novices, the curious and the desperate who had found themselves washed up in The Loophole. I tried to approach the problem from another angle.

'I was in here a few nights ago with a friend of mine, Wal— Wilma Riley.'

Amanda rolled here eyes. 'Oh, her! I know one shouldn't speak ill of the dead but ... Rank amateur, she was. Looked as though she hadn't been near a decent clothes shop for years. The word fashion had passed her by. I'm sorry, I don't wish to be rude about your friend, but she dressed as though she was a pantomime dame.'

I nodded as though in agreement. It wasn't a topic I wished to discuss. I was no expert. Women's fashion is rather a closed book to me. I just knew when they looked nice and that's about it. A simple soul am I.

'Did you know her well?'

Amanda shook her head. 'Not really. She'd only been coming here a few months. She seemed a decent sort, I suppose. She usually met up with a dark-haired piece, sits in a corner in a huddled tête-à-tête, not much interested in anyone else. Not very sociable. You get types like that.'

'Is this other person tall, slender with long dark hair?' I remembered the creature with whom Walter Riley had an altercation just before we left the club.

Amanda shrugged. 'Yeah, that sounds like her. She's called Helen. She's not very friendly. Don't know much about her.'

I looked around the room. 'Is she here now?'

'She hasn't been in for a few days at least,' Amanda said, her eyes not leaving my face. 'I should know, I manage the place. I'm here every night.' She smiled wryly. 'I'm one of the fixtures and fittings.'

'Is there any way I could get in touch with this Helen?'

Amanda smiled coquettishly, leaned forward and placed her hand on my knee causing a certain paralysis in my lower limbs. 'Now why would you want the mysterious Helen when you've got me here and now and in the lovely flesh?'

I tried to ignore the gentle squeezing of my knee cap. 'I just need to see her, to ask her a few questions, that's all.'

The squeezing stopped, the hand pulled away sharply and the smile vanished. 'You're a copper, aren't you?' Amanda's voice suddenly lost its sexual allure and was replaced with a deeper, more aggressive gruffness of tone.

'Not exactly,' I replied awkwardly, tugging at my tie.

'What the hell's that supposed to mean?'

I reckoned there was no point in prevaricating or coming up with some flimsy excuse. I'd peddled enough lies for one day. It was best if I told the truth now. 'I'm not with the police,' I said evenly. 'I'm a private investigator. I'm trying to find out who was responsible for Wilma's murder.'

'You don't think this Helen had anything to do with it, do you?

'I don't know. I just think that she might be able to help.'

'Is this on the level?' Amanda's voice was almost masculine now, all the feminine artifice had evaporated. It seemed so surreal to hear a man's rather coarse tones emerging from that beautiful feminine face.

'Yes.'

'You got a card? Some ID?'

I flicked one of my business cards out of my wallet and passed it to Amanda. She scrutinized it closely as though normally she was used to wearing spectacles and then grinned at me coquettishly, as she slipped the card down her cleavage.

'Well, Mr John Hawke,' she said at length, the seductive female tones fully reinstated, 'leave the matter with me a while. The girls here are quite a close knit community, for obvious reasons. We look after our own. I'll see what I can ferret out. I'll get in touch if I hear anything. OK?'

'As soon as you can would be good.'

Amanda touched the back of her wig. 'Well, it shouldn't take long to find things out. Say tomorrow late afternoon, around four. Come round to my place. It'll be more private. This place has ears.'

'Sure,' I said, with a nervous smile. I saw the sense of her suggestion, but I was just a little apprehensive about being alone with her on her own territory.

'Give me another of your cards, John.' Her eyes flickered with amusement. She was actually enjoying herself. Now she knew exactly where she was with me, she was taking pleasure in playing with me, keeping me uncertain as to her motives.

I passed her a card and she scribbled her address on the back and returned it to me. 'Around four,' she said, suggestively. 'A secret assignation. I like that. Quite exciting, isn't it?' She wriggled with delight.

I nodded with false agreement.

'All right, Jonathan. I'll get on the case and see you at my place tomorrow. Bring roses.'

'I'll be there,' I said and slipped off my stool ready to leave, when Amanda leaned over, very close to me and smiled sweetly. 'Take care of yourself, John, darling. I'd hate anything untoward to happen to you. Goodbye,' she said, leaning forward and kissing me lightly on the cheek.

SIXTEEN

Despite Johnny Hawke's strong assurances and protestations, Susan McAndrew was not really satisfied with his story about Peter. Her doubts nagged at her as she went about her duties at the Charing Cross Hospital. The niggling suspicion that perhaps he was not telling her the whole truth, that he was covering up for Peter, grew in her mind as the day progressed until it developed into a strong conviction that she had been sold a pack of lies. Why would the lad ring up Johnny rather than just land on his doorstep? Where else had Peter to go in London? She answered the questions herself, shooting holes through Johnny's story in the process. By the time she had reached the end of her long shift at the hospital, Susan was not only convinced that she had been conned, but she was angry with herself for having believed Johnny in the first place.

As she was grabbing her coat and bag from her locker, her friend Tilly approached with a weary sigh.

'What a shift. I don't think I've sat down since I arrived here at God knows what time this morning.'

Susan responded with a sympathetic smile and nod.

'Would you like to join me in a cup of tea and scone in the canteen before you hop off for some shut eye?' said Tilly. 'I've got some juicy tittle tattle about Dr Brewis and I'm bursting to tell someone.'

'I'd love to, but something rather urgent has come up. I've got things to do.'

'Oh, not bad news, I hope.'

Susan pursed her lips. 'I hope so, too. Maybe tomorrow, eh? Save the Brewis story for me then.' She leaned forward and gave her friend a peck on the cheek and then headed briskly for the door.

As she might have guessed there was no one at home at Hawke

Investigations in Priory Court. After ringing the bell for some time and then tapping on the glass panel, Susan tried the door on the slender chance that it might be open. There was no joy. Of course Johnny's absence might well be quite legitimate: he could be out there on the streets of London trying to catch criminals or following up clues. She just hoped he wasn't in a bar somewhere, soaking up the booze with a little boy by his side.

Then she had an idea: Benny's café. Where else would Johnny take a hungry young boy but his mate's café, an Aladdin's cave of paste sandwiches and iced buns? Well, it was a possibility, a strong possibility, she told herself and with a determined spring in her step she set off to find out if she was right.

By the time that Susan had turned the corner into Dean Street she had convinced herself totally that Peter was with Johnny and he was deliberately hiding the fact from her. On seeing the illuminated windows of Benny's café, she developed a strong desire for surprising that lying toad, John Hawke – to catch him red-handed with Peter. It would give her great satisfaction to see his jaw drop and then hear him try and splutter out some feeble explanation. The windows of the café were steamed up and despite pressing her nose against the glass, she couldn't see inside. Disappointed, she entered.

The place was quiet. The lunchtime trade had dispersed and there were only a few elderly customers inside. Sadly, there was no sign of Johnny or, more importantly, Peter.

Benny was at the counter chatting with a red-faced fellow in a shabby raincoat who was settling his bill. Out of habit, the café owner glanced up to greet the new customer with a smile. When he saw who it was, the smile froze on his lips and his eyes flickered nervously.

Benny's behaviour was evidence enough to satisfy Susan that she was on the right trail. His obvious discomfiture at her arrival spoke volumes. She waited for the red-faced man to depart before she approached the counter.

'Hello, Benny,' she said. Her manner was friendly, but her eyes told a different story.

'Miss McAndrew. How nice to see you. It's been a long time ...'

'Where are they?'

Benny frowned. 'Pardon?'

'Johnny and Peter, the little boy Peter. I know they are together. Where are they?'

Benny's stomach began to churn uncomfortably. He hadn't expected this. What was worse, he was no actor. He knew that he couldn't handle subterfuge. Whatever story his mouth came out with, his face would tell the truth. And yet he was aware that he had to carry out the charade. He had to try at least for the sake of Johnny and Peter. This woman, nice though she was, represented authority and that meant that Peter would be taken away. He couldn't allow that. Johnny would never forgive him. He would never forgive himself.

'I'm sorry, I don't—'

But Susan McAndrew, further angered by her belief that she had been right all along about Johnny and Peter, was in no mood for prevarications. She leaned over the counter, her face coming close to Benny's. 'You know exactly what I mean. Where is the boy?' she snapped, loudly enough to attract the attention of the few customers in the café, their faces turning towards her in surprise and interest. 'I am sure you don't want me to bring the police here to get him.'

It would be the last thing she would really do, but Susan wanted to scare Benny into coming out with the truth.

'What boy?' Benny asked lamely, still prevaricating because he couldn't think of anything else to say.

'Look, Benny. You know who I mean. Peter Blake. I mean him no harm. Remember I was responsible for his evacuation to Devon, in the care of my sister and her husband. I need to know where he is.'

In the back room beyond the counter, the subject of their conversation was spying on the scene. He had been disturbed from his washing-up duties by a woman's raised voice and had opened the door slightly to see what was happening. Peering through the narrow gap, he was shocked to see Nurse McAndrew, Mrs Booth's sister, in conversation with Benny. The scene froze his young heart. He began to shiver with fear.

What was the nurse doing here? He answered his own question. She's come to take me back. They've all lied to me. Even Johnny. They don't want me here. I'm just a nuisance. They mean to take me back to Devon … or put me in another place. In an orphanage or maybe even a prison. He trembled at the thought.

The mixture of fear and indignant anger prompted a silent flow of tears, misting his vision. He bit his lip hard in an attempt to stop his crying. And then the horrible truth came to him again but this time with greater clarity: Johnny had lied to him. The man he liked most in all the world; the man he trusted most in all the world; the man he had wanted to be with most in the world … had lied to him.

It was all clear to him now. His contented little dream crumbled and he slumped to the floor in despair.

Beyond the door, Benny was giving the performance of his life. His head was constantly shaking in the negative as he tried to fend off Susan's allegations.

'I really can't help you. Honest. Why not sit down and I'll get you a cup of tea. I can see you are upset.'

'I don't want a cup of tea. I just want to know where Peter is.'

'Well, he's not here and neither is Johnny. You can see that with your own eyes.'

Instinctively, as if to test Benny's assertion, she glanced around the café. As she did so the customers who had been her rapt audience, swiftly returned their attentions to their own varied business.

'What's beyond that door?' Susan said at length, after she had scanned the premises.

Benny twitched. 'That door?' He felt his mouth go dry. 'It's just my kitchen.'

Susan moved around the counter. 'May I see?' It wasn't a question for which she was going to wait for an answer.

'It's just my kitchen', mumbled Benny, making a feeble attempt to bar her way, but she brushed past him with ease and pushed the door open. The room beyond, the cramped little area where Benny cooked up his breakfasts and lunches, was empty. Two gas stoves were laden with empty pans and a pile of washed plates and dishes were stacked haphazardly on the draining board ready for drying but there was no one in the room.

Benny squeezed into the room behind Susan and gave a little gasp when he saw that it was empty. Peter had done a disappearing act. He didn't know whether to be glad or worried. Meanwhile, Susan had scooped something up from the shelf below the sink. It was a children's comic. After a brief examination of it, she waved it under Benny's nose.

'Since when have you taken an interest in Tiger Blake and his comic book adventures, Benny?'

Benny's mouth opened but his brain had seized up. It was a question that he could not answer.

'We both know that Peter is a great fan of Tiger Blake, don't we?' said Susan. 'I think it's time you came clean and told me the whole truth, my friend.'

When Peter reached Tottenham Court Road, he stopped running and fastened up his coat properly. He'd had the good sense to take a ten shilling note from Benny's coat which had been hanging at the back of the kitchen door. He felt a little guilty about that, but he reasoned that Benny hadn't been straight with him, he had lied to him and so was a bad man.

So here I am again, thought Peter ruefully, alone and unwanted in the great big city. Well, this time he would not make the mistake of trusting anybody. This time he really was on his own and he would stay that way. He turned right towards Cambridge Circus, walking briskly, as though he had a purpose, which he didn't have, except perhaps, he told himself, to get as far away from Prior's Court and Johnny Hawke as possible.

Soon he was swallowed up by the conflicting currents of pedestrians.

S E V E N T E E N

After leaving The Loophole Club, I'd taken myself off to the quiet waters of Enfield where Mrs Sandra Riley resided. I wanted to chat further with her about Walter in the hope that I would pick up something which might bring a spark of illumination to the mystery of his death. Sometimes clients are more relaxed, more careless on their home ground. I was sure that the delightful Sandra hadn't told me all. If necessary I had to go in there and prise the information from her.

I found the house down a quiet tree-lined street about a mile from the underground station: the epitome of hushed suburbia. The house was actually a bungalow; detached and bijou in appearance, fronted by a neat lawn and well-tended flowerbeds. However, what really caught my attention was the black Wolseley car parked outside. I was fairly certain the car did not belong to Sandra and therefore she had a visitor – a very interesting visitor.

I took a note of the car's registration number and then made my way up the path and peered in at both bay windows. There were net curtains to restrict my view but I could see that the rooms at the front were used as bedrooms. I made my way down the side of the house and round to the back. There were lights on in one of the rooms there and I could hear voices. They were raised and discordant. Again net curtains hindered my view and I could just make out two figures, but not their faces. However it was clear that one was Sandra and the other was a man. He seemed to be doing most of the talking. Although I could not hear what he was saying, he spoke forcefully and with a tone of menace in his voice. Sandra was upset. When she responded, she was in full Joan Crawford mode with the occasional dramatic sob and gasp.

The conversation lasted a few minutes and then the man made for the door as though his business was over and he were about to leave. I felt like a theatregoer who had arrived very late for a performance, only able to see the closing moments of the play before the curtain came down. What made it doubly frustrating was that I had no idea what the two leading characters had been talking about.

As the man reached the door, he stopped suddenly and picked something up from a little table. It shone in the artificial light. It looked like a glass dish. He held it out and then casually let it fall onto the dark wooden floor. I heard the sound of smashing glass followed by the cry of anguish from Sandra Riley.

With that the man left the room and Sandra sank down into an armchair. I made my way to the front of the house in time to see the visitor leaving. He was a short, thick-set fellow enveloped in a dark double-breasted overcoat; he wore thick horn-rimmed glasses and a large Homburg was perched precariously on his head. He looked quite a comic figure as he strode purposefully and rather pompously down the path towards his car and he might well have raised a smile from me if I had just encountered him in the street, but after witnessing his performance with Mrs Sandra Riley I didn't smile.

After he had driven off, I waited a few minutes before approaching the front door and ringing the bell. It took some time before there was a response. Perhaps Sandra thought that her unpleasant visitor had returned and she was not about to allow him back in to smash another glass ornament. Eventually the door opened and Sandra stood before me. She had repaired her make-up and, although she still looked a little strained and tearful, the casual observer would not have noticed. However, she could not hide her surprise and unease when she saw who her visitor was.

'Mr Hawke.'

I raised my hat. 'Just thought I'd call round for a little chat,' I said smiling.

For a moment I thought she was about to close the door on me, but she rallied to the occasion and invited me in. She led me into the sitting-room which was furnished in the same smart, immaculate and chic style that Sandra herself affected. The cushions on the cream three-piece suite were beautifully plumped up and looked as though no one had ever had the nerve to sit on them and spoil their pert appearance. As I say, everything about the room was perfect, straight out of a magazine, apart from one thing: there was a shower of glass on the parquet floor by the door, vicious shards of crystal glistening in the subtle light created by a rank of table lamps.

'A little accident,' she said responding to my raised eyebrows as I stepped over the glass detritus. 'I was just about to sweep it up when you rang the bell.'

I said nothing but headed for the plumpest cushion on the sofa and sat on it heavily. Despite her other preoccupations, I noticed that Sandra winced slightly at such desecration.

I sat back and lit a cigarette. 'Who was he?' I asked, blowing smoke in the air.

She shook her head as though puzzled by my query. She wasn't puzzled by my query. She knew exactly what I meant.

'Who was who?' she said as casually as she could, passing me an ashtray. I mustn't be allowed to drop ash on the floor. Glass bowls were a different matter.

'The gentleman I saw leaving as I arrived. Darkish, shortish, thick glasses. Driver of a black Wolseley.'

Sandra Riley knew the game was up. There was no point in denying the fellow's existence.

'Oh, him. An old friend of Walter's. He just popped in to offer his condolences.'

She was lying of course, but I decided to play along for a while. 'An old friend, eh? Who is he?'

'Does it matter? What has this got to do with his murder?' She sat in the chair opposite me.

'If he is an old friend of Walter's, he may well harbour some notion about who might want to kill him or at least have an opinion concerning the motive.'

She shook her head, too vigorously for my liking, and then added an indulgent smile. 'I can assure you he'd have no idea. He hasn't seen Walter in years. As I said, he was an old friend.'

'He …? This person has a name, I trust.'

'I'm not going to tell you his name. I don't want him to be involved. I can assure you that he had nothing to do with Walter's death.'

It was time to end the charade. It was bad enough having a mystery at one end of the case without the complication of a duplicitous client.

'You're lying, Mrs Riley. I'm fairly certain that your visitor was not an old friend. Certainly his behaviour was not friendly. You see I happened to have witnessed the scene with the glass bowl. I was watching through the window.' I indicated with my arm. 'His actions looked more like a threat than an expression of condolence.'

For a moment Sandra Riley was stunned into silence. Then she turned her gorgon eyes on me. 'You bastard,' she said with vehemence. 'How dare you spy on me?'

'I do many things in search of the truth. Now are you going to tell me who your visitor really was and what he wanted?'

'It was personal and private business and no, I am not going to tell you. What is more, I am dispensing with your services as of now, Mr Hawke. I want you to stop your investigations immediately.'

'My, he did frighten you, didn't he?'

She didn't rise to the bait. 'You may keep your fee, but I want you to drop the case. Leave my house now. I never want to see you again.'

I was sure that her anger was a smokescreen hiding the fear she felt as a result of the visit from the friend with the horn-rimmed glasses, but I was equally certain that whatever I said now would not affect her resolve to cut me adrift. I had been sacked from jobs before but never because the client was worried that I was getting near to the truth, that they were frightened of some threat. It seemed to me, as my rusty clockwork brain whirred furiously, that it would be best if I seemed to concur with Sandra Riley's wishes and leave, agreeing to drop the case. I had no intention of relinquishing the case, of course. I was a terrier and I had my bone and no one was going to make me give it up.

I smiled my little patronizing smile and rose from the chair. 'If you are sure that's what you want …?'

She nodded curtly. 'Just go,' she said and I detected a slight tremor in her voice.

And so, 'Just go' I did, but I couldn't help feeling strangely pleased with this sudden development. I just had to discover what that little white rabbit of a man, Bernard France, secretary to Sir Robert Gervais, was doing visiting the widowed Mrs Riley, giving her a tough old time and breaking a glass bowl.

It was growing dusk when I arrived back in the centre of London. I made my way to Benny's, my feet taking me automatically there while my mind did a cerebral juggling act with the facts and ideas I harboured regarding the Riley case. Before I knew it I was standing outside the café. The blinds were drawn and it was closed. I knocked hard on the door and after a while I heard a noise within and then, with a click of the latch, Benny was standing before me. He did not have to say a word for me to sense that something was wrong. His pale face registered sadness and dismay.

'What is it?' I said as Benny ushered me inside.

'Come up to the flat,' he said quietly.

This subdued Benny was not the fellow I knew.

'What is it?' I asked again. And then a thought struck me. 'Where's Peter?'

Benny did not respond directly. He just sighed heavily.

On entering the small-sitting room of his flat, I saw Susan McAndrew sitting there, her hands toying nervously with a handkerchief. She looked as though she had been crying.

'What the hell's going on?' I demanded, my anger stemming from frustration.

'Peter's gone,' said Susan.

I sank into a chair. What was it old Shakespeare said about troubles not coming in single spies?

Between them, Susan and Benny told me what had happened, how Susan had arrived to challenge Benny about Peter and the boy no doubt misjudging the situation, thinking he was going to be hauled back to Devon or worse, had done a bunk. Done a bunk, God knows where.

They had contacted the police but while they had been sympathetic they didn't hold out much hope. There were too many runaways in London as it was. Peter was just another poor little sod added to the list.

I was too tired and too dispirited to get angry. But fatigue did not prevent me from getting more depressed. The fact that there was nothing practical we could do to bring Peter back cut deep into my soul.

E I G H T E E N

Harryboy was getting bored with Rachel now. She had been quiet, sullen almost, all day. He assumed that this martyred performance was just because he had knocked her about a bit for being too cocky. He couldn't be doing with her petulance. It was about time that he dumped her. There were plenty more eager little tarts in the pie shop. Apart from her attitude, she didn't look so good now anyway and, besides that, he wasn't sure he believed her 'time of the month' story either. The more he thought about it, the more he was convinced she was putting him off. Either she was making him pay for having the nerve to slap her about a bit or she had gone off the bouncing bedsprings routine. Either way she was no use to him as she was. Yes, he was convinced that he had his shilling's worth with Rachel from the valleys. The time was rapidly approaching when he would get rid of her.

However, his main concern at the moment was his dwindling supply of cash. He needed to organize a significant injection of funds and for that he'd probably need Rachel. He mulled the situation over as he sat in the pub that evening sipping a pint of beer without much enthusiasm. Rachel was in the Ladies powdering her nose, yet again. He had lost count of the times she had felt the need to adjust her make-up during the day. So she had a black eye? So what? She wasn't marked for life. Stupid bitch.

He dragged his mind back to his money problem. He certainly wanted greater pickings than he'd got from the off-licence a couple of nights ago. And it had to be cash. He didn't want to have to go round some of his old haunts seeking out a fence to bargain with for a measly payout. He wanted real crinkly notes and clinking coins. As if to underline his thoughts, there was a sudden lull in the bar and he heard the cash register clang shut.

He glanced at his watch and cursed. It was just after eight. He'd left it late for tonight. He'd just have to try his luck with a few pedestrians with the aid of his lady friend. At least she'd come in useful there.

Rachel returned, looking as miserable as she had when she left. A little spark of anger ignited within Harryboy, but he quelled it. That could wait. At the moment he needed her. He'd deal with the sad cow later. A couple of days or so. That's all she'd got. And then she'd be dead meat.

Literally.

She sat beside him hardly acknowledging his presence.

'You want another?' he asked, pointing at her empty glass.

She shrugged.

He grabbed hold of her wrist so hard that she winced. 'Stop playing this game, lady. I asked you if you wanted a fucking drink. Now answer me. Answer me properly.' He spat the words out in a low vicious monotone.

Rachel's body stiffened, her eyes trying to avoid Harryboy's face. 'Yes, yes, I'll have another drink,' she said, desperately trying to control the hysteria in her voice.

He dropped her arm and pushed his way to the bar. She was aware that an elderly couple in the corner had observed the little scene, but as she glanced over at them, they averted their gaze. Apart from the entertainment value it was none of their business. They certainly didn't want to get involved. Well, who would? No one could help her, but herself. She had got into this mess by herself and that was the only way she would get out of it. She glanced over at the bar. Harryboy was still waiting to be served. She looked with hatred at the bullish little figure with the arrogant tilting of the head, the back of his neck pressing against the collar of his shirt, causing a thick fold of flesh to bulge out.

On impulse, she got up and moved in the opposite direction, squeezing her way through the smoking haze and the crowd of customers towards the door. No one seemed interested in her desire to pass. Caught in conversations, the customers needed asking more than once to let her by and then they did so reluctantly, indolently, barely pausing in what they were saying as they moved slightly to ease her passage. She had to push and squeeze past intransigent bodies to make any progress. Somehow the closer she got the further the door seemed to be as though it was deliberately shifting away from her, like an optical illusion, preventing her escape. She felt her heart thudding against her ribs and her legs began to give way as she pressed harder against the sea of bodies. 'Mind those bleedin' elbows, darling,' squawked one indignant punter as she scraped by him. The harder she pushed, the tighter they seemed to pack themselves. She began to whimper with frustration and now heads began to turn as she continued to force her way through.

Rachel knew that any moment Harryboy's thick hand could land on her shoulder and drag her back. Her own hand reached out in desperation for the brass handle of the door. It was like a mirage before her. Her arm was fully extended and yet it was still beyond her reach. One extra shove and ... at last her fingers gripped the cold metal. She held it tightly and with a small thrill of excitement she pushed the door open. Suddenly, she felt the fresh cool night air on her face. With one last effort she passed through the door. At last she was outside in the welcoming dark.

Rachel gave a sigh of relief and found herself leaning against the wall, sobbing involuntarily. She allowed herself the luxury of the tears for a few seconds before she remonstrated with herself. Enough of this, she told herself brusquely. You have to get yourself well away from here and as quickly as possible.

Pulling her coat about her, she began to walk briskly, her heels making sharp click-clacking sounds on the pavement. Her heartbeat was still rapid, but she managed to smile.

Freedom beckoned.

Rachel had reached the corner of the street a few yards up from the pub when she felt the hand on her shoulder. Involuntarily she turned round. As she did so, cold liquid splashed in her face. She could tell it was gin.

'I thought you wanted a drink,' said a voice in the blackness. 'Here am I spending good money on you and you decide to go walkies.'

She knew that it was pointless to try and invent an excuse, so she said nothing. She just mopped the gin from her face with her handkerchief.

'Cheers,' Harryboy said. It was too dark to see his features clearly, but she could tell from his voice that he was grinning. He cast the glass into the gutter where it smashed into tiny glittering pieces.

Grabbing hold of her arm so hard that it hurt, he began to walk her down the street away from the pub. 'Now that you've had your little drink, it's time I set you to work.'

James Dolan had been putting off going home since he left the bank. Just at the moment, his domestic life was not particularly enjoyable to say the least. His wife's sister had come to stay and the two women were making his life intolerable. They had joined forces to organize his life, upset his daily routines and belittle and ridicule him at every turn. They had turned him into a downtrodden lodger in his own home. His protests and requests went unheeded or were greeted by bouts of sarcastic laughter. The situation was exacerbated by his position at the bank. As the manager, he was respected, even feared by his workforce. They deferred to him for all decisions and sought his advice on the most trivial of matters. In the bank he was king, but at home he was derided and abused. That was why he had taken to staying in the city on the pretence of attending a series of meetings – 'secret meetings concerning the war effort' – to avoid going home so early. In reality, he grabbed a bite to eat in a café and then sat in a pub nursing a pint of beer while he attempted *The Times* crossword, passing the evening away in quiet contentment until it was time to catch the tube train home. He was aware that the harridans waiting for him to return had probably guessed he was lying. They would have smelt the alcohol on his breath and put two and two together. However, it didn't seem to bother them. It gave them more time to plot and plan to make his life more miserable. Sometimes when he heard the German planes overhead, he wished they would make a direct hit on number 11 Bradley Avenue.

Glancing at his watch, his heart sank. It really was time for the tube. With at least half the crossword incomplete, he stuffed the paper into his pocket, drained the glass of beer and left the pub.

It was a chilly night and he pulled up his coat collar against the cold. A bright, newly minted sharp-edged moon creamed the streets in a pale-yellow light. Knowing now that the best of his day was over, Arthur turned down the little side street that would eventually lead him to the Tottenham Court Road tube station, and eventually home.

He was preoccupied with his own miserable thoughts when he saw her – the solitary woman standing on the corner of the next street. Oh, no, he thought, not another prostitute. He hated being accosted by them because he never quite knew what to say. He had no desire to go with one – well, he had two women at home and that was enough for him – and yet he didn't want to be rude to them because he was aware that many of them had turned to this profession out of desperation, by dreadful circumstances brought on by the war.

However, he knew he had to pass her to reach his destination and so he prepared himself to utter his usual polite but rather pathetic reply: 'No thank you very much.' When he was within ten yards of the woman, she began to sway and then stagger as though she was afflicted with some strange malady and then with a little cry, she collapsed to the ground.

Shocked, James Dolan glanced around him. There was no one else about. The street was deserted. He couldn't just walk on by. The woman might be very ill and in need of urgent medical attention. It would be on his conscience for ever if he ignored her, that dark shape on the pavement.

With some trepidation, he approached the woman. She lay very still. He stood over her, just glimpsing her pale features. Her eyes were closed and her face was bruised. He could not tell if she was breathing or not.

'Hello, my dear. Are you all right?' he said, knowing it was a stupid question, but he really didn't know what else to say. She made no response. His heart fluttered with apprehension and he knelt down beside the inert figure and attempted to turn the young woman round on to her back. As he did so, he heard a rustling movement behind him. He hadn't time to turn around to see what had caused it before he felt a sharp stabbing pain on the back of his head. For a split second his world flashed white as though someone had shone a very bright light in his eyes and then darkness consumed him. He crumpled to the pavement unconscious.

Harryboy gave a guffaw of triumph. 'Very neat. Very neat,' he crowed, wiping the specks of James Dolan's blood from the butt of his pistol with a handkerchief. 'You can get up now, darling. Your performance is over.'

Stiffly Rachel Howells pulled herself to her feet while he rifled James Dolan's pockets, extracting some loose change and a wallet. 'Very nice,' he grinned, pulling a selection of notes from the wallet before casting it aside into the gutter. 'A very nice haul. There's well over ten quid here. You did good, girl. A couple more of your fainting performances tonight and we'll be set up for quite a few days.'

Rachel said nothing. She just gazed down at the unconscious figure of James Dolan. He lay on his back, his glassy, unseeing eyes staring up at her. He looked like a nice man, she thought.

N I N E T E E N

Strangely, despite the recalcitrant springs of my mattress, I slept well. In fact I had hardly closed my eyes before I drifted off into a thankfully dreamless sleep. However, I woke early feeling depressed and uneasy. I got myself ready for the day with zombie-like movements, determined not to switch my brain on until I'd got a clean collar around my neck and sucked in the first fag of the day.

When I was ready and all the woes, responsibilities and problems of my life began to seep back into my consciousness, I groaned. Above all, I felt desperate about Peter. This time around Fate or whatever that lottery which runs our lives is called, had not even allowed me the chance to really help the little blighter.

With a headache, a sour grin and leaden feet I took myself off to Benny's in the futile hope that Peter had returned to his fold.

As I entered I could see that Benny had some other issue on his mind. After he had passed on the news about Peter that there was no news about Peter, my little Jewish friend leaned over the counter, and with a crooked finger drew me towards him.

'They're in again, Johnny.'

I shook my head in bewilderment. 'What are you talking about?' I murmured.

'That couple I told you about. That poor girl and the bully of a boyfriend. You remember. I said that she was in trouble. Well, they're in again.'

Vaguely I did remember what Benny was talking about but I could not see why he was making such a fuss. My expression must have reflected what I was thinking for he threw his arms in the air and spluttered in frustration.

'They're in again and you should see the girl's face. It's black and blue. I tell you, he's been beating her. I am sure of it. The man's a villain.'

'You can't be sure, Benny. She might have been in an accident.'

'Accident! Oh yes, she ran into his fist. That kind of accident. I know these things.'

'What do you want me to do? Arrest him?'

Benny threw his hands up again. 'The girl needs help. Call yourself a detective!'

'All right. All right. Show me where they are and you can get a full fry up on the go for me.'

Benny led me to a table and whispered in my ear. 'They're over there, in the corner by the window.'

Casually, I glanced around, my gaze quickly settling on the couple that concerned Benny so. The man had his back to me but I could see the girl quite clearly and Benny had not been exaggerating. Her face was a mess. She was heavily made up, but the make-up did not disguise the damage done to her face, which was puffy and bruised. Her nose was swollen and she had a black eye. Her expression was one of total misery. Her sad, darting eyes reminded me of an animal in the zoo, trapped in a barren cage far away from its own natural environment.

The couple weren't talking, but from the man's posture and actions I could tell that he was relaxed. He was eating with great enthusiasm, shovelling the food into his mouth at a rate of knots.

This first impression suggested that Benny was right. The guy was a bully and had been knocking the girl about, but she was still with him either by choice or under some kind of duress. However, there was nothing I could do about that. I had no powers in such a situation.

Suddenly the man stood up and without a word made his way to the lavatory, leaving the girl playing with her piece of toast. On his departure her face relaxed a little but the desperate sadness in the eyes remained.

Benny gave me a little push. 'Now's your chance. Go and speak to her.'

'What am I supposed to say? Benny, whatever's going on over there is a private matter until the girl decides to do something about it. I can't just barge in like some tin pot knight in shining armour and save the day.'

Benny shook his head in frustration. He knew I was right and this inability to do anything to help the sad creature was upsetting to him.

'Can't you even offer her a lifeline?' he said.

I sighed resignedly and rose from my chair. Checking that the bully boyfriend was not on his way back from the lavatory, I made my way to the girl's table. She looked up in surprise. Close up I could see that beneath the puffiness and bruising she was actually very pretty.

'Sorry to interrupt,' I said awkwardly, tugging absent-mindedly at my tie, 'but I'm a private detective. It's my job to help people, especially when they can't go to the police. If ... if you ever feel the need for such help ....' I handed the girl one of my business cards. She looked at it and then back at me. I smiled and for a brief moment her features softened. It never struck me at the time what she made of this one-eyed fellow in a crumpled suit and dingy shirt leaning over her, offering help.

'Keep it safe,' I said. 'Any time you need me.'

For a moment she looked apprehensive and then seemed on the verge of saying something, but suddenly her faced clouded with concern and eyes flickered nervously. Benny had been right. This girl was frightened.

I touched her shoulder and gave it a gentle squeeze. 'I mean it,' I said quietly. 'Any time.' With that I left her and returned to my table.

I had just sat down when Bully Boy returned from the lavatory. This time I was able to get a good look at him. He was indeed a nasty piece of work. He was short and stocky with a pug nose and a cruel basilisk stare. He swaggered rather than walked across the room. Apart from the unpleasantness of his demeanour, there was something else about his face that troubled me.

I had seen it before.

Somewhere in the back of my brain bells were ringing, but for the life in me, I couldn't tell why.

'What did you say?' Benny whispered in my ear with some urgency. I told him.

'Well, I suppose it's better than nothing.'

'Under the circumstances that's all I could do.'

Benny gave me a reluctant smile. 'I guess you're right,' he said, placing his hand on my shoulder. 'Thank you, Johnny.'

'Now then, there was talk of breakfast ...'

'Coming up.'

Benny hurried off to the kitchen. I sat back and casually cast a glance across at Bully Boy and his girlfriend. He was hunched up staring out of the window smoking a cigarette. Even this simple activity had an air of aggression about it. The girl sat submissively, nervously fiddling with her cutlery. Briefly, our eyes met and a fleeting half smile touched her lips and then quickly she looked away.

Under normal circumstances I would have tried to follow them when they left to see if I could help the girl, but these were not normal circumstances.

I trudged back to my office and rang David Llewellyn at Scotland Yard. I gave him the registration number of the car that the White Rabbit had been driving that I'd noted down outside Sandra Riley's bungalow the day before.

'Can you get me details of the owner? I believe his name is Bernard France. I'd appreciate his address,' I asked.

'Ah, you've got a lead at last have you?'

'I could have. I'm not sure.'

David didn't press me for further details. 'Well, I'll do a bit of digging on your behalf and get back to you.'

I managed a weak grin. 'Thanks.'

I spent the morning numbing my brain by tidying the office and sorting out some paperwork. I was also visited by a new client, a timid little fellow, who wanted me to find his daughter. Apparently there had been a row and she had walked out. I sensed that's she'd be back after she'd cooled down but I took details and assured him that I would get on to the case as soon as my current investigation was completed.

Around noon, David rang back. It wasn't good news.

'It's a government car. That's all I can tell you. The rest is restricted information, so it must belong to someone fairly important. Who is this Bernard France? You want to tell me about it?'

'Not just now. It's a bit complicated. Have you heard of Sir Robert Gervais? '

'Can't say I have. Sorry.'

'I seem to be heading for culs-de-sac all the time on this case.'

'You sound really down, man.'

I told him about Peter.

'That's a bugger,' he said gently when I'd finished. 'Let's hope the boy has a change of heart and turns up on your doorstep again.'

'Yes,' I said, not wanting to extend the discussion. How likely was it that Peter would return when he thought I had betrayed him and was ready to turn him over to the authorities?

I thanked David again and replaced the receiver.

Well, I mused, the White Rabbit is involved in the Riley case in some way. I needed to find out more about him. No doubt I would not receive any further help from Sandra's brother, Captain Eddowes. I'm sure Sandra would have told him that she had sacked me and he was not to have anything more to do with me. All I had to go on was the fellow's name, the fact that he worked at the War Office and was private secretary to some chap called Sir Robert Gervais. Surely that was enough to set me going. However, there was obviously a ring of security around these fellows which would be hard to get through.

Well, I thought, as I reached for my hat and coat, perhaps I could put a hold on that line of enquiry until I'd seen Amanda. She or rather he might have some information that would take me further in this case. I reckoned I could do with a drink to help me sort my ideas out and hot water over tea leaves or chicory was not going to do the job: I needed something stronger.

The Velvet Cage is my favourite night-time haunt. I love the dim lighting, the smoke, the busy chatter and the jazz. They wrap themselves around me like some comforting security blanket, inducing a mild amnesia so that you can for a while forget all the slings and arrows of outrageous fortune and just enjoy the boozy, fuggy, toe-tapping moment before passing through the swings doors to grim reality once more. However, in the middle of the afternoon, the place is like a mausoleum. There are few customers, no music and little atmosphere. It lacks its night-time charm. It struck me then that this place had something in common with its strange sister, The Loophole Club. The place felt cold and lonely and smelt stale when I walked in. It could have been a different establishment altogether from its evening persona.

Well, I was here now: I'd better make the best of it.

I bought myself a double Scotch from a dull, uninterested barman whom I'd not seen before and slipped into one of the darker booths.

I took a sip of my drink, allowing the liquid to roll around on my tongue before allowing it to slip away to warm my innards. It felt good. And after a couple more sips, I started to relax.

Nevertheless, my mind kept going back to the possible motive for Walter's death – Walter's murder. I was convinced now that it was a deliberate targeted murder. He knew something did old Walter. He knew something dangerous and so he was silenced. But what did he know? Some gossip, some secret he'd picked up at the War Office? Surely not, they were on our side. They wouldn't kill a chap if they thought he might blab in the wrong places. Would they? I'd rather not let my thoughts wander down that particular thoroughfare at the moment; it was too dark, too unpleasant, too frightening.

I drained my glass. Time for another. I must keep the old brain cogs well lubricated. My glass replenished by the same dull barman, I returned to my booth and my cogitations.

I thought back to that evening in The Loophole and the tall woman with whom Walter had had an argument. There was something very serious going on there. It wasn't simply a bitchy spat. This Helen creature held a key to the mystery. I felt sure. Well, I had my own agent chasing up that particular strand of the case. I glanced at my watch. I was due to visit Amanda in a couple of hours. Hopefully, I would learn more then.

Amanda lived in a shabby block of flats in the area behind Kings Cross Station. I arrived five minutes before the appointed time and rang the bell. I had no idea how she would answer the door. Would she, I wondered, be dressed up to the nines in her cocktail dress all ready to skip off to The Loophole Club, or would I see the real Amanda in jacket, shirt and trousers as the man of the house.

As it turned out, I saw no one because no one answered the door. After several minutes of persistent ringing, I knocked loudly but this elicited no response either. She might be late, I supposed. (I couldn't help thinking of Amanda as a 'she'.) Her enquiries could have taken her longer than expected. Or she could have changed her mind about helping me and was refusing to answer, hoping I'd go away. Well, I wasn't going to go away without finding out more. I peered through the letter box but all I could see was a small featureless dimly lighted hall. There was no sign of life. Then I simply tried the handle of the door and to my surprise it opened with ease.

Glancing about me to check there was no one about, no one to see what I was doing, I entered Amanda's flat.

I found her in the living-room. She was sitting on a dingy settee, dressed in slacks and a cream blouse. Her eyes stared at me in surprise, shock even, as I entered. They were wide and glassy and they didn't move. Neither did her tongue, which was lolling out of the corner of her open mouth.

Amanda was dead.

She sat erect on the sofa, her wig slightly askew and her face registering terror, looking like an exhibit in the Chamber of Horrors at Madame Tussaud's. The scarf tied around her throat clearly indicated that she had been strangled. A silent death.

Obviously in trying to trace this Helen character, she had got too near the flames and had been burned. A wave of sadness and guilt swept over me. It was my fault that she was dead. If I hadn't asked her to find out about the mysterious individual I'd seen with Walter Riley she would still be alive, swanning around The Loophole Club in her finery. I was partly responsible for her death. That made me angry. Not with myself but with the bastard who had killed this poor, sad creature and valued her life so casually.

The growing feeling of anger was added to the mix of the emotions which were spinning around in my brain. No matter how corny or clichéd the sentiment, I wasn't going to let them get away with this.

Then, luckily, my professional concerns took over from my theatrical pronouncements, and I began to search the flat for clues. It was clear that in a short space of time Amanda had discovered the whereabouts of Walter's associate and indeed maybe more incriminating evidence. That was why she had been silenced. In searching her flat I might be able to discover something that would help me find her too. Obviously, the killer would have given the place the once over, but by necessity it would have been a hasty procedure and possibly not as thorough as it should have been.

I was wrong. It was very thorough. There was nothing I could find which would help me trace the killer in any way. I searched through the drawers, the clothes – a strange mix of dresses and men's suits – Amanda's handbags, anything that may contain some clue. I drew a blank.

Then an idea struck me. Where did Amanda keep her private

information? I thought back to our conversation in The Loophole Club the previous day. When I had given her my card. Where did she put it for safe keeping? Not in her handbag. No. She slipped it discreetly inside her brassiere.

I gulped and stared at the cold corpse sitting on the settee with the wild staring eyes and errant tongue. My blood ran cold. And then my eyes focused on the cream blouse she was wearing and the swell of her chest where her artificial breasts pressed against the material producing a convincing feminine curve.

The thought of unbuttoning the blouse and feeling inside the dead body of a transvestite was not only bizarre in the extreme but it made me feel rather queasy. There was something of the necrophiliac about it.

But I had to do it.

Thank God, no one could see me – otherwise I would be locked up in a pervert's prison for life.

With nervous fingers, I unbuttoned Amanda's blouse, while avoiding looking at her wide terrified eyes. As I pulled back the blouse to expose her brassiere, the action caused Amanda's body to slide sideways and fall onto the arm of the sofa.

I pulled back in shock. It was as though Amanda was objecting to such personal interference.

I stared at the frozen figure for a moment and then with the admonishing utterance, 'Get a grip, Johnny!' I resumed my task.

Slowly, I slipped my hand into the left hand cup of her brassiere. It was a strange sensation. At first my fingers came into contact with some material which I took to be a kind of sponge and then I felt a piece of paper. My heart gave a leap and a sly grin fought its way onto my lips. I extracted the paper and standing back from the dead body I examined it.

The sheet which had been torn from a small notebook, was folded in two. I opened it out and written there in neat handwriting was an address. I could only hope that this address would lead me to the murderer.

TWENTY

Peter had run out of money. He sat hunched up on a ramshackle bench, one of those that still remained along the Embankment, staring miserably into space. He wanted to cry but he couldn't. He had tried to cry, thinking that the tears would ease his distress but they would not come. It was as though they had dried up within him.

He didn't know what to do. He was beginning to wish that he hadn't left Devon, hadn't come to London and hadn't trusted Johnny. It had all been a big mistake. But he knew he couldn't go back. Not now. The previous night he had slept under one of the bridges, but it had been cold and uncomfortable and there had been rats. At one point he had woken from his uneasy slumbers to find one of the filthy creatures scampering over him, so close to his face that he could see its beady eyes. He shuddered at the thought.

He had spent his last few coppers on a cup of tea from a tea stall further down the Embankment. The man running the stall had taken pity on the bedraggled youth and given him one of the previous day's left-over cakes. 'It's a bit dry, but if you dip it in your tea, it'll taste fine,' he'd said. Peter had taken his advice and indeed the cake did taste good.

One thought that was edging its way into his mind, and one that he was trying desperately to ignore, was the realization that there were only two options open to him now. He could give himself up – find a policeman and tell him the whole story. Then he'd be carted off to an orphanage somewhere. Or he would have to steal. If he didn't, he'd starve. He really didn't want to become a criminal but the alternative was far worse. If only he was grown up, he could get a job and earn some money and look after himself. As this thought passed through his mind, it prompted another. Perhaps he could earn money by washing-up. He quite enjoyed it when he was at Benny's place. The thought of Benny sent a cold nostalgic shiver down his spine. For a brief time – having his breakfast with Johnny in the little café and helping out in the kitchen – he had been the happiest he had ever been. Why had it to end so suddenly? Now he found himself crying. The tears had crept up on him unawares and they rolled down his cheeks leaving clean tram lines on his otherwise grimy countenance.

He sniffed and wiped his face with his sleeve and forced his mind to go back to his idea. Perhaps the nice man at the tea stall would pay him to wash up for him. That would get him enough cash to buy food at least. A phrase that Mr Booth was often repeating about the house came into his mind: 'beggars can't be choosers'. Peter hadn't quite understood it at first but now he saw the sense of it. In essence he was a beggar and he didn't have much choice – he couldn't be a chooser. That's how he saw it anyway.

Well, he'd give it a try. The chap could only say no. Even if he refused, he might feel sorry for Peter and give him another of his stale cakes as a kind of compensation. With brisk determination, Peter wiped the last of the tears away and retraced his steps along the Embankment until he reached the tea stall. It was doing a brisk trade and Peter hung back until there was a lull. Tentatively he approached the counter. The owner didn't see him at first and Peter had to attract his attention by manufacturing a little cough.

'Hello again,' the man said, a faint smile on his lips. 'You going to be a regular?'

'I've come for a job,' said Peter.

The man laughed. 'Have you now.'

'I'm very good at washing-up. Please let me do your washing-up.'

Suddenly the man's expression grew serious. The boy really meant it. This was no childish joke.

'I don't need no one, son,' he replied, after some thought. He gazed down at the scruffy scrap of humanity and saw that he had been crying. He felt sorry for the lad. It was clear that he was a runaway of sorts and in sore need of help. 'I does me own washing-up.' He was about to add that he hardly scraped a living for himself from the tea bar as it was and that he couldn't afford to take on any help but he couldn't bear to verbalize such a depressing thought.

'Oh, please,' said Peter. 'I'd work hard and you wouldn't have to pay me much.'

The man scratched his chin and gave the situation some thought. Eventually he nodded his head. 'Tell you what, I'll give you a trial. Thruppence an hour and see how you get on.'

Peter beamed. 'That's great. I won't let you down.'

'Come round the back and I'll let you in. You can make a start right away.'

Peter scampered around to the back of the stall where his new employer admitted him into the cramped interior. Within minutes he had a tea towel around his waist and was dipping numerous pots and plates in lukewarm sudsy water, a smile on his lips.

As the tea-time trade faltered and dwindled, it came time to shut the stall up for the day. The owner, who had told Peter to call him 'Dave' handed over the requisite number of coins for Peter's services. 'There's yer wages. You done well, lad,' he said.

'Can I come tomorrow?'

Dave sighed. 'The truth is I can't really afford to keep you on full time. I barely make enough for meself, let alone payin' out wages.'

Peter's face fell. Another disappointment just when things seemed to be looking up.

'Let's say I give you a couple more days' work and then I reckon you gotta move on.'

It was something of a reprieve and Peter nodded his acceptance with good grace.

'Righto. Now we start early in this establishment. I'll need you here by six thirty in the mornin'. Do you think you can cope with that?'

Again Peter nodded.

'Good lad. See you then, eh?'

Peter pocketed the coins and slipped on his coat. 'Thank you, Dave. See you tomorrow.'

'Six-thirty sharp,' said Dave, holding the door of the stall open.

Taking this as his cue to leave, Peter made a swift exit. Dave watched him as he disappeared into the gloom of the night. He felt sure the boy would turn up the next day. He had to if Dave's plan was to work.

TWENTY-ONE

Another day. Another hotel room.

Rachel pulled back the net curtain and stared down at the dingy side street. Across the way workmen were busy demolishing the shell of a row of bombed premises. The masonry wavered briefly before crumbling and crashing thunderously into the cavern that had once been the heart of the building. But the noise and the rising clouds of dust and debris failed to impinge themselves on Rachel's consciousness. Her mind was elsewhere, dwelling on her own dilemma – her own crumbling fortunes. Strangely, although she still had the ache of fear deep within her, the fear of Harryboy and her enslavement to him, she was also bored. Was this how her life would pan out now? She was caught on the grim conveyor belt of long time-wasting hours until the evening before they could commit some crime that would enable them to eat well and move on to another hotel.

Harryboy was lying on the bed smoking and reading the newspaper. For the moment he seemed content and that offered Rachel some respite at least. Nevertheless she was very unhappy. She leaned her forehead against the cool glass of the window and sighed.

Harryboy's antennae came into play. He looked up from his paper and an unpleasant frown manifested itself on his forehead as he turned his gaze on Rachel.

'What's wrong with you?' he snapped, stubbing out his cigarette in the ashtray on the bedside table with some petulance. 'Pining after your boyfriend?'

'Boyfriend! I–I don't know what you mean? What boyfriend?' She was genuinely puzzled by this outburst. She'd never mentioned Will to him. He belonged to her old life in Mumbles.

Harryboy cast aside the paper with an angry gesture. 'Don't give me that. Do you think I'm stupid? D'you think I'm blind?'

Rachel shook her head in confusion. 'Honestly, I don't know what you're on about.'

'So you *do* think I'm stupid.'

''Course not,' she replied quickly, her heartbeat quickening. She recognized that aggressive, whining tone of voice and what it signalled. Was he trying to pick a phantom quarrel so he had an excuse to beat her up again? Please, God, no.

'I have no boyfriend but you. You know that,' she added, hoping that affirmation would quell Harryboy's growing annoyance.

'What about the one-eyed bloke in the café this morning? I saw you chatting with him. Smiling and simpering. Nothing gets past old Harryboy you know. I've got the *two* eyes.'

'I don't know the man. He … he just came over to the table.'

'What did he want? Was he trying to pick you up?'

'No. No, he … he....'

'Yes? What did the bastard want?' Harryboy was shouting now, his eyes wide with fury. Rachel realized that this outburst had been building ever since he'd seen the detective chap come to their table. Harryboy had probably been concocting wild stories in his head about what really happened, his anger festering and growing all the while.

'I've never seen the man before. He was a stranger.'

'But you took a shine to him though, didn't you? I saw your smile.'

'I was being polite. He … he just asked if I'd got a light. I just smiled politely. What else could I do? We don't want to draw attention to ourselves, do we?'

'He wanted a light, did he?'

'Yes.'

'Liar! He wanted you. He tried to pick you up. My girl! And you smiled at him. Smiled at him like you were easy meat. Just like you smiled at me the day *I* picked you up.'

Rachel shook her head. 'No, no. You've got it all wrong. It was out of politeness. I smiled out of politeness. He means nothing to me.'

Harryboy was off the bed now and advancing on her, a thin sheen of sweat glistening on his furrowed brow. The long slow fuse had reached its target. Now it was about to explode.

Rachel cringed and cowered before him, knowing what to expect. 'You're nothing but a cheap tart,' he bellowed, his face contorted like a furious gargoyle. He raised his fist ready to strike.

It was then that something snapped inside Rachel. No one had ever called her that before. She knew she wasn't a cheap tart. She had more self respect and dignity. Emboldened by this certainty, she stood up and faced him.

'I am not a cheap tart,' she said quietly emphasizing each word with firmness.

Harryboy sneered. 'Yes, you are.' And he hit her across the face with the back of his hand. Fireworks exploded before her eyes and she stumbled backwards, just managing to keep her balance by grasping hold of the chest of drawers. From the corner of her eye she spied a small glass ashtray on the chest. Instinctively and with great speed she snatched it up, swung round and brought it crashing down towards Harryboy's head.

He dodged sideways to avoid the blow but he wasn't quick enough and it struck him on his right temple. He staggered back on to the bed with a cry, a thin red rivulet of blood trickling down his brow. Harryboy was in a kind of double shock. He never expected the silly bitch to retaliate and he never expected to be wounded. Gingerly he sought out the cut with his fingers. When he examined them and saw the blood glistening there, his rage increased. He jumped from the bed and hurled himself at Rachel. This time he wasn't going to beat her senseless: this time he was going to kill her.

A strange calming coolness had now settled on Rachel and she was able to anticipate Harryboy's clumsy actions. With ease she managed to dodge him as he blundered towards her, lashing out once more with the glass ashtray as she did so. This time she caught him on the side of his head. The ashtray thudded against his ear. He gave a yelp of pain and dropped to his knees, clasping his hand to the wounded area. She slid by him and made her way to the door. Harryboy's jacket was hanging on a hook there. An idea flashed fiercely into her mind. With grim determination, she grabbed it, reached inside and pulled out his gun. It felt heavy in her hands, but, as she gripped it tightly, pressing the cold metal against the skin of her palm, she smiled, and her eyes lit up with excitement. It felt good to hold. And it gave her the upper hand.

By now, Harryboy was on his feet again. At first he did not notice that Rachel had his gun. He moved sluggishly towards her, breathing heavily, his anger now at eruption level. And then he saw the glint of metal in her hand and he stopped in his tracks.

'Get away from me,' Rachel said. On the surface her tone was measured, calm and unemotional, but inside she was sick and frightened. Here she was holding a loaded weapon and, God help her, prepared to fire it if necessary. She suddenly realized how far she had strayed from the innocent girl she had been only a few days before. Now she was tainted and this monster standing before her was responsible.

Harryboy responded with a nervous laugh. 'What d'you think you're going to do with that, eh?'

'I'm going to shoot you, if you come any nearer.'

Harryboy laughed again, but it was unconvincing merriment. Rachel could see the uncertainty and indeed the fear in his eyes. The crazy tart might just be telling the truth.

'Don't be a fool, baby. You don't want to kill me. OK so I was a bit rough on you, but that's no reason to … behave like this. Come on put the gun down. We can sort this out …'

He took a step nearer to her.

She flinched but did not step back. Instead she thrust the gun towards him in a threatening manner.

'I warned you,' she said firmly, but Harryboy could see that her hand was shaking now.

It's all show, a little voice in his head advised him. The silly cow wouldn't dare pull the trigger. Look how terrified she is. Already her bravado is ebbing away. Go get her, Harryboy. Take her and then teach her a lesson that she'll never forget.

He did as the voice told him. He rushed at Rachel, his arms outstretched to grab the gun. But before he could reach her, she fired the pistol. There was a sharp crack like the snapping of a piece of wood and then he felt a searing pain in his left arm. He found himself flung backwards onto the bed again with blood pouring from the wound in his left upper arm. In reality, the bullet had only nicked the flesh and had ended up lodged in the padded headboard. But Harryboy didn't know this. He believed he had been seriously wounded. The thought of this and the severe pain he felt prompted him to retch at first and then the dark clouds of unconsciousness rolled in swiftly and invaded his senses. He fell back on the bed in a dead faint.

The room thundered with the noise of the demolition work across the street, the noise pounding in Rachel's brain. She didn't move for some seconds. She couldn't. The enormity of what she had done rooted her to the spot. She thought that she had killed Harryboy. She stared with horror at his inert body lying on the bed.

What had she done?

Tears sprang to her eyes, but they were not tears of sorrow for the man on the bed, but for herself. Oh, how far she had travelled down the dark corridor of immorality and corruption. Now she was a murderess.

She dropped the gun with a short disgusted cry as though it had suddenly caught fire in her hand.

Her thoughts now focused on escape. She must get out of there. As far away as possible. She dragged her coat from the chair beside the bed, snatched up her bag and headed for the door. As she did so, Harryboy groaned and shifted his position on the bed. She glanced back at him and to her surprise saw that his chest was rising and falling in a slow regular motion. So he wasn't dead after all. This realization brought mixed emotions. She was glad that she hadn't committed murder but she was sorry that the rotten bastard was still alive.

Suddenly, another thought struck her. She retrieved Harryboy's jacket from the floor where she'd dropped it and extracting his wallet from the inside pocket, she scooped out all the cash and thrust it into her bag.

'You owe me, you bastard,' she said, addressing the comatose Harryboy, who lay there, bleeding quietly.

With that she slipped her coat on and left the room.

TWENTY-TWO

On leaving Amanda's flat, I walked for some time, cudgelling my brains, trying to sort out what I should do for the best. I was reluctant to get the police involved. Involved in what? All I had was an address. That wasn't exactly water-tight proof of anything, was it, Johnny? Oh, well, there was a body, of course. I had to do something about that. I didn't want Amanda, poor pale dead Amanda, to be left undiscovered for days. She deserved better than that. I slipped into a telephone box and adopting a croaky cockney voice, I made an anonymous call to the police informing them of Amanda's murder. Before I was bombarded with questions, I replaced the receiver and wandered out into the dusk.

One thought burned itself into my brain as I lay in bed that night. Surely, I told myself, I had got my hands on the address of the murderer. The crumpled slip of paper that I had taken from Amanda's dead body bore the words '12 Studely Mansions, Kensington'. It must be that whoever dwelt here had not only done in Amanda but had been responsible for Walter Riley's death also. Could it really be Helen, the creature I had seen arguing with Walter that first night at The Loophole Club? Another transvestite? This case grew crazier by the minute. What on earth could have been the motive? Why would a little clerk with an unusual peccadillo become the target for a murderer.

However, while that area of the investigation was still shrouded in fog, it certainly seemed clear that in trying to discover more about the lovely Helen, poor Amanda had found herself in shark-infested waters. She had come across something that she wasn't meant to know, had got too close to the truth and for her pains had been bumped off before she could tell anyone. And the truth was …? Well, that was a question I wasn't as yet capable of answering.

The previous evening I had pored over my *A to Z* of London and had eventually located Studely Mansions at Bedford Gardens, Kensington. As a detective I was pleased with my deductions, but I wasn't certain what I was to do with the information. My immediate thought was to gallop around there, storm the citadel and then.... Well, yes, Johnny, what follows the 'and then'? What do you do 'then'? Break the door down and stomp in there guns blazing? I think not. This is not a Hollywood movie. You are not Tom Mix. Remember, the killer is likely to have guns too. And for certain they'd be bigger than mine. The situation needed handling with more subtlety, and sadly that's not a commodity I have in great quantities.

I needed to sleep on it to help me gain some perspective. Unfortunately, eight hours of tossing and turning in a darkened room didn't help. The morning light brought no clarity to my uncertainty. So I did what I always do in these circumstances: I followed my gut instinct.

I dressed hurriedly, swilled down a scalding cup of coffee and was out on the street in quick sticks. On an impulse I hailed a taxi and told the driver to take me to Bedford Gardens, Kensington.

I sat back enjoying the luxury of a taxi ride. My usual mode of transport was the bus, tube or, inevitably, shanks's pony. The income of a young private eye in London does not allow one to use a taxi cab as a matter of course. But this was a special job and I had been paid for my services. Also, as I had allowed my instincts rather than any carefully conceived plan to dictate my actions, I could give my brain a rest and view the world from the back of a moving vehicle. I must admit that the grey panorama of London which swept by me at speed was no less depressing seen through the window of the cab than it was when I pounded the pavements. It was just slightly more surreal as though I were watching a depressing newsreel film on a very small screen.

However things did improve a little as we entered the environs of Kensington. There were fewer buildings boarded up or damaged and fewer pedestrians crowding the streets. When we drew up on the corner of Bedford Gardens and I emerged, the air did smell a little sweeter. After the taxi roared away, I stood on the pavement taking in my bearings. It was a short, quiet road with a few smart cars, shiny emblems of wealth, parked neatly by the kerb, and some very grand-looking town houses at one end – the end where I was standing. Just before the corner at the bottom of the road I spied an imposing block of flats – very modern, very chic, built less than ten years ago. This must be Studely Mansions. Elementary, my dear Watson.

I sauntered along in a casual manner, puffing on a Craven A, making my way towards this compartmentalized Xanadu. I wondered how much it would cost a month to rent one of these fur-lined hutches. Probably what I paid annually for my place. I passed through the impressive revolving door and found myself in a large marble hallway. A concierge in a claret coat was standing at a mahogany desk and on seeing me he raised a deferential eyebrow.

'Can I help you, sir?'

'I'm here to visit someone. A business acquaintance. He lives in flat twelve.'

'Ah, Mr Webster.'

I beamed. 'That's the fellow.'

'Shall I buzz him to let him know you are here?'

'Oh, no. I want this to be a surprise.' I gave my deferential friend a knowing wink. His expression suggested that such facial tics were not appreciated in Studely Mansions.

'His apartment is on the first floor, sir. The elevator is over there to your right.'

'Thank you. I'll take the stairs.'

I wasn't a fan of lifts at the best of times – stale smelling, confined, claustrophobic cages – but they certainly were to be avoided when making forays into enemy territory.

The place was starkly modern with clean lines and a touch of Hollywood glamour – the sort of place Fred Astaire would visit in his attempts to woo Ginger Rogers. Less elegantly than Fred I tripped up the staircase and found myself on the first floor. Flat 12 was easy to locate. A large cream anonymous door with the gold number twelve emblazoned on it gave the game away. Now I was here, what was I to do? I was reminded of the times as a little boy when I would go to the sweet shop although I had no money and gaze through the window at the tempting confectionery beyond my financial grasp. Here I was with my face up against the pane again. It really would be foolish to press that shiny but discreet doorbell. It could lead me into a lot of trouble.

And so what did I do?

I pressed the doorbell.

A discreet mellifluous ring resounded somewhere beyond the door. I scurried away to the end of the corridor, dropped to my knees and hid behind a large mahogany stand which supported a luxuriant display of artificial flowers. Peering around the side of the stand, I waited. The door opened and eventually a head appeared, glancing up and down the corridor for a fleeting moment before disappearing again. I had only the briefest glimpse of his features but recognized them. It was my old friend the White Rabbit. I felt a tingle of excitement.

In my brain I heard the sound of a satisfying click as another piece of the jigsaw slotted into place. As I was pondering the implication of my discovery, I heard the elegant wheeze of the elevator and the gentle clunk as it reached its destination: this floor.

With speed, I swivelled round the mahogany stand, changing position so that now I couldn't be seen by anyone leaving the elevator. The doors swished open and one passenger emerged: a smart-looking gent wearing a grey belted raincoat carrying an impressive briefcase. He made his way along the corridor, fishing out his door key and entered the flat next door to number 12.

Well, I told myself, with some satisfaction, either the White Rabbit lived a double life as a Mr Webster, or he was using his flat for some reason. Either way he was heavily involved in the Riley and Amanda murders. Oh yes, I was making headway. I was about to smile at this thought when I felt an arm grab me tightly around the throat.

The pressure on my windpipe was so great that for a moment I thought I was going to pass out. My eyes watered, my vision blurred and I made a strange involuntary gagging sound with my mouth as my knees began to sink beneath me. It is at times like this when your brain screams at you, warning you not to give in. Fight back, you dummy, it yells. Fight back or you're a gonner. The panic and adrenalin that this call to arms stimulates combine to give you a brief moment of superhuman strength. With a force I didn't know I had, I gave my unknown assailant the mightiest thump in the ribs with both my elbows. I heard a sullen grunt in my ear and his grip lessened. That was all the leeway I needed. I thumped him again and managed to pull myself free of his fierce embrace. Spinning round I found myself facing the red-coated concierge. Now his complexion matched his uniform.

'I know your sort,' he gasped, his eyes aflame with anger. 'I got you tagged the moment I set eyes on you. A ruddy thief. Sniffing around for booty, eh?'

He rushed me, but I sidestepped him.

'You won't get away, you bastard. I've called the police.'

He said no more because I smashed him as hard as I could in the face with my fist. Blood fountained from his nostrils and he fell backwards, eyes flickering wildly, his head crashing against the mahogany stand. His mouth moved silently in some unspoken curse before he slithered to the floor, out cold. I rushed forward and saved the artificial flower arrangement from tumbling to the ground. Wincing from the pain of my bruised knuckles, I made a quick exit. I raced down the marble staircase – more like Groucho Marx than Fred Astaire – and through the revolving doors to fresh air and freedom. I couldn't help but be amused. I've lost track of the number of scrapes and tight corners I'd found myself in, but I had never been accused of being a thief before. Despite the throbbing knuckles, I found myself chuckling at the comic irony of the situation.

As inconspicuously as I could, I hurried down the street. I had just reached the corner when I saw a police car swing round the bend, no doubt on its way to Studely Mansions to apprehend a potential thief.

TWENTY-THREE

When Harryboy Jenkins slowly regained consciousness, he became aware of a fierce throbbing pain in the upper region of his left arm. It was a pulsing ache that seemed to be in rhythm with his own heartbeat. It took him some time to remember exactly where he was and what had happened before he had blacked out, but as the ceiling above him gradually slid into sharp focus it all came back to him; the gunshot, the pain, the enveloping darkness. Without moving from his prone position on the bed, his fingers gingerly sought out the source of his pain. He grimaced when he felt the dampness of his shirt over the wound. He was still bleeding.

With a throaty rasping curse, he slowly raised himself from the bed and moved over to the wash basin. He gazed back at himself in the pitted mirror: his face was ashen and dark circles had formed beneath his eyes, but what concerned him most was the large spreading badge of blood on his sleeve.

Carefully, he removed the shirt and examined the damage. The skin was ruptured and was weeping blood gently, but the wound was not deep or serious. He was convinced there was no bullet in there. Luck had been on his side and he'd survived with just a nasty gash. He heaved a sigh of relief and grinned back at his own reflection.

He bathed his arm, wiping away all the blood, patted it dry with a towel and then poured a little whisky from his flask into the wound as a form of antiseptic, before taking a swig himself. The burning liquid made him choke and his body shook with a coughing fit. He swore. Then, tearing a strip from one of the bed sheets, he made himself a rough makeshift bandage which, after several attempts, he managed to tie around the damaged area, using his teeth to pull one end tight.

He sat on the edge of the bed as a wave of weariness swept over him. It was as though his brain needed to shut down. Without thinking, he curled himself up into a tight ball and surrendered himself to sleep once more.

When he awoke, it was morning. Slowly and stiffly he raised himself up from the bed and splashed his face with cold water. His arm still throbbed but it bothered him less now that he knew it was just a flesh wound and that no serious damage had been done. He shaved and got dressed. Now that his concern for the injury had evaporated, a new emotion began to grow within him. Anger. Incandescent fury. Again he swore, this time with loud vehemence as he remembered Rachel and what she had done to him.

He paced around the room like a caged animal, calling her all the foul names he could muster from his extensive lexicon of swear words. It wasn't his wounded arm that preoccupied him now but his wounded pride. By God, she was not going to get away with it. No one messed with Harryboy Jenkins without paying dearly for it. Oh, yes, she would pay and pay in fucking spades. As his frustrated anger grew, beads of perspiration began to drip from his brow.

He would find her. Wherever that bitch had gone to earth, he would find her.

He picked up his gun from the floor where Rachel had dropped it. Holding it again gave him pleasure and calmed his racing heartbeat. He felt whole once more and the furrows faded from his brow and his lips curled into a satisfied smirk. He picked up his jacket from the back of the chair and put it on, slipping the gun into his left inside pocket. It was then that he noticed his wallet was missing. A chill of panic ran up his spine. In desperation, he searched the jacket, pulling out the linings of all his pockets. It was to no avail. The wallet was not there.

He swore and sat on the bed, wiping the sweat from his forehead. Then, remarkably, he spied it, on the floor beside the dressing table. He snatched it up and examined it. It was empty. All the cash was gone. For a while he stared at the compartments where crisp notes had once nestled and then suddenly he laughed. It was a strange, sneering laugh which was layered with menace rather than humour. This was another nail in Rachel Howells' coffin. Not that she needed one. She was gonna be dead meat anyway. He would see to that, no danger.

He felt in his trouser pockets and dragged out some coins and a crumpled ten shilling note. Well, he wasn't completely broke and, best of all, he had his gun. That would solve most of his problems.

Some ten minutes later Harryboy Jenkins was out on the streets of London. He walked with determination, his pugnacious face set in a cocky smile. He had a very busy day ahead.

It was early afternoon when Harryboy walked into the little tobacconist's shop in Felshaw Court, a narrow thoroughfare up from the Embankment near Waterloo Bridge. He'd been watching the premises for fifteen minutes or so. Trade was desultory. Three customers only in the time he'd been on watch. No doubt early mornings, lunchtimes and evenings were the busy periods when the workers would pop in to stock up on their fags. Now was the quiet time. He was sure he'd picked the right target. Everyone smokes. Tobacconists were little gold mines.

With his hat pulled low over his face and his coat collar up, he bustled in, turning the sign round to 'Closed', before drawing down the blind on the door. The tobacconist's shop was of the old type with glass cases displaying various kinds of pipes as well as racks of cigarette packets, pouches of tobacco and little tins of snuff. The air was filled with the rich aroma of strong tobacco and the feeble gas lighting bathed the tiny premises in a pale yellow light which lent the place a quaint Victorian atmosphere.

The woman behind the counter, a plump lady in her late forties, hadn't looked up at first when Harryboy had entered for she was concentrating on her knitting, but when the light dimmed with the closing of the blind, she jerked her head in his direction. She saw the silhouette of a short, broad-shouldered man, standing near the counter, his face in shadow.

'What d'you think you're doing?' she demanded indignantly, climbing off her stool and leaning forward over the counter.

'This is what I'm doing,' said Harryboy, pulling the gun from his pocket and aiming it at the woman.

'Jesus wept,' cried the woman with annoyance rather than fear. 'What have I done to deserve this?'

'Shut your mouth and empty the till.'

'Empty the till,' she repeated the words slowly, as though she wasn't sure she had heard them correctly.

'That's it, missus,' snapped Harryboy, advancing on the counter. 'I want your money.'

'Well, you can't have it. It's mine. Hard-earned cash and it's mine. So take your little gun, cowboy, and sling your bloody hook.'

'This is no joke, lady. I said empty the till. Now be quick about it or I'll shoot you dead and take it myself.'

'Shoot ... me ... dead.' Again she repeated the words in a derisory mimicking fashion. 'Who the hell do you think you are? Al bloody Capone?' She gazed at the gun and sneered. 'You little bastard,' she snapped. 'Do you think I'm going to hand over my takings to a slimy little spiv like you?' She emitted a harsh, rasping laugh. 'Shoot me dead then. Go on, you'd better get on with it, sonny boy. 'Cause you'll get no money out of me while I'm still standing. If Hitler's bombs can't shift me, I damned if I'm going give in to a spineless creep like you.' She glared at Harryboy, her pale features suffusing with indignant anger. Suddenly she thumped her fist down on the counter. 'Go on,' she cried, 'get out of it, before I call a policeman.'

Harryboy hadn't expected this reaction. Usually the gun brought instant submission, but the lady tobacconist had chosen the wrong day to retaliate, to challenge him. He had already been humiliated by his girlfriend and his ego was still smarting about that; he wasn't about to take another dose of the same from this old bag. Her defiance only inflamed his anger.

'You talk too much,' he said matter-of-factly before pulling the trigger.

The lady tobacconist gave a gurgling cry of surprise as, her arms flapping wildly, she fell backwards, crashing against the shelves, dislodging a small avalanche of cigarette packets as she did so. Briefly her eyes widened with shock and surprise behind her spectacles before they closed forever as her body slumped to the floor.

Harryboy gave a little satisfied chuckle as he moved around the counter to reach the till. It was brimming with cash. There were few notes but handfuls of silver coins. He began scooping up his spoils and filling his pockets. When the till was empty, he added a few packets of cigarettes to his haul, stuffing them in his overcoat pockets. As he was about ready to leave he gazed down at the dead body of the lady tobacconist, her features now in twisted repose, her spectacles halfway down her face.

'Stupid cow,' he said with disdain and then left the shop.

TWENTY-FOUR

Muffled against the cold October morning, which was still murky and uninviting, Dave Roberts, the tea bar owner, arrived early to set up his stall for the day. He wasn't looking forward to what he perceived would be quite a dramatic episode which was destined to take place that morning. That's if the little boy Peter reported for his washing-up duties. And he had no reason to believe the lad wouldn't. He was desperate enough. Dave wasn't happy about the situation, but he hoped that he was making the best of a bad job. After all, he kept telling himself, I'm acting in the young un's best interest – though he doubted whether the boy would see things in the same light.

As Dave approached the tea bar, his figure looking like a squat phantom hurrying along the Embankment in dark relief against the gradually lightening sky, he spied the boy standing by the parapet, hugging himself against the cold,

'He's here already,' muttered Dave to himself, as he quickened his step.

The boy stepped forward as he recognized his new employer.

'Mornin', son,' Dave cried cheerfully. 'You're a keen one.'

Peter nodded and smiled.

Dave picked up the small crate of milk left by the door, unlocked the premises and switched on the lights. 'Once I got this old boiler going, it'll warm the place up and then we can start brewing the tea. Won't be long before we get a queue of punters.'

While Dave busied himself with the boiler, Peter stood by the door, eyeing up the left-over cakes from the previous day.

'Help yourself to one, if you like,' said Dave, observing the boy's avaricious glances. 'The new ones won't be here for another hour.'

Peter did not need to be told twice. He snatched up one of the buns and, all decorum abandoned, almost swallowed the thing whole. His cheeks bulged and his mouth moved furiously as he munched his way through the cake. He had spent some of his wages on fish and chips the night before, but sleeping rough again – this time in a shop doorway as he had done when he first ran away from his mother – had enhanced his hunger pangs.

With a grunt and a muttered swear word, Dave pushed up the recalcitrant hatch by the serving area which formed a canopy over the front of the stall, allowing the cold morning air in. Dave shivered involuntarily. 'Co-or, it's parky out there. OK, lad, grab a cloth and wipe down the counter and then swill those pots out and put them to drain.'

Peter swallowed the last of the cake and set about his allotted tasks.

Dave surreptitiously glanced at his watch. It was just after 6.30. Sandy said that he'd come along just after 7.30. He'd got to make sure he kept the boy occupied until then.

Within ten minutes the first customers began arriving, melting out of the early morning mist like grey shadows. They were a mixed bunch: a number of overalled workmen, some smartly suited business types, and the odd serviceman, all desiring a hot brew to wake them up properly and prepare them for the rigours of the day. Within half an hour there was quite a large group assembled around the serving hatch. Many were Dave's regulars who exchanged chit chat and repartee with the proprietor. By now Peter was at his washing-up duties. A smile touched his pale and tired features. He was happy to have his hands in warm water again, being useful to someone.

By 7.30 the red streaks of dawn were fading from the sky and a bright, sharp autumn day was in prospect. London was fully awake now. The traffic roared past the little tea bar and the Embankment was thronged with pedestrians most of whom hurried by, each wrapped in their own concerns. Very few people dawdled along. This was the time of day for going or returning with a purpose. From time to time Peter would glance over his shoulder to catch a view of the passing show, the shady cavalcade that paraded by, but he failed to see the imposing figure of PC Sandy MacGregor materialize out of the crowd and approach the tea bar.

Sandy touched his helmet in gentle salute as he peered over the counter at Peter. He raised a quizzical eyebrow at Dave who responded with a decisive nod. PC MacGregor made his way around to the back and let himself inside. As the door opened, Peter looked up in surprise. He thought perhaps it was the delivery of today's cakes, but instead, it was a large policeman in a shiny cape. So big was he that he had to remove his helmet in order to stand up straight inside the cramped quarters.

He smiled kindly at Peter, but the boy's heart froze. He knew instantly that the policeman had come for him. He knew that look. That kindly but serious expression. Dave must have told him. Ratted on him. He was trapped. There was no way of escape this time.

'Hello,' said the policeman, bending down so that his face was on a level with Peter's. 'What's your name?'

'It's Peter.'

'Hello, Peter. I'm Sandy.' He held out his hand and Peter shook it tentatively. 'Where do you live?'

Peter looked at the broad, sympathetic features of the policeman and then at Dave who turned his head away with a guilty sigh and began wiping down the counter absentmindedly. Peter knew that it was pointless to come up with a set of lies. They knew. Of course they knew. So he said nothing but concentrated all his efforts in fighting back the tears which he did quite successfully.

PC MacGregor ruffled Peter's hair. 'Run away from home, have we, eh? Why was that then?'

For a moment Peter remained silent. He didn't know what to say … where to begin. At length he said, 'I was unhappy.'

'Were your mum and dad hitting you, being nasty to you?'

Peter shook his head. 'I've got no mum and dad.'

'I see.' PC MacGregor stood up and turned to Dave Roberts. 'You did right to report this. He's obviously been sleeping rough.'

Dave looked embarrassed and avoided Peter's censorious glance.

'Well, lad,' said MacGregor, his tone taking on a sterner, more official tone. 'You'd better come along with me to the station and we'll sort you out. Can't have you wandering the streets with no one to look after you, can we?'

To Peter there seemed to be a world of misery and discomfort in the phrase 'we'll sort you out'. He knew what that meant.

'I'm all right, thank you. I don't need no help.'

'Let me be the judge of that, eh?' said the policeman matter-of-factly.

'What about my job here? Can't I just stay and help Dave?'

'A lad of your age should be in school, learning, not washing pots.'

'The policeman's right lad,' said Dave gently. 'This isn't the place for you.'

Peter said nothing. The feelings of disappointment and betrayal – yet again – overwhelmed him.

'Come on,' said PC MacGregor stepping forward and placing a hand on Peter's shoulder. 'Pop your coat on and let's be off, eh?'

'Are you going to put your handcuffs on me?' asked Peter, glancing at the shiny bracelets clipped to the policeman's belt.

'I don't think that will be necessary,' observed PC MacGregor with a gentle smile.

Within minutes Peter was being steered along the embankment by the large constable towards the local police station. A blood-red sun was peeking over the jagged contours of the city, bathing its streets in a fiery glow.

The elation that Rachel felt after she had left Harryboy unconscious in the hotel room soon evaporated. She may have got away from the bastard and taken all his money, but now she didn't know what to do. Here she was all alone in an alien city not only on the run from a killer but no doubt also wanted by the police as an accessory to robbery and murder. In a few short days her life had splintered and shattered. Her dream of coming up to London and finding happiness and glamour had turned into a nightmare.

One thing was certain: she would not go back to Wales. She would not go home. She could not face them now. It was too late for going back. It seemed to her that the events of the last few days had effectively severed all links with her past life. She was a different woman now. Tainted and immoral. No, she had made her bed and now she must lie on it.

She walked and walked, pounding the pavement as she turned matters over in her mind, trying hard to control her emotions and to stop her thinking about Harryboy and what would happen if he caught up with her again. That was unlikely, wasn't it? In a city of a million strangers, the odds of bumping into that twisted bastard again were infinitesimal. Surely? She tried to convince herself of this but failed. The harder she tried to blank his face from her mind, the stronger it became, as though by some magical force he had imprinted his image permanently on her brain. Occasionally a figure would emerge from the crowd, swaggering towards her, trilby pulled low and she would halt in her tracks with heart-stopping terror thinking he had caught up with her, only to realize as the man got nearer that he looked nothing like Harryboy.

After a while, she took herself in hand and found a room in a small guest house near the British Museum, a bolthole where she could rest and hide away until she decided what to do. She bought a small bottle of gin and drank it quickly, seeking alcoholic oblivion. Putting her head under the covers, she soon got her wish. If the truth be known, it wasn't just the alcohol which had carried her off into a deep, dreamless sleep, it was also the stress and anguish she had suffered over the last few days – ever since she had met Harryboy Jenkins.

She slept peacefully for almost twenty four hours.

The next day, she woke in slightly better spirits. Time away from that demon had done a little to heal the large wound, but it would take much more than time to make her whole again. She breakfasted at a small place in Russell Square and then made her way to Oxford Street to buy herself some new clothes and visit a hairdresser to have her hair cut and dyed. She was desperate to change her appearance – to become a new woman. It was a cosmetic way of sloughing off her past.

When the hairdresser had finished, she looked at herself in the mirror. Her face was still blotched with bruises but now her mousy brown hair fell about her face in glossy blonde curls. For the first time in her life, Rachel Howells thought she looked pretty. She even smiled back at herself.

It was while she was paying the hairdresser that she came upon the little card in her handbag. At first she was puzzled by it and then she remembered. Of course, it had been given to her by that kind chap with the eye patch in the little café in Soho. He had offered to help her. He had sensed that she was in trouble and was concerned. On reflection he seemed the kindest person she had encountered since she arrived in the city. She read the card carefully: John Hawke, Private Detective, 7 Prior's Court, off Tottenham Court Road. Then she placed it back in her bag having made an important decision.

TWENTY-FIVE

Within a few hours of his 'little adventure at the tobacconist's' as Harryboy thought of it, he had visited Bourne & Hollingsworth where he bought himself a new suit and then he'd taken rooms in a reasonably smart hotel near Hyde Park corner, where he redressed his wound. He was feeling good again. He had some money in his pockets, he had a nice gaff and he was as free as air. And he didn't have no silly tart tagging along with him to complicate his life.

However, the particular silly tart he had in mind occupied his thoughts. His arm, which still throbbed unpleasantly, was a constant reminder of her treachery. He had some unfinished business with her and until that was dealt with – until *she* was dealt with – he wouldn't be fully at ease. He wouldn't be able to relax and get on with things until he'd shown her a lesson – the final lesson. The bitch would make the ultimate sacrifice for what she had done. However, there was one little problem, he had to find her first, didn't he? London was a big place. He knew from personal experience how easy it was to lose yourself in this sprawling city.

But he had an idea.

It was late afternoon as he sauntered down Dean Street and entered Benny's café. Unlike the mornings, at this time of day the place was quiet with only a few customers. The little Jewish guy who ran the place was leaning on the counter idly perusing the crossword in some newspaper. He looked up as Harryboy entered and took a seat. On catching sight of his new customer something like a frown flitted across the old boy's features before he picked up his order pad and made his way to Harryboy's table.

Smiling in what he considered a charming manner, Harryboy ordered a pot of tea and bun. Benny took the order in a businesslike manner but without returning the smile. He remembered this brute all right. He was the bully with the pretty girl – the one he had told Johnny about. Now he was on his own. Why was that? What had he done with the girl? He hoped, maybe, that she'd had the sense and the guts to leave him. The alternative scenario didn't bear thinking about.

He returned some minutes later with the order. Harryboy smiled at him again. 'I was wondering if you could help me, chum,' he said touching Benny's arm. Benny flinched.

'You want a pastry, perhaps?'

Harryboy shook his head. 'No, nothing like that. A bit of information is what I'm after. I'm trying to locate someone. A customer of yours.'

'A customer …' Now Benny was really puzzled.

'Yeah. A young bloke with an eye patch.'

Instinctively Benny said, 'Oh, you mean Johnny.' He blurted it out without thinking. He could have bitten off his tongue as soon as the words had escaped his lips.

'Johnny, eh? Yes, that would be the bloke. I need to get in touch with him urgently.' His fingers clamped themselves tightly around Benny's arm so that he flinched. 'You can tell me where I can find him, can't you, eh?' Harryboy's voice remained calm and polite but there was an undertow of menace that chilled the café owner.

Benny shook his head nervously. 'I don't know him really. Just his name. He's just a customer. I don't know where he lives.'

Harryboy shook his head in mock dismay. He knew that this Jewish fellow was lying. He could see it in his eyes. If he didn't know this Johnny character he wouldn't be so edgy – so frightened. 'Now I just want to know where I can find Johnny, that's all. It's not asking much, is it? A little piece of information and in return I'll leave you and your nice little café alone.'

Harryboy smiled sweetly and hooded his eyes.

With a determined effort, Benny wrenched his arm free from Harryboy's grasp. 'Look mister,' he said, somewhat breathlessly, his heart pounding against his ribs, 'I told you I don't know this feller apart from his name. I can't help you. This is a café not an information centre. Now I suggest you drink up your tea before it gets cold.' Before waiting for a response Benny swung round and hurried away, his whole body shaking.

Harryboy gave a tight grin. So, the old fool wants to play it the hard way, he thought, as he bit into his bun. Well, I'm happy to oblige him. It's obvious he knows where this Johnny hangs his hat and he'll tell me. No doubt about that. I'll just have to be more persuasive.

A few minutes later, Harryboy having finished his snack moved to the counter and threw a few coins down. Benny, who had been pretending to sort out some items in the cash drawer, looked up nervously. Harryboy touched the brim of his hat with his forefinger. 'See you,' he said pointedly and flashed his unsettling smile before he left, leaving the door ajar.

Benny waited a few moments before grabbing the telephone and dialling Johnny's number. There was no reply.

It was dusk and the blackout blinds were being drawn. Standing across the street from Benny's café, Harryboy could see that the old fool was about to shut up shop for the day. Trade had run dry. There had been no customers for at least fifteen minutes.

Skittering his cigarette end into the gutter, Harryboy sauntered across the road and entered the café. It was as he had determined, empty apart from the proprietor who was busy wiping down the tables with a damp cloth. Benny looked up as he entered, ready to turn away this latent customer with a 'sorry we're closed' but on seeing Harryboy he froze, mouth slightly agape.

Harryboy leaned against the door and smirked. He was pleased that his presence had obviously unnerved the little Jew. 'As I was saying ... about this feller with an eye patch.'

'Leave my premises now,' snapped Benny, rallying himself. He could feel his heart beating faster than a castanet but he wasn't going to be intimidated by this two-bit hoodlum. 'You're trespassing. Get out now or I call the police.'

Benny's flourish of bravado amused Harryboy all the more. The smirk broadened and then quite suddenly it disappeared. 'You're gonna call no one,' he said quietly, slipping the revolver out of his coat pocket. 'And if you don't tell me what I need to know, you'll never be calling anyone ever again. Do I make myself clear?'

On seeing the gun pointing at him, Benny paled. 'Look, I told you before, I don't know this man.'

Harryboy fired the gun. In the empty café it sounded like an explosion, the noise echoing and reverberating around the room. The glass case on the counter which had housed a few limp pastries had shattered into a thousand fragments.

Benny moaned at his loss.

'You next,' said Harryboy, stepping forward quickly and grabbing Benny by the collar and pushing him against the counter so hard that he cried out in pain. When Harryboy placed the barrel of the gun to his forehead, Benny almost fainted with the shock.

'Now then,' snarled Harryboy, his face close to Benny's, as he pressed the gun barrel hard against skin, 'tell me where I can find this Johnny character …'

TWENTY-SIX

After seeing two uniformed officers spill out of the police patrol car and hurry into Studely Mansions, I hurried away in the direction of Kensington High Street where I caught an underground train. For what seemed like hours but was in fact two fairly short tube journeys, I found myself face to face with sardined humanity, rattling along down a dark snaking tunnel in a crowded metal tube with the brim of a bowler hat in my eye and a ladies umbrella prodding my backside.

With relief, some time later I emerged into the throng of pedestrians on Tottenham Court Road. As I walked along, I began smiling to myself as I replayed the comic drama in which I'd taken a starring part at Studely Mansions. I felt sorry for the diligent commissionaire and for his busted nose and the headache he would no doubt be nursing now, but I was also pleased with myself for getting out of a tricky situation with Houdini-type élan.

On my way home, I considered my next course of action. I had to find out more about Mr Bernard France and to see if the mysterious Mr Webster was the real identity of the male *femme fatale*, Helen. I reckoned another visit to The Loophole Club was on the cards in the hope that I'd see Helen again.

However … what did that Scottish chap once write about the best laid plans?

On reaching the office of Hawke Investigations, I found my door slightly ajar. Someone had broken the lock. To be honest, this would not have been a difficult thing to do. The feeble Yale contraption could easily be demolished with a hair grip or a nail file. What surprised me was the fact that someone had taken the trouble to break into Hawke Towers in the first place. There was nothing of any value in there worth stealing. However, it struck me, as I peered through the crack into my darkened office, that perhaps my intruder had another motive other than theft.

What now, I pondered, as I slipped through the door quietly. I stood on the threshold of the room allowing my eyes to get used to the dim light provided by the fading daylight falling through one small grimy window while my nerves tightened and the hairs on the back of my head bristled. Nimbly I crossed to my desk and withdrew my gun from the top drawer.

I stood in the darkness and waited. And then I noticed the sound. A gentle regular whispering sound. It seemed to be coming from the armchair across from my desk. And indeed, as my eyes grew further accustomed to the gloom, I could make out a vague shape in the chair. That's all – just a vague shape, sort of draped there. Whatever it was, this was the source of the sound and, as I drew nearer, I identified the noise: it was heavy breathing. Heavy breathing ... or, to be more precise, gentle snoring. I leaned in close and saw that the chair was occupied by a young woman who seemed to be fast asleep.

Quietly, I closed the door and switched on the desk lamp. My visitor was undisturbed by my actions. I put my gun back in the desk drawer, relieved to dispense with it, slipped off my coat and then took a closer look at my visitor. In the harsh beam of the lamp I could see that she was more girl than woman. Now that I was able to observe her features clearly, I recognized her. She was the girl from Benny's café. Her hair was different, lighter and done in a different style but there was no doubt in my mind that she was the nervous creature with the bully of a boyfriend that I'd spoken to in the café. And by Jove, he was a bully, if the bruises on her face bore witness of his treatment of her. I clenched my fists in a brief spasm of anger. There was nothing I hated more than a man hitting a woman.

She must have taken me up on my offer of help. Why else would she be here? I could imagine her turning up at my office in some state of distress, only to find it closed. In desperation, she broke in and waited for me to return. Whatever the circumstances, it was a refuge for her and, like Goldilocks, she had fallen asleep while the Daddy bear was out.

I slipped through into my living quarters and put the kettle on. Five minutes later I carried two mugs of coffee back into the office. My visitor was still snoozing contentedly. As gently as I could I nudged her awake. Her eyes flickered and then with a slight stretch of the body and a half-hearted yawn, they opened. It took a moment for her to remember where she was and who I was. Then she sat up with a start.

'Oh,' she said, with a mixture of surprise and despair, speech not coming to her readily in her still dazed state.

'Coffee,' I said cheerfully, proffering one of the mugs. 'I took the initiative of putting some dried milk and one spoon of sugar in it for you.'

Gingerly she took the mug and cradled it between her hands. 'Thank you,' she murmured and tried to smile.

'I don't usually offer refreshments to burglars you understand, no matter how pretty they are, but then they don't often fall asleep on the job in my office,' I observed wryly.

'Oh, I'm not a burglar. I ... I didn't take anything.'

'I was only kidding. Relax. Take a drink and then you can explain everything.'

She struggled to manufacture a smile and almost succeeded before taking a drink of coffee. 'That's nice,' she said.

Hot watered down chicory mixed with artificial milk has never approached the category of 'nice' to my taste but I know that in certain circumstances it can be sort of comforting and I reckoned for her this was one of those circumstances.

'Now, you know my name, John Hawke, but I don't know yours.'

'It's Rachel. Rachel Howells.'

'Pleased to meet you, Rachel. Cigarette?' I flipped open my pack and offered it to her. She took one and we both lit up. I could see that the coffee, the fag and the gentle treatment of male nurse Hawke were having the desired effect. She was mentally and physically relaxing. Her posture softened and the worry lines that creased her brow had eased.

I sat cross-legged at her feet. 'Now then, tell me all about it.'

'Oh, goodness. I don't know where to begin.'

'Well, at the beginning is usually a good place to start.'

'I know ... but when was the beginning? When did the nightmare start?'

'I'm not good with nightmares. I'm more of a practical chap. When did the trouble start?'

'I suppose when I met Harryboy.'

'The bruiser you were with in the café? Harryboy ... you mean Harryboy Jenkins?'

She nodded. 'That's the bastard.'

I thought I knew his face from somewhere when I saw him in Benny's. Then I was unable to make a connection. But now that Rachel had mentioned his name ... That triggered my memory. I'd seen his ugly mug on the blurred photograph that David had shown me, the one of the deserting soldier who had killed a policeman. I reckoned this girl was lucky to be alive.

'Go on,' I said gently.

'I've run away from home, you see. From Wales. I was being stifled there. I could see myself heading for a boring marriage with a boring chap and never experiencing any excitement in my life.'

'Excitement is over-rated.'

'I'm beginning to think so, too. I realize now how stupid I was just arriving in London with nowhere to go and not knowing a single soul. I thought it would be so simple. Get a job, shop work or something, find a room somewhere and then enjoy myself.'

I reckoned girls like Rachel arrived in London every day. Despite the war or maybe in some perverse way because of the war, they saw the capital as a kind of Shangri-La. So much decorum and restraint had disappeared since the autumn of 1939 and ironically there was a strange sense of freedom pervading the streets of the city. It was legitimate to let your hair down and have a good time for you never knew when your number was going to be up. The crowds, the bombed buildings, the threat of air raids seemed attractive compared to the dull routine of provincial life. I understood that. Of course I did. Or *I* wouldn't be here.

'I met Harryboy in a café on my first day. I say met him, but really he picked me up. He seemed a nice enough chap at first ... Well, not nice I suppose, but ...'

'Exciting?'

Rachel nodded glumly. 'What a fool I've been.' Her eyes moistened and she bit her lip.

'It's too early for tears, my girl. If you start crying now, I'll never hear the end of the story.'

She sniffed and smiled.

'He treated you badly, this Harryboy,' I suggested, attempting to get her back on track again. 'Rough stuff.'

'Rough stuff, yes. At first he was kind to me. He had a wad of cash and didn't mind spending it. But he could change in a minute. He'd smile and give you a hug and next thing you know ...' The memory of what he had done made her catch her breath and her lips begin to tremble. I reached out and touched her hand, but she pulled it away sharply.

'Don't be nice to me,' she said breathily. 'You'll only make me worse.'

I nodded, blowing smoke away from her towards the ceiling and waited for her to continue.

'You see, Harryboy ... well, he's a crook. A killer.'

I said nothing and waited for her to continue.

'When the money was beginning to run out, he tried to steal some more ... from an off-licence in the Old Kent Road. There was this copper ...'

'PC Alan Reece, a young chap, married with two kids. Harryboy shot him.'

Her eyes widened with surprise and she leaned forward. 'You know about it?'

'Yes. Your boyfriend is a deserter from the army and he's killed before.'

'I knew it,' she cried, burying her head in her hands. The sobs were silent but they shook her whole body.

I drained the last of the coffee down and waited for her tears to subside. 'So where is he now?' I said at length.

'I don't know. We were staying at a little hotel on Shaftsbury Avenue and he started getting violent and so I shot him.'

This girl was full of surprises. 'You shot him!' My voice went up a register. 'You mean he's dead?'

'No, no. I just wounded him in the arm. But I wish he was dead. He's an animal. I meant to kill him. If I hadn't shot him he would have killed me. I could see it in his eyes. When he loses his temper there's no controlling him. He has ... he has no morality, no conscience. So I shot him ... and then I ran for it. Now I don't know what to do. I don't feel safe. I feel terrified. I just know he'll come after me. He wants me dead. I'm sure he won't rest 'till he's done me in. And then I remembered you and your card. You offered me help.'

'So I did.' I said slowly, wondering exactly what kind of help this girl expected me to offer. This really was a police matter now. If her boyfriend had just been a nasty bully boy I could have given her some protection, but he was something more than that. He had killed at least two men. However, if she was right and Harryboy was after her, the police may well try to use her as bait to catch him. This was a situation I wouldn't want to inflict on anyone.

Rachel looked apprehensive as I deliberated over these points. 'Please help me,' she said quietly without emotion.

'This is a big city, Rachel, it's very unlikely Harryboy will find you. It's needle-in-haystack time. But there is one way you can be sure of being safe.'

Her face brightened and she looked eagerly at me. 'What's that?'

'Go back home. Go back to Wales. You'd be safe there. Go back to your old life. You've had a taste of London and it disagreed with you—'

She shook her head wildly. 'No! No, I couldn't go back. Not after what's happened. I couldn't face it. Not there. No nasty creep like Harryboy is going to drive me away. If you won't help me I'll have to find some other way.'

I sighed wearily. Her response was the one I'd expected. Despite all that had happened to the girl she was still starry-eyed about the city as though this great mass of buildings and teeming population would somehow make life bearable, interesting and even fun.

I knew that I'd have to help her – I couldn't leave her walking the streets while her maniac boyfriend was seeking her with a gun in his pocket but I wasn't sure *how*.

As it turned out Fate took a hand in events.

'Well,' I said, 'for starters, you can stay the night here and then we'll sort out some plan of action for tomorrow—'

I was interrupted by the jangling of the telephone. I rose and reached for the receiver.

'Johnny, is that you?' The voice at the other end was breathless. I recognized it immediately. It was Benny. He sounded in some distress.

'Yes, this is Johnny. What is it Benny? What's the matter?'

Before I could catch Benny's reply, another voice spoke to me. Not on the telephone –in the room.

'Put the phone down. Put it down now!' It demanded.

I turned in the direction of the voice and there in the doorway as large and as ugly as life was Harryboy Jenkins. He was grinning and pointing a gun at me.

TWENTY-SEVEN

I replaced the receiver slowly. As I did so I could still hear the tinny voice of Benny shouting at the other end until with an abrupt click he was silenced as the phone rested on its cradle. For some time the three of us in the room stood still like a bizarre tableau in an *avant garde* drama and then Harryboy turned to the cowering figure of Rachel. She had pushed herself as far back in the chair as she could, her eyes wide with terror as her worst nightmare came true.

'Hello, darling,' Harryboy said, a sarcastic leer staining his features. 'I bet you thought you'd never see me again, did you?'

'Would you care for a cup of coffee?' I said nonchalantly, leaning casually on my desk. I wanted to direct his attention away from the girl in an unthreatening manner. I didn't like the way he was pointing the gun at her, his finger taut on the trigger.

With a sharp, robotic movement, Harryboy turned and focused his baleful eyes on me. 'If there's one thing I can't stand it's a comedian, especially a pathetic comedian.'

'Tea, then?' I said, smiling enough to show my teeth.

He then did something I was just not expecting. He rushed forward. With the speed of a lizard he came towards me and struck me across the face with the gun. My head exploded and I literally saw stars. They whizzed and fizzed before me like they do in the cartoons before my knees received urgent messages from my brain to give way. With an inarticulate expression of surprise, I sank to the floor. Through the haze I saw Harryboy standing over me.

'You shut your fucking mouth or I'll shut it for good. I got unfinished business with this tart here and I don't want any smart interfering nonsense from you. Is that clear?'

To emphasize his point, he hit me again. Boy, was I a glutton for punishment. And I remembered, inconsequentially, I was right out of headache pills.

Reluctantly, I said nothing. I just nodded and mopped the trickle of blood that was running down my cheek with a handkerchief. I was learning my lessons the hard way. Rachel had not been exaggerating when she had called this son of a bitch a maniac. He was top of his class in that department. I could see from his eyes that he had lost touch with reality. He was in his own righteous, immoral world where he was king and whatever he thought or wanted to do was the right thing to think or do.

He grabbed hold of Rachel's arm and dragged her from the chair. At first she didn't struggle. For the moment she had retreated within herself. Limply her body obeyed him as though she were a rag doll, but once she was on her feet she suddenly seemed to comprehend the danger that she was in. With a strangulated cry which seemed to be a complex mix of anger and fear, she flexed her body and brought her fist round and thumped Harryboy's left arm with some force. He gave a snort of pain and released his hold of her. That, I assumed, was his wounded arm.

His moment of distress gave me an opportunity. Girding up what loins were still in working order, I struggled to my feet and lunged at him. Oh, but he was a slick one was this Harryboy. He had regained his equilibrium very quickly and, with great agility, he sidestepped my advance. I blundered into nothingness.

As I attempted to steady myself, I heard the sharp cracking sound of a gunshot and a bullet whistled past my ear. I was in no doubt, this was no warning shot: it had been meant for me. I did the sensible thing and stood still, raising my arms in surrender.

'Get over there and sit at your desk or I'll blow your stupid head off your shoulders,' snarled my unwelcome visitor through gritted teeth. He was like an unpredictable wild animal who could charge you at any minute. I knew it would be foolish to disobey him or say anything smart. That would only enrage him further. This was a fellow who reacted emotionally to every situation, the thought processes following lamely behind. I was very keen to keep my stupid head and so, without a word, I obeyed his instructions.

Rachel had by now collapsed back into the chair and was quietly sobbing to herself. For her, it would seem, the bleak nightmare continued.

For a moment Harryboy stood perfectly still like an unpleasant exhibit in Madame Tussaud's Chamber of Horrors. In the harsh half light provided by the table lamp his eyes glittered eerily in his pugnacious face. What he was thinking only a highly qualified psychiatrist could hazard a guess, but whatever it was, I knew it was something unpleasant. At length, he turned his attention back to Rachel. 'Now lady, let's see you on your feet and no funny business this time.'

Rachel raised her head a little and I could see from her pale complexion and fearful expression that all the fight had gone out of her. As far as she was concerned Harryboy had won. With the stiff limbs of an automaton, she got to her feet and stood by him.

'That's better. That's a good girl,' said Harryboy and suddenly once more his face broke into that wide unpleasant grin.

Rachel said nothing but just stared at her feet dumbly.

'Right, you and I are going to leave now. We have a little unfinished business together. You're coming with me, away from all the goodies, so I suggest you say your last farewell to your boyfriend.' He spoke in a dreamy, childlike way which was somehow more frightening than his aggressive stance. His body relaxed and he shifted rhythmically from foot to foot like a little boy who was waiting for a treat.

Momentarily, Rachel flashed a frightened glance at me. A kind of desperation had taken hold of her. 'Don't hurt him, please,' she begged.

Rachel's plea served only to amuse Harryboy further. He knew now that he was complete master of the situation, him and his little gun. He almost rose in stature with pleasure at the thought of it.

He raised the gun and trained it on me. I felt my mouth go dry as though it was filled with sand.

'But, sweetie,' he said in a mocking baby-type voice, 'you've got to let lickle Harryboy have some fun. Just one lickle bullet that's all. Just one lickle bullet … right through his lickle heart.'

He raised the gun higher. Rachel screamed and then the world seemed to go mad.

There was another gunshot. I held my breath and prayed.

Nothing happened. I felt no pain.

I blinked and then realized with relief that the bullet had missed me. I gazed around the room in shocked puzzlement and then I saw

Harryboy. He was lying face downwards on the floor. The back of his head was wet and shiny with blood. Standing over him wielding a large iron bar was the proprietor of Benny's Café.

'I knew this would come in useful one of these days,' Benny said, trying to grin and failing. However he was far from amused. I could tell from his shaking hand and his hoarse voice that he was mortified at what he had done.

'Oh, Benny,' I said with a sigh, 'you've saved my life. Now I'll never hear the end of it.' I went over to my agitated friend and gave him a hug.

'Thank you,' I said.

He steadied himself and nodded, recovering a little 'You got any whisky in the place? Now that's a silly question,' he said.

I nodded and retrieved a bottle and glass from my desk drawer. I poured Benny a generous slug which he downed in one go.

Rachel was kneeling by the prostate figure of our friend Harryboy.

'Is he dead?' she asked in a way that told me she hoped that the answer would be in the affirmative. I knelt down by her and took Harryboy's pulse. It was still there, faint but persistent.

'He's just concussed.'

'Thank goodness,' said Benny with relief. 'I want no man's death on my conscience no matter what kind of devil he is.'

'Well, this devil is a multiple murderer so if you had killed him you'd have saved the hangman his job.'

'Everyone to their own profession. I run a café. Cakes and pastries I can do. Executions ... pah! Now, you got any more of that whisky?'

I poured Benny another glass and then he told me how he happened to arrive at my place in the nick of time with an iron bar.

' ... and so with his bullying threats ... he shot up my place ... he managed to get your address out of me. When he'd gone and I'd pulled myself together ... I didn't know what to do. Such a state I was in. Then I tried to ring you but you put the phone down on me. I reckoned the brute had already got to you. So I grabbed my coat—'

'And an iron bar.'

'I keep it behind the counter to warn off spivs when they come around causing their bother. I took a taxi – that's one shilling you owe me – my poor old heart pounding, and just got here in time.'

'You certainly did. Another few seconds and you'd have been dusting off your black armband, my friend.'

Benny shook his head and closed his eyes. 'Don't make me think of it, Johnny.'

I collected another two glasses from my living quarters and poured some more whisky. I took one myself and gave the other to Rachel who had gone very quiet and was sitting on the chair again staring at the floor. I touched her shoulder. 'It'll be all right now,' I said softly.

Benny, who, with the aid of the alcohol, was rapidly returning to his normal demeanour, tapped Harryboy's arm gingerly with his foot. 'What you going to do with this beauty then?'

'Something fairly quick before he regains consciousness,' I said snatching up the telephone. I rang David Llewellyn on his home number.

'I'm just in the middle of my evening meal, Johnny. Can't this wait?' he said with some chagrin when I told him that I needed his help urgently.

I assured him that it couldn't wait. 'That's the nature of something that's urgent,' I said sarcastically. 'I have a desperate killer here for you. A certain Harryboy Jenkins. The guy who did for the young policeman the other evening.'

'Is this on the level?'

'Yes.'

'Right, boyo, I'll be round there straightaway.'

'Bring some big bobbies too. He's rather a handful.'

'They won't arrest me will they?' asked Benny genuinely concerned, after I had replaced the receiver. 'I've been a law-abiding citizen all my life ... now this.' He gazed down at the inert form on the floor, the blood from the wound beginning to trickle onto the carpet.

'They're more likely to give you a medal.'

For a moment Benny almost believed me.

'I reckon the best thing is for you to skedaddle now. There's no need for you to be involved in the matter. Nor Rachel, for the time being at least. Would you take her back to your place, Benny, eh? Give her some of your home cooking and a bed for the night and we can sort things out in the morning.'

Benny nodded in agreement, but glanced uncertainly at the girl who seemed somewhat bewildered by the train of events.

I gave her shoulders a squeeze. 'Come on Rachel, you go with

Benny. You'll be safe with him. He'll look after you until I've dealt with Harryboy. The worst is over now. This monster's heading for the scaffold.'

She gazed at me dreamily and a ghost of a smile manifested itself briefly on her pale features.

'OK, Johnny.' She leaned forward and kissed me on the lips.

It was the nicest thing that had happened to me in a long while. And I found myself kissing her back.

As I felt her body lean in to mine, I realized with some embarrassment that it was time to withdraw. I was taking advantage of a damsel who was not only in some state of distress but who had just gulped down a triple whisky.

I gave her shoulders another squeeze and gently manoeuvred her in the direction of Benny who was gazing at me with a bemused expression. I avoided his glance. We both knew that under different circumstances I would have carried on kissing.

'I'll call around in the morning,' I said, as they departed.

Left on my own, I took another slug of Johnnie Walker and then directed my attention to my unwanted comatose guest. I turned him over on to his back. He was now breathing easily and his features were in repose. He looked as innocent as a new born babe – apart from the revolver which he was still clutching in his right hand. I relieved him of the weapon and placed it on my desk. I didn't know how long he'd reside in the land of dreams but I reckoned it would be safer if I bound his hands together in case he regained consciousness before the police arrived.

I glanced round the office looking for something suitable to tie him up with but without success. I wasn't really an avid collector of rope or manacles. Then I remembered I had some thick twine in the kitchen drawer. If I doubled that, it would probably do the trick until David clapped some handcuffs on him. I went retrieve it. I pulled the twine out and examined it. It would just about do, particularly if it was secured very tightly.

When I returned to my office, I knew something was wrong the moment I entered the room. It didn't take me long to determine what it was. The body of Harryboy Jenkins was no longer lying on the floor in front of my desk. It had disappeared. All that was left was the patch of blood which glinted in the light. Harryboy was not the only thing that was missing: the gun that I had so casually and carelessly left on my desk had gone too. I gave a silent curse. How could I have been so stupid? My first thought was that Harryboy had come round and done a bunk, but I soon readjusted this thought as I heard a noise in the shadows behind me.

Here we go again I thought, as I spun round to see the lumbering shape of Harryboy moving towards me. Even in the dim lighting I could see by his hazy expression and the lazily hooded eyes that this brute had not fully shaken off the cloak of his concussion. He had all the speed and aplomb of a drunken sleepwalker. Quickly I stepped forward and snatched the gun from his grasp and gave him a mighty thump to the chest. Without a sound he crumpled before my eyes like some conjuror's illusion, reverting back to his comatose state on the carpet at my feet, his bleeding head staining another area. Oh, if all my enemies were so easily disposed of.

I wasted no time in binding his wrists with the twine and then secreting the gun in my desk drawer.

Pouring myself another snifter of Johnnie Walker, I sat at my desk and waited for the cavalry to arrive.

I had not long to wait. David Llewellyn turned up on my doorstep some fifteen minutes later, in the company of his Detective Sergeant, a chap called Sunderland, and two bobbies. Because of Harryboy's condition they would have to take him to hospital to have him attended to before they could dump him in a cell at the Yard. He would have to be in perfect health before they could hang him. He was handcuffed and hauled down in his unconscious state to a waiting patrol car by Sunderland and the bobbies. David told them to wait there until he'd had a word with me and established the facts of the matter. He not only had a word with me but he also finished off my bottle of Johnnie Walker.

'I'd better warn you at the outset,' I said, 'that I'm not going to tell you everything. I'm protecting a couple of innocent people who have been hurt enough. Be happy you've got your man.'

'I'm always happy when I've got my man,' said David. 'I'm just intrigued as to how this nasty piece of work ended up bleeding on your rather threadbare carpet.'

'We professionals have our secrets,' I said wryly. Then I gave him a sketchy adapted version of what happened in my office. No names were mentioned and David did not press me on the matter.

When I'd finished, David stroked his chin thoughtfully. 'You realize, boyo, that if I didn't know you were as straight as a die, you'd be coming along with me to occupy a nice little cell at the yard. On paper you're a mighty suspicious fellow.'

'On paper I'm many things,' I mused. 'Like a one-eyed reject.'

'Now don't go for the sympathy angle or I will slip the cuffs on you.'

We exchanged smiles.

He rose to go, but before he did he leaned forward and patted me on the back. 'Good man,' he said warmly. 'I'll be in touch.'

TWENTY-EIGHT

After David had departed, I slumped down in my office chair and lit up a cigarette and found myself grinning. It has to be said that the grin was of a seriously ironic nature, but nevertheless it was there, plastered on my tired features. I was contemplating the notion that no one could accuse me of having a quiet life: runaway girls seeking my help, maniac killers invading my office, transvestite murderers on the loose and an errant orphan to worry about. My life at present was a rich tapestry indeed. However, the thought of Peter quickly wiped the smile off my face. Where the hell was he? In some cold doorway somewhere ... or worse?

I knew it was pointless contemplating his fate but I let my mind have its way for a few minutes before I reined myself in and turned it to more practical matters: the Riley murder case. I weighed up the recent evidence I'd gleaned. Most of it related to my friend, Bernard France, The White Rabbit. (1) He worked at the War Office and it was likely he would know of, if not be acquainted with, Walter Riley. (2) I had seen him warn off Mrs Riley. (3) I had seen him at the address I had found on the dead body of Amanda from The Loophole Club. (No doubt she had been warned off too, but in a far more serious manner.) (4) He drove the same kind of motor car used in the murder of Walter Riley.

Even Dr Watson could come up with a conclusion using these facts. All I needed now was proof to link him to the two murders. And a motive would be useful too.

I lit another cigarette and watched the smoke spiral up into the darkness beyond the beam of the lamp. It seemed to me that another visit to Studely Mansions was called for. This time I needed to get inside the apartment and do a little snooping.

With this thought and rough plan of action, I dragged myself off to bed with the knowledge that I would have to rise very early in the morning if I was to catch the worm.

At 7.30 the following day, somewhat bleary of eye and fatigued of body, I had positioned myself along Bedford Gardens in Kensington, with a clear view of the entrance to Studely Mansions. I reckoned Mr White Rabbit would be at his desk at the War Office by half-past eight and so would leave the apartment around eight o'clock. Sometimes, fate smiles kindly on me and indeed my friend France, or was it Webster? along with his thick horn-rimmed glasses, appeared on the steps of the building just before eight o'clock. He stood there as though waiting for a bus, while sniffing the air in a twitching White Rabbit fashion as though it offended him. Shortly after his appearance, a black Wolseley drove up and the commissionaire got out. I was delighted to see that it was not the fellow who had called the police and I'd had to bash in the face. He, no doubt, was at home nursing a broken nose. His replacement, a much younger, thin-faced fellow, saluted as he handed over the car keys to the White Rabbit. He had obviously retrieved the vehicle from some hidden underground parking place. Within seconds, the White Rabbit was in the car, revving up and shooting away down the street.

The commissionaire stepped into the road and saluted once again. While he was concentrating on his obsequious duties, building up bonus points for what he hoped would be a large Christmas tip, I slipped behind him, my hat pulled well over to the left to help obscure my eye-patch, which was always a give away in situations like this. No doubt he had been informed about the one-eyed intruder and to tackle anyone with an eye-patch who came anywhere near the building.

I was through the doors and up the stairs before he had re-entered the building. Getting out may not be as easy, I told myself as I reached the first floor, but I would have to face that revolving door when I came to it. With my trusty hairgrip, I quickly effected an illegal entrance to flat 12.

My, but it was sumptuous inside. I waded through the thick pile carpet into the sitting-room which was very Hollywood: a fusion of black, white and cream with large lamps on mirrored side tables.

Sumptuous indeed it was, but also rather barren. There were no little personal touches that gave individuality to the room, no sense of the character or personality of the owner.

I thought of my own dingier, cramped quarters. A detective scouting around there unhindered, picking up items hither and thither, rummaging through my untidy but revealing drawers, would soon have a fairly full and clear picture of the occupant. Not here though. This apartment was sanitized and neutered.

I wandered into the bedroom which was decorated in a similar style with one wall housing a run of mirrored wardrobes. Sliding back the doors, I peeked inside them. The clothes were split into two sections: men and women. The men's clothes, predominantly smart formal suits, were obviously made for a shortish, broadish chap: Mr France, no doubt; while the ladies clothes, mainly evening wear, were long and slinky and were for someone taller and leaner. I doubted if there was a Mrs France. My guess is that these belonged to Helen. I had certainly seen her wear something of the sort at The Loophole Club. Ah! Perhaps she was Mr Webster. There were other feminine items in the chest of drawers – bracelets, necklaces, underwear and various bottles of perfume.

There was a large cream telephone on the bedside table by the bed. Next to it in a silver frame was a black and white photograph of a beautiful, dark-haired woman. It was Helen from The Loophole Club. I picked it up and studied it closely. She was beautiful as a woman, but I also knew that this character was a transvestite and, as I gazed at the photograph, I tried to erase all the feminine touches from the face – the long hair, the lipstick, the mascara – to unearth the male face beneath, as it were. I laid the photograph on the bed and cupped my hands around the face, blanking off the dark tresses. Slowly the man emerged from behind the artifice. And I recognized him. I had seen him only once before in the flesh – as a man that is – but now I saw him again. I sat for some moments on the bed to let the implications of my discovery sink in.

Eventually I moved into the bathroom. Here in the cabinet over the sink there were two sets of shaving equipment. Of course there were.

Further scrutiny of the apartment revealed little else of interest and so after making sure I was leaving the place exactly as I'd found it, I left.

*

As it happened I was able to slip out of Studely Mansions without any problem. Things were going my way today for a change. The thin-faced commissionaire was studying the pages of what looked like some sporting rag as I breezed by his desk. I suppose he might have looked up if I had been entering the building, but he wouldn't be expecting a man with an eye patch to be leaving the premises.

After my little bit of detective work I felt hungry. I thought a breakfast at Benny's was in order and I set off for Kensington High Street underground station at a brisk pace while I juggled about the new pieces of information in my mind, shifting them around the puzzle canvas until I slotted them in neatly. By the time I'd reached Dean Street, I was quite convinced I had solved the Riley mystery. However, that was only part of my problem. Proving my case would be rather more difficult. One thing was sure: I needed to visit The Loophole Club again.

On entering Benny's Café, I found the proprietor ensconced behind the counter, now minus its glass display case, smiling broadly as though he hadn't a care in the world. Just then the door of the kitchen opened and Rachel, wearing a smart apron, came out carrying a trayful of breakfasts. She hesitated a little when she saw me, smiled nervously and then went on her way to distribute the victuals to the hungry customers.

'Have you met my new waitress?' said Benny, the smile broadening.

'I think so,' I said evenly.

Benny eyed me defensively. 'She needs a job: I need the help. A good arrangement, eh?'

'A good arrangement,' I repeated. It seemed to me that Benny had managed quite well without the aid of a waitress before. This was the old boy being generous again. He had a heart of gold but made great efforts to conceal the fact. However, he also had a soft spot for a pretty face and a womanly figure.

'It's just a temporary, you know …until she finds herself a proper job.'

'In the meantime you take it easy.'

He grinned. 'You could say that. I trust our violent friend is in police custody this morning?'

I nodded and reassured him that neither he nor Rachel would be involved further in the nasty business.

Benny's grin broadened. 'That's a blessed relief. Now, what can I get you? The usual fry up?'

'Why not?' I made my way to a small corner table and picked up a newspaper someone had left behind. I flicked through the pages filled with the latest trials and tribulations of our sorely tried nation. After a while Rachel came and brought me a mug of tea. 'Your food won't be long,' she said.

'Thanks.'

'How … how did things go after … after we'd left you last night?'

'Fine. You've nothing to worry about. Harryboy's safely in the hands of the police. He's no threat to you any more.'

At this news her face brightened considerably. 'Really?' she said breathlessly, as though she was having great difficulty in believing that her luck had changed.

'Really,' I repeated, squeezing her arm.

She leaned forward and kissed me on my cheek. 'Thank you, Johnny.'

I could smell her, the sweet fresh aroma of soap and powder and my face tingled where her lips had been. Once again I felt that not unpleasant feeling of excitement in my stomach, like a very small musician playing the xylophone with my intestines. She had gone before I could respond. Somewhat embarrassed I looked around to see if anyone had noticed this gentle display of affection but everyone seemed involved in devouring their breakfast or deep in some hushed conversation. Shaking my newspaper, I returned to the small print.

I was a little dismayed when it was Benny who delivered my food a few minutes later. I had hoped it would be Rachel.

'I saw that kiss,' he whispered, his face split from ear to ear with a smile of delight.

'She was showing her gratitude.'

'Oh, so that's what it's called these days.' He paused, pretending to examine his tea cloth before continuing, 'She's a nice girl. And pretty. You could do a lot worse …'

One of Benny's missions in life was to get me married off to 'a good woman'. I know he meant well, but I reckon if I was going to have a wife or a girlfriend, I wanted to have quite a large say in the matter. Any time a girl showed any interest in me or vice versa, Benny was all ready for calling the banns.

'You got any brown sauce in this establishment?' I said, ignoring his banter.

With a smirk, he reached over to a nearby table and plucked up a bottle of sauce and plonked it down by my plate.

'Enjoy,' he said with a chuckle and left me to eat my food in peace.

When I had finished Rachel returned to collect the crockery. 'I was wondering if I could call on you to do me another favour,' she said, scooping up my empty plate.

'If I can.'

'Benny's helped me pick out a few addresses from the paper for lodgings. I want somewhere cheap but respectable. I wondered if you'd go with me while I looked at some of the places. Help me decide. You'd be much better at it ... more experienced like.'

'I'm not so sure about that. When do you want to do this?'

'Benny says I can go now.'

I looked over at the beaming rascal leaning on the counter.

'Does he?'

'What about it, Johnny?'

'Sure. Get your coat.'

Most of the addresses were in the Marylebone area, down dreary streets with nondescript names. Suspicious women stuck their unsmiling faces around half-open doors to peer at us disapprovingly. I'd manufactured the story that I was Rachel's brother helping her to find lodgings in London but it didn't really win the hearts of these domestic dragons. They saw fancy man, boyfriend and trouble tattooed across my forehead and for the most part we were turned away. Where we were invited in to inspect the room and facilities, I wouldn't have wished the accommodation on my worst enemy. Damp and decay were the strongest architectural features, with grey bed linen, mouldering wallpaper and cracked window panes. We had all but given up hope when I noticed a sign in the window of a smart looking villa in an avenue in Lisson Grove.

Two women appeared in response to my manly knock on the door. They could have been twins from their age, dress sense and identical grey hair which each had tied in a neat bun atop their head. They were in fact sisters. Unmarried sisters with smooth unlined faces which seemed to suggest that they took the sorrows of life with a certain ease or resignation. I was to learn that it was their faith that had helped to ease their way down the rocky road of existence. And it was probably their faith and general belief in the goodness of man that allowed them to accept my story about being Rachel's protective brother. They looked on us benignly and invited us in. Their parlour, spick and span with shining wood and gleaming glass, was like a Victorian museum, complete with aspidistra in the window and a well-polished harmonium in one of the alcoves. Miss Evelyn and Miss Edith Horner bade us sit down and provided us with a glass of sherry each.

Rachel, I thought, while I sipped my sherry, you have beached up on a fine shore here. These ladies were perfect. The room was small but in the same tidy and pristine shape as the parlour. One cooked meal a day was part of the deal and the rent was ridiculously small. Rachel glanced at me with raised eyebrows. I gave her the nod of assurance.

The Horner sisters seemed as pleased with the transaction as we were.

'It will be so pleasant to have someone young about the place,' observed Miss Edith Horner, while her sister nodded in agreement.

Financial matters were settled and Rachel arranged to move her meagre possessions in that evening.

'That is marvellous.' Rachel said, once we were outside again. 'It'll be like two grannies looking after me,' she giggled.

'Wasn't it that kind of life you left Wales to escape?'

'In a way. But I don't think they'll suffocate me or be judgemental.'

'As long as you are a good girl.'

She stopped and turned quietly towards me and gazed up into my eyes. 'You might not think so, Johnny, but I *am* a good girl.'

She squeezed my hand and, Goddammit, I blushed.

We crossed Park Road and found ourselves strolling in Hyde Park. For a crisp and sunny day in autumn, it was a very pleasant experience. Although the amber sun generated little warmth that was discernible, it gilded the bare trees and the damp scrubby grass in such a way that it lifted one's spirits. Rachel had been quiet for most of the trip but now in the park she seemed to relax and began to talk about her experiences with Harryboy. It was an ugly tale. It was clear that Rachel regretted falling in with him so easily and was ashamed at how gullible she had been.

'I suppose you think I'm a yokel from the sticks,' she said earnestly when she had finished her recital.

'We're not all as smart as paint in London, y'know. We can all make mistakes when we encounter cunning snakes like Harryboy Jenkins; and I reckon you paid for yours the hard way.'

Instinctively she touched her face where the bruise was still visible. 'I've certainly learned a lesson. I won't be so stupid again.'

Suddenly, she grabbed my hand and rushed forward. 'Look!' she cried, tugging me forward. 'Down by the lake. Someone is feeding the ducks. I love ducks.'

And like a teenager she scampered forward towards the water's edge with me in tow. I'm sure that for all the world we looked like a courting couple.

If only life was that simple.

TWENTY-NINE

Harryboy Jenkins gradually grew conscious of muffled sounds and a sensation of bright lights before he was capable of opening his eyes. He was aware of other sensations too: the feel of starchy, stiff sheets about his aching body, the smell of antiseptic assailing his nostrils and, above all, the herd of elephants stampeding in his head. He tried to remember what had happened and where he had been before he lost consciousness. With infinite slowness he was able to piece together the various fragments of memory that were floating around his brain like the debris of a shipwreck and reconstruct a kind of out-of-focus movie of the events of the previous night. He remembered a man with an eye-patch, probably a pirate, a woman crying and most of all the sudden, searing pain at the back of his head. He didn't have to remember that: it was still there.

Gingerly, he prised his eyes open and struggled to bring them into focus so that he could take stock of his situation. He was in a bed in a pale featureless room; a bright sun was shining through the window creating shifting shadows on the wall and, in the distance, he could hear voices, while from beyond the window came the muffled purr of traffic. He was in hospital. That was it. He was in a hospital and was being treated for his head injury.

On coming to this conclusion, his energy waned and he found himself drifting back into sleep. The corners of his vision darkened and his thoughts began evaporating, leaving a void behind them. He licked his dry lips and tried to fight against it, digging his nails into the palms of his hands in a desperate attempt to keep himself awake. He needed to know more – like how the hell he had got here in the first place. The nails dug deeper. He rallied briefly, his eyes widening again, just long enough for him to glimpse the figure sitting on a chair by the door. He seemed to be dozing, head nodding, and he was cradling some dark object in his lap. Harryboy strained to bring the thing into focus. It was a helmet. A police helmet! This feller was a policeman. So the coppers had got him after all. They had come to arrest him for what he'd done to his brother. But it had been an accident! He had explained that a hundred times before. Although, in his heart of hearts, he knew he was responsible. He knew he was guilty. He had to get away. He had to escape. To get somewhere safe. He had to go where no one would find him. Yes! He had to get back to the hideout. The sheriff's men would never catch him there. That's what he'd do. He'd escape and go there, to the hideout.

With this resolution firmly fixed in his mind, he gave up the struggle to keep a grip on consciousness and he slumped back into a deep sleep once more.

The constable by the door was indeed dozing and had not witnessed his charge's brief resuscitation. However, he was roused sometime later by the cries and whimpers of the prisoner as he tossed and turned in a disturbed sleep. Hesitantly, the policeman rose from his chair and made his way to the bed. Harryboy's brow was wet with perspiration and his body shifted awkwardly beneath the covers but he was imprisoned in a deep sleep. He was muttering words and phrases over and over again like a mantra. The constable withdrew his notebook and pencil and proceeded to write down what the man was saying. After all, it could be important, although it did seem to be the ramblings of a delirious mind.

He scribbled down in neat handwriting: 'Got to get to the hideout. My hideout. Get away from the sheriff's men. Jack will never find me there.'

'Don't know what the inspector will make of that load of nonsense,' the constable murmured to himself, as his charge lapsed into silence once more as a strange calm seemed to overtake him.

'That boy is more than feverish; he's in a real bad way: he needs medical attention,' observed Sergeant Woodcock rubbing his chin as a visible sign of his consternation. 'I don't want to be responsible for a death in my station. We need to get a doc to look at him.'

PC MacGregor who had brought Peter into the station nodded in agreement. The boy had begun behaving strangely ever since he'd taken him from Dave's tea bar. He'd barely said a word, even when questioned and had begun shivering involuntarily before they had reached the police station. Sergeant Woodcock had contacted the appropriate authorities about the runaway but was told it would be at least twenty-four hours before they could send an official down to take custody of him and try to find a place for the boy in one of the orphanages. 'They are bursting at the seams. We have more of these children than we can handle,' he was told by a stern-voiced woman at the other end of the telephone. As a result Peter had spent the night in the cells. Despite being treated kindly and offered some food, he had retreated into himself, curling up into a defensive ball on his makeshift bed and slipping into a deep sleep. Peter really had no control over his actions. His mind had taken over and feeling battered and shocked after all the terrible experiences he had undergone in the last few months it sought a way to escape. It did this by shutting down.

The sergeant ran his fingers over the hot, damp forehead of the unconscious boy and then turned to his constable, a grim, grey expression on his features. 'Get Dr Glover here, as fast as you can!' he said.

Doctor Glover, who was used to treating old lags when he was summoned to the police station, was surprised to find a ten-year-old boy in a high fever lying in one of the cells.

'He's a runaway,' explained Sergeant Woodcock. 'Probably been living rough along by the river. God knows what he's picked up. By the look of his face, it could be scarlet fever.'

Doctor Glover knelt down by Peter and felt his pulse and then, extracting his stethoscope from his bag, he pulled open the young boy's shirt to reveal a fine red rash there. He listened to his heartbeat 'I reckon your diagnosis is correct, Sergeant. Has he vomited?'

Sergeant Woodcock shook his head. 'He's done nothing but shiver and sleep.'

Glover pulled back one of Peter's eyelids to reveal only the bloodshot white beneath.

'We need to get him into a hospital fast. If he isn't treated quickly, this could develop into rheumatic fever.'

'Right,' said Sergeant Woodcock hoarsely, shocked at this diagnosis. He'd lost a brother to rheumatic fever and he knew what a killer it could be. 'I'll get on to Charing Cross Hospital straight away. Get them to send an ambulance.'

He turned at the door of the cell and glanced down at the small, curled figure on the bed. 'Poor bugger,' he said, and then hurried away.

THIRTY

There was a black wreath on the door of The Loophole Cl
I arrived around nine o'clock. It was, no doubt, placed th
token of respect for Amanda. I wondered who would reall
for her. Her? I knew that it really should be 'him' but I coulc
but think of Amanda as anything other than a woman. I rec
would have approved of that.

The club was packed and smoky which was fine by me
enough of a sore thumb as it was, dressed in male attire; th
lighted, crowded room afforded me a little camouflage. I st
the door and surveyed the place. It was quite bizarre and
rather like (I would imagine) attending an annual general mee
the pantomime dames association. With the exception of a fe
convincing ladies, most of the men there were dressed badly, c
made-up and wrongly shaped: they made terrible women. B
thing struck me forcibly: they all seemed happy. The air wa
with cheery chatter and laughter. I couldn't remember the last
laughed – for the right reason.

To my dismay, there was no sign of Helen, tall, slinky I
Eventually I squeezed my way to the bar. I battled across the
and secured a stool, sardined between a large fat apparition
black shiny evening dress and a thin fellow in a WAAF uniform.
parties ignored me, as did the lovely creature who was se
behind the bar. It was the same person who had served me th
time: I recognized the stubble. I suppose a chap in a suit is r
persona non grata in an establishment like this. However, eventu
the barman deigned to come over. I ordered a Scotch on the roc

'Is Helen in tonight?' I asked casually, as he slapped my d
down on the counter.

'Who?'

'You know, Helen. Tall, long black hair. Friend of Wilma Riley's.' I waved a ten-shilling note provocatively as bait.

'Oh, her. I haven't seen her, but she often leaves it late till she comes in, when things have quietened down a little.' His hand crept towards the note.

'What do you know about her?'

The barman's eyes narrowed suspiciously and he pulled back. 'This is a private club. We don't ask questions here. Understand?'

I nodded. I understood. I placed the ten-shilling note on the counter. 'Just give me the wink if you see her come in, eh? I have a message for her.'

Without a word, he picked up the money and went off to serve someone else. I lingered over my Scotch for the best part of half an hour while I surveyed the room in an apparently casual manner. There was no sign of the lovely Helen.

It looked as though I was in for the long haul and so I had no alternative but buy another drink. I made it a tonic water. This was easier on my wallet and I wanted to keep a sharp brain tonight. One of the things I'd learned since I'd been doing this job: never get squiffy when you're meeting up with a murderer.

By ten o'clock the club had quietened down a little but it was still busy. Somehow the blitz and the danger of further bombing had done away with people's bedtimes. What was the point of getting into bed before midnight, if you've only to get up again to rush down to the shelter an hour later? You may as well stay up.

And then she came in. Or rather made an entrance. She swanned slinkily down the stairs as though she was attending a Hollywood premiere. I was reminded of the newsreel pictures of Vivien Leigh posing and pouting at the opening of *Gone With the Wind*. No pushing and shoving through the throng to get to the bar for Helen. The crowd parted like the Red Sea, numerous envious eyes appraising her as she did so. This character made a remarkable woman. She was tall, shapely and had the most deli-cate feminine features. It was as though Nature had been undecided which sex to dole out in the womb and this borderline amalgam had emerged.

She sat on a stool at the other end of the bar and ordered a drink. Another customer, in a flowery red dress and a disappointing wig

came up and offered her a cigarette. Helen ignored her, extracting her own packet of cigarettes and lighter from her small clutch bag.

I noted with chagrin that the bartender failed to earn his ten bob by giving me the nod to indicate that Helen had arrived, although I suppose I would have been a very dim fellow indeed not to notice such an entrance. I was still involved in a waiting game. I knew it would be too dangerous to try and speak with Helen in the bar. I was sure that if I did, a scene would ensue and before long I would be surrounded by a group of angry transvestites baying for my blood – the blood of a bloke in male attire invading their patch and causing trouble. I was relying on Helen's bladder to give me a break,

It took fifteen minutes before she felt the need to visit the powder-room. Before then she had been approached by numerous customers, each paying court in their own way. Helen had a strange magnetism – I could see that even from where I was sitting. It was both alluring and excitingly dangerous. I remembered how I had seen the flash of anger in her eyes on the first night I had visited the club when she had the argument with Wilma Riley. Helen was not a creature to tangle with; and yet I had to tangle with her.

Eventually she slid off her stool and made her way to the powder room. I followed in what I hoped was a discreet fashion. Once inside the dingy, ill-lighted lavatory, I slammed the door behind me. Helen was just about to enter one of the cubicles but the noise caught her attention and she turned to face me. A sardonic smile twisted its way on to her flawless features.

'I wondered how long it would be before we met properly, Mr Hawke.' The voice was husky and feminine. Helen remained in character.

'You know my name. I think it's about time I knew yours. Your proper name, that is. The one you were born with. And it's not really Mr Webster.'

The smile broadened. 'I don't think so. There would be no point now.'

'Why did you kill Walter Riley?'

'My dear Mr Hawke, I did not. I would never sully my own hands with murder.'

'You're lying,' I said, though something told me that he was telling the truth – or at least a version of it.

'You'll have to prove it and quite honestly I don't think that you

181

are in a position to do that.' He opened his clutch bag and pulled out a small pistol. 'Dinky little thing, isn't it. Petite but very deadly.'

'So you're going to kill me now, eh?'

'Not unless I absolutely have to. I abhor violence and I certainly do not want to be directly involved in the unpleasant business of your demise ... if at all possible. But of course that is up to you.' The eyes flashed, clearly signalling the threat in that final phrase.

'What are you going to do then?'

'You and I are going to leave the club together. You will come along with me like a nice little detective.'

'Where to?'

'Ah, let's say that will be a surprise.'

'OK,' I said amiably. 'Let's go.' I half turned to open the door when I felt the gun in my back.'

'Not that way, Mr Hawke. You are a naïve fellow, aren't you? You don't think I'd trust you to behave sensibly if we went back into the club.' Suddenly his smile vanished and his features darkened. 'This way,' he snapped, tugging my arm and nodding towards the back of the room where there was a door marked 'Emergency Exit'. Lifting his foot up he kicked hard against the push bar on the door and with a sharp crack it swung open allowing a blast of cold air to gust in.

'Out we go, Mr Hawke. You first.'

I stepped out into an alleyway with Helen close behind me. It was very dark out there and the dim lighting from the open doorway and a pale moon provided the only illumination. I soon felt the stab of the pistol barrel in my back once more.

He marched me down to the end of the alley to where a Wolseley saloon was parked. I could see a vague silhouette on the driver's side. As we drew nearer, the figure moved, the door swung open and someone emerged. Even in the gloom, I recognized the fellow. It was my old friend, the White Rabbit.

He, too, had a gun. He, too, aimed it at me. Now I was really starting to get worried, when suddenly the world exploded. I felt a searing pain on the back of my head and with flashing lights the world turned into a negative: the blacks were white and the whites were black. And then all was blackness as I found myself sinking down to embrace the hard wet pavement.

When I regained consciousness with a very neat throbbing ache at the back of my head, I found myself lying on the rear seat of a moving car. As all my senses returned, I realized that my hands had been tied behind me. Sliding my feet forward, with a determined effort I managed to drag myself up into a sitting position. While carrying out this awkward procedure, I gave an involuntary gruff exclamation which alerted the driver, the only other occupant of the car, of my return to consciousness. I could see his features in the driving mirror. They were illuminated ghoulishly by the dashboard lights creating a frightening reflection rather like an animated woodcut. As I suspected, it was the White Rabbit himself: Bernard France.

'Ah, the sleeper awakes,' he said smoothly, ramming the gear lever in to a higher gear. The car jolted and I almost slid sideways back into my recumbent position.

'Where is Helen ... or should I say Sir Robert Gervais.'

'He is no doubt enjoying himself back at The Loophole Club. I have taken over his duties now.'

'And what are your duties?'

'Oh, don't be so naïve, Mr Hawke.'

Those few simple words, spoken in a soft, lisping sarcastic manner not only informed me of the fate that awaited me, but blew away much of the fog that had surrounded this mystery. Within seconds, so much became clear to me. Not every detail of the picture was clearly in focus, but my tired mind could see the whole. If what I believed was true, it was a chilling scenario.

'So it was you who killed Walter Riley, wasn't it?'

'Of course it was,' came the smooth reply. 'And now I'm going to kill you.'

THIRTY-ONE

Nurse Susan McAndrew peered through the porthole window into the small side ward and saw the flushed face of the little boy peeping over the white crisp sheets in the hospital bed. A lamp by the bedside illuminated his haggard features. There was no doubt: that was Peter all right. He looked so lost and tiny, so vulnerable lying there that Susan felt a lump materialize in her throat. But she reminded herself that she was a tough and experienced nurse and she soon dismissed it with a sharp shrug. Anyway, she told herself, as she entered the room, she should be rejoicing and happy. At least the lad had been found. It was only by chance she had overheard one of the other nurses saying that a young homeless boy had been brought in suffering from scarlet fever and that he had been living rough. Susan hoped against hope that it was Peter and now she saw that it was.

She ran her cool hand over his feverish brow. His eyelids fluttered momentarily but they did not open. She checked his progress chart at the end of the bed. His temperature was worryingly high. Slipping her hand under the covers, she found his wrist and took his pulse. It was slow and weak. 'Come on, lad, fight it,' she said, leaning over him. 'You can do it if you really want.' And then it struck her that he might not want to fight it. So far his short life had been one of disappointments and hardship, suffering what he saw no doubt as a series of constant betrayals by adults in whom he had put his trust. Maybe he'd had enough. This thought sent a chill of dismay through her.

She realized that she would have to inform Johnny about the situation, but perhaps she would wait until she'd had a chance to talk to the doctor treating Peter to find out what his chances of survival were. With a final glance at the sleeping boy, she left the room quietly with a bowed head.

In another part of the hospital, Harryboy had been propped up in bed by a sturdy nurse who was spoon feeding him some hot soup. The whole procedure was observed by a grim-faced constable who remained in the shadows at the far side of the room. Harryboy sipped the soup as a baby would, nodding his head forward automatically with each mouthful, apparently not fully conscious of his actions. His mind was still fogged and the world was strange and threatening to him. However, simple but determined thoughts remained with him and were dominant: he had to get away, to escape from his captors, the goodies. He wouldn't be safe until he made it back to his hideout. They'd never find him there. He would be safe. As he contemplated this simple idea he allowed himself a little smile between spoonfuls. He just needed to wait until he was strong enough to make a move. He was sharp enough to pretend he was more fragile than he was – another smile – allowing himself time to recover and then he would act – then he would escape.

He'd finished the soup and the nurse wiped his chin just as his mother had done. His eyes widened and he stared at the nurse. It wasn't his mother, was it? No, of course not. What would she be doing helping the goodies?

'All done. That's a good boy,' said the nurse, placing the tray on the bedside table, before turning to the policeman. 'Would you give me a hand to settle him down? He's quite a weight.'

The policeman nodded and strode over to the bed. He lifted Harryboy forward while the nurse pulled away the pillows and arranged them so that her patient could lie flat. Once down, Harryboy turned on his side and slipped very quickly into a deep sleep, heading for a dream in which he reached the dark and cosy confines of his hideout, safe from all those that wanted to hurt him. As he slept, his mouth shifted slowly into a grim smile.

THIRTY-TWO

'So, you do all his dirty work for him then,' I said with apparent calm, belying the fact that my heart was doing an energetic rumba in response to the notion that I was going to be killed by Bernard France, alias the White Rabbit, any time now.

'I look after him,' France replied, curtly.

'Sir Robert Gervais ... alias Mr Webster ... alias the lovely Helen.'

I saw France's head twitch nervously at the recital of these names.

I grinned because now I knew. The curtains had parted and revealed the truth. Now I understood the mechanics of their strange partnership. I had no notion of how it had evolved, but it was clear that France and Gervais were involved in a kind of dark and dangerous Jeeves and Wooster relationship. Gervais, head-strong and reckless, no doubt a trait fostered by his privileged background, followed his passion for dressing up in women's clothing whatever the risk, while France trailed behind mopping up the mess and ensuring his noble master's indemnity – even to the point of murder.

'Sir Robert Gervais,' I repeated, smoothly. 'You are his protector. You make sure that his secret remains a secret. You "arrange things" when there is a danger of exposure.'

France did not respond, but his head twitched nervously.

'You must love him very much,' I said.

I was obviously spooking my captor. The truth when clearly expressed verbally was a little too close for comfort for him. 'Shut up,' he barked, and shifted awkwardly in his seat before stamping his foot down on the accelerator. The car jerked forward at speed and then suddenly, with a screech of tyres, swerved around a corner, throwing me down onto my side again.

'I thought the idea was to kill me. Carry on driving like this and we'll both end up dead.'

'Shut up!' he cried again, his voice strident and emotional.

'Oh, that's one thing I can't do. And why should I? I've nothing to lose. If I'm going to hell in a handcart, I want all the answers first. Why did you kill Walter Riley?'

'You tell me, Mr Knowall.'

'I think Walter found out that the voluptuous Helen, the *femme fatale* of The Loophole was in fact one of the bigwigs at the War Office where he worked. This posed a threat that had to be dealt with.'

'He tried to blackmail Sir Robert. The situation was untenable.'

I raised an eyebrow at this news. I had never taken Walter for a blackmailer; he seemed very much the victim. But then, of course, push a worm so far and inevitably he will turn. I remembered the altercation that first night in The Loophole Club when there had been such a heated conversation between Wilma and Helen. It all made sense now. Wilma had been demanding money to keep quiet. No doubt he had ideas about feathering his own nest so that he could leave Sandra.

'And Amanda,' I said, after a moment spent digesting these thoughts, 'I suppose she came too close to discovering the truth as well, did she?'

'She got in the way.'

'And so you murdered her.'

'She posed a threat to Sir Robert. I couldn't allow that. He is much too important a person.'

'As I said, you must love him very much.'

'Of course I do. I don't expect you to understand. He is a wonderful man and his work for the government is vital to the war effort.'

'But your loyalty goes beyond that, caring about his welfare, doesn't it, Bernard? You don't just love him … you are *in* love with him.'

'You make it sound so sordid. It is far from that. I don't expect you to understand. It is not a sexual thing. It transcends all that bodily function stuff. But, yes, you are right: I care for him more than I can say. He is like a god to me. To be in the same room as him is a privilege. I would do anything to protect him and he knows that and relies on me.'

'He orders you to kill people.'

'He does not need to. I know instinctively what to do.'

The man was crazy, of course, but there was something disturbingly touching about his perverted loyalty. I never cease to wonder at the range and strength of emotions that can be harboured within the human breast.

'And so now you know instinctively that I should be bumped off.'

There was a pause before France replied with a simple, quiet, 'Yes, of course.'

The sudden lack of emotion in his voice chilled me to the marrow.

We picked up speed again and my captor swung the car down a narrow cobbled alley. The vehicle reverberated noisily as it thudded over the uneven surface as though it was being bombarded with rocks. We had long since left any main roads behind and had been driving down a complicated series of back streets. There were tall industrial premises closing in on us from either side and I could see the vague outline of something that looked like a crane up ahead, its silhouetted gantry reaching high into the night sky. I guessed that we were down somewhere near the docks.

'And now *I'm* in the way,' I said, attempting to maintain the flow of conversation.

'Not for long, old boy. Not for long,' came the sneering reply.

Without warning, the car slewed to a halt, the tyres crunching on the gravel. I looked out of the window and confirmed that I had been right. We were by the docks: there were cranes, warehouses and in the distance the murky glitter of the river, the ripples caught by the pale half moon.

Bernard France got out of the car and came for me. Gun in hand, he opened the back door and dragged me outside, my hands still tied securely behind my back.

'Another body floating in the Thames,' he said stoically, waving the gun in the direction of the water. 'Come along, Mr Hawke, time for your midnight swim.'

'You didn't tell me Sir Robert would be joining us,' I said, nodding my head in the direction of one of the warehouses in the shadows behind us. France was momentarily distracted by my desperate ploy and against his better judgement, he turned his head to look over towards the shadows as though he expected to see his friend, Sir Robert Gervais standing behind him.

This gave me just a second, but a second was all that I needed. I let fly with my foot with great force and, as it turned out, with great accuracy. My target was the White Rabbit's genitals. My shoe hit bull's eye. With a sharp yell, a kind of bizarre parody of Tarzan's yodel, France bent double in pain and sank to his knees.

Within a heartbeat I was running for cover, towards one of the dark buildings to my left. I'd never thought about it before, but having one's hands tied behind your back does slow you down. You run like a drunken man in a strange loping fashion because you can't swing your arms to help propel you along and steer a straight course. So despite all my efforts, I stumbled and zig-zagged rather than sprinted off into the darkness. I had just about reached the corner of the building when a shot rang out and a bullet zinged by me. It was too close for comfort.

I glanced behind me and saw that France was already back on his feet and heading in my direction. It gave me a little crumb of pleasure to see that he was limping badly. My blow must have been particularly accurate.

I slipped around the corner into pitch darkness. I was down the side of a low one-storey shed, with boarded-up windows. It had long been deserted. Keeping to the wall I felt my way towards the far end. The ground was uneven and littered with large stones and other unidentifiable debris. Once or twice I stumbled and nearly fell down, not being able to steady myself with my arms. If only they were free! And then I crashed into what I later surmised was some sort of water butt and winded myself. I ricocheted backwards and my cry of surprise helped France to pinpoint my location in the blackness and another bullet came my way. I ducked down and pressed on still using the wall as my guide. Within seconds I had reached the far side of the building and was out of the shadows and into the moonlight. I had to think fast. We could go on circling this particular building all night like characters in a cartoon until eventually France caught up with me and then ... Bang! Bang! Goodbye Johnny. I could hear him behind me, his heavy footfalls and his even heavier breathing growing louder. He was gaining on me.

I crossed over to the next building, an exposed figure in the pale rays of the moon. Exposed enough for the White Rabbit to take another shot at me. His aim was getting better. I felt the bullet whistle past me. I struggled down the far side of the building, wading now through tall, damp grass which seemed to cling like tiny hands to my trousers, dragging me back. Halfway along there was a door. On the off chance, I gave it a shove. It responded slightly so I shoved even harder ramming the door with my shoulder. It creaked and moaned and then suddenly it gave way and sprang open. Pushing the door wide, I slipped into the pitch blackness, a crazy plan forming in my mind.

Placing myself directly behind the door, I waited. I was sure that old White Rabbit would have seen me come in. I just hoped he would behave as I expected him to.

Thank the Lord he did.

I could hear his laboured breathing before I caught sight of him through a narrow crack in the door. He was still limping and his face was wet with perspiration. Gingerly he touched the door, pressing it open a little further and then he stepped forward, standing on the ·threshold, his gun pointing into the darkness.

Now it was my time to act. With all my might, I hurled my weight against my side of the door, forcing it to slam shut or as shut as it could do with a short man standing in the way.

The door hit France head on. I heard a cry and a gunshot and through the crack I caught a glimpse of him as he fell backward, landing flat on the ground. Pushing the door open with my foot, I ran outside, ready to kick the living daylights out of my captor, but he lay still on the ground, not moving a muscle. At first I thought he must have hit his head on a stone or something very hard and was concussed. But that wasn't the case. As I knelt down beside him, I could see a dark shiny wet patch on his overcoat around the midriff. And it was spreading. Then I noticed his right hand, the one holding the gun. It was twisted inwards, the barrel of the gun pointing towards the spreading stain. I had caused the man to shoot himself. The force of the door hitting him must have snapped his hand back against his stomach as he pulled the trigger.

Indirectly I had been responsible for his death, but I reckon I wasn't going to lose much sleep about it.

As a frosty October dawn made its presence felt over London, an orange sun slowly rising over the bomb-damaged contours of the city, I was sitting in the office of Detective Inspector David Llewellyn at Scotland Yard telling him of my night's adventures.

Cradling a mug of hot coffee in my hand, I gave him a full account of the Walter Riley case, even including my frantic attempts to cut my bonds after Bernard France had shot himself. I had in fact found an old oil drum and by rubbing the rope against a rusty jagged lip, I managed to fray it sufficiently for me to slip free. The whole arm-aching procedure took about twenty minutes – far longer than it does for those tough guys in the movies.

After that I had scooped up France's body and placed it in the back of the Wolseley and driven to Scotland Yard where I waited for David to arrive. He had been dragged from his bed a couple of hours earlier than usual because of me and he wasn't in the best of humours.

'In essence, Bernard France confessed to two murders: Walter Riley and the person you call Amanda,' said David, jotting down the information in his notepad.

I nodded. 'I don't know her real name.'

'Don't you mean his real name? He is a bloke, isn't he?'

'If you say so.'

'What I don't get,' said David, running his hand through his hair, 'is Sir Robert Gervais' actual involvement.'

I shook my head. 'I don't pretend to fully understand the relationship here but France was much more than Sir Robert's secretary. He was his self-appointed protector ...'

'His lover?'

I shrugged. 'Possibly. He obviously loved Gervais. He killed for him.'

'To protect his secret: that he likes dressing up in women's clothing.'

'He lives dangerously for such a prominent person, visiting The Loophole Club on a regular basis, dressed as Helen. Discovery of his unusual proclivity—'

'His perversion, more like.'

'Discovery would bring scandal to anyone, but to a fellow in such a privileged and important position as Sir Robert it would destroy him. He had a bolthole in Kensington, a flat in Studely Mansions; he rented it under the name of Webster. He shared it at times with France. This was where he keeps his dresses.'

David pulled a sour face. 'Do you think that he sanctioned these murders, or did France act off his own bat?'

'Well, old Sir Bobby was fairly well involved in trying to do away with me. Whether he would have pulled the trigger … I don't know. In essence, he was just being the delivery boy: passing me on to his guardian angel. I think he relied on France to keep his life clean and simple and free from unpleasant ripples, rather like employing a homicidal butler. However, I don't think he would ever give the precise instruction for someone to be killed. He didn't have to. France knew instinctively what to do.'

David gave a tight grin. 'It's all rather bizarre, boyo. I feel a little out of my depth here. I have no trouble with the straightforward murder merchant, but men who dress up as women and use their lovers to kill for them …' He shook his head in despair. 'This bloody war.'

'I don't think this is something you can blame on old Adolf Hitler. I reckon you'll find this sort of thing has gone on through the ages.'

'Not in Wales, it hasn't!'

David was only half in jest and I smiled indulgently.

'What now?'

'You'll need to make a statement for us detailing all you've told me, including your encounter with Sir Robert dressed as a woman. Then we'll have to bring him in for questioning. Let's hope he wears a suit.'

I walked back to Prior's Court. I thought the fresh air would clear my head and help to revive me. It had been a long weary night and I was about done in. However, it was strangely pleasant to make my way through the early morning streets, watching the city and its inhabitants brace themselves for a new day. The pedestrians hurried by me *en route* to work, or returning home after a night shift some-where. No one seemed to dawdle. Everyone had a purpose and, it seemed, a vigour to carry it out. Except me. I hadn't the energy but to stroll along, smoking a cigarette as I did so. The sky was blue, the air was crisp and the sun was dazzlingly bright and for some inex-plicable reason I felt relaxed.

Well, I pondered, I had reduced my series of problems by one. The Walter Riley case had been solved after a fashion and the murderer had met a fitting end. I would leave David and the powers of Scotland Yard to deal with Sir Robert Gervais. I didn't feel sorry for the man because however much he distanced himself from the killings, he knew about them and whether directly or indirectly, he had sanctioned them. The tragedy was that the whole business stemmed from a quirk of nature. Dressing up as a woman may be odd, but it wasn't a cardinal sin. There are far worse activities being carried out in this blighted city, but slipping on a brassiere and a dress, if you are a man, does invite blackmail with all the nasty repercussions that brings.

I would in due course contact Sandra Riley out of courtesy and inform her of the facts. After all, she did employ me in the first place, even though she also dismissed me later, but that under duress after she was threatened by France. However, the main thing on my mind now was getting home, making myself a strong cup of tea and then going to bed for a long sleep; then I could face the other complications in my life.

THIRTY-THREE

It was time to move. He'd waited long enough in this bed being spoon fed by his mother, who also had taken him to the toilet as though he couldn't wipe his own backside. He'd been doing that for years. But he'd been clever. He'd pretended to be weak, which he wasn't. He was all right now, strong enough to escape, and he'd be even better when he got back to his hideout.

With grim determination, Harryboy pulled himself up into a sitting position in the bed and called out to the dozing constable in the corner of the room.

'Here, mate. I need a pee.'

The policeman roused himself from his sleepy reverie and grimaced. This wasn't bloody police work, was it? Being a glorified wet nurse. Looking after a little turd like Harryboy Jenkins and helping him to piss into a bottle. That's not what he joined the police force for: to be a bloody nanny to a murderer. He'd rather be directing traffic. Reluctantly he retrieved the heavy china bottle from under the bed and handed it to Harryboy, who had already pulled back the covers in readiness.

'Ta, mate.'

Harryboy took the bottle from the constable and then without hesitation smashed him hard across the face with it. The policeman fell to the floor with a strangulated cry, a mixture of shock and pain. Blood gushed from his nose and a cut on his forehead. Harryboy jumped out of bed and aimed a second blow, this time on top of the policeman's head. The bottle cracked hard against his skull and he lay very still, the life seeping out of him.

Harryboy emitted a childish tuneless whistle as he set about divesting the policeman of his clothes. The constable was somewhat

194

taller and slimmer than Harryboy, but he managed to cope with the uniform. Harryboy stripped off his own pyjamas and with lively enthusiasm pulled the policeman's trousers high into his crotch so that they didn't hang too long over the boots, which to his surprise were almost a perfect fit. It was all a big dressing-up game to him. His pleasure was increased when he discovered a large penknife in one of the pockets of the policeman's tunic. He opened it up, caressing the blade. 'Nice and sharp,' he muttered to himself in a sing-song voice. His smile grew wider. This was an ideal deterrent for anyone who tried to prevent him from reaching his hideout.

Ten minutes later, Harryboy Jenkins was dressed for the street in what he considered was his 'great disguise.' He slipped on the policeman's long grey raincoat which had been hanging by the door. He glanced in the mirror and looked at his face. He was very pale, with very dark circles under his eyes, but apart from that he looked his old self, more or less. But, unfortunately, there was the blood-soaked bandage on his head. He couldn't walk around with that on show. However, he knew that it might be dangerous to take it off. His brains might fall out. He giggled at the thought. The image of a squirmy sponge plopping out of his head onto the floor amused him greatly. Slowly he looked around the room for inspiration and saw the policeman's old trilby under the chair on which he'd been sitting.

'You won't want that anymore, will you? Now that you're dead,' he chortled, addressing the inert figure by the bed, whose head was now encircled with a halo of blood.

Snatching up the hat, Harryboy Jenkins placed it gently on his head and then carefully pulled it down so that the bandage was completely covered. He adjusted the brim in order to shade part of his face and then grinned at his reflection in the mirror. Now he was ready. Now he could escape. Now he could go to his hideout where no one would ever find him.

He pushed open the door and glanced down the corridor. There was no one about. He slipped out of the room and hurried off to the left not knowing whether this would lead him to the exit or not. He had discovered by keeping his ears open and catching fragments of conversations while lying in his bed pretending to be asleep that he was in Charing Cross Hospital, but he'd no notion of the geography of the building. That didn't bother him though; he knew that luck was on his side.

Just as he reached the end of the corridor, three gossiping nurses bustled round the corner. They were chirping away and laughing, so engrossed in each other's company that they did not give Harryboy a second glance. This pleased him so much he couldn't help but have another little giggle. He'd become invisible. He next encountered an ancient porter, struggling along with a mop in a galvanized bucket.

"Scuse me mate, I got myself a bit lost,' said Harryboy in a cheerful manner. 'Which is the way out of this place?'

With a sigh, the porter put the pail down, relieved to have a reason to unburden himself briefly and, with hand signals and gestures, gave Harryboy a very detailed description of how to reach the entrance foyer.

'Ta, mate,' said Harryboy and hurried off.

He had reached the ground floor and was well on his way to freedom when his luck ran out. Some distance away from him, he saw one of the nurses and the doctor who had been treating him. They surely would recognize him if he attempted to pass them by. He was well aware that he looked a bit odd in the ill-fitting raincoat and the trilby clamped to his head. He would attract their attention immediately. They'd only to catch a glimpse of his mush and the game would be well and truly up. On impulse, he opened the nearest door and ducked inside. He found himself in a small private side ward similar to the one he'd just left. In the bed was a small boy who roused himself from his slumbers at Harryboy's entrance and with some effort sat up.

'Johnny ...,' croaked the boy dreamily, rubbing his eyes.

Suddenly an idea struck Harryboy. A brilliant idea, he thought. He even chuckled at the thought of it.

'Yeah, yeah. It's Johnny,' he replied. 'I've come for yer. Time to leave, sonny. Let's have you out of that bed now. C'mon.'

Like an automaton Peter swung his legs on to the floor and stood unsteadily wondering what to do next. Harryboy came over to him and spied the boy's clothes folded neatly in the open cabinet by the bedside. He snatched them up and thrust them at the boy. 'Here get these on and hurry.'

Peter gazed up at the man in the large hat, his eyes gradually coming into focus. 'You're not Johnny.'

'No, no. I'm not Johnny, but he sent me to get you. C'mon kid. Get yer skates on.'

Harryboy was convinced that taking the boy along was one of his greatest brainwaves. If the hospital authorities were searching for him, and probably by now they would be, they wouldn't look twice at a man with a little boy. Father and son. He could walk the corridors with impunity with the lad by his side.

Reluctantly and with great awkwardness, Peter shrugged off the pyjamas that the hospital had provided and began to struggle into his old clothes. Tired and still ill, everything seemed slightly out of focus to him and he felt very hot and clammy all over. Reality had somehow become a heated dream for him. He stopped from time to time thinking that he was going to faint, but he persevered. He so wanted to see Johnny again. Whatever the consequences. In his fevered thoughts, he had come to the conclusion that despite everything Johnny was his only real friend in the world. He should have trusted him. He would trust him now.

'For Christ's sake, get a move on,' snapped the man fiercely as Peter fumbled with his shoe laces.

'Yes, I'm coming,' he mumbled.

Eventually, Harryboy helped the boy into his grubby gabardine and they were ready to leave. Peering through the porthole window into the corridor, Harryboy checked that for the moment the coast was clear and then man and boy emerged from the room.

'Keep your head down, boy, and hold my hand,' Harryboy snapped.

'My name is Peter,' he said, slipping his hand into the stranger's – the man who had come from Johnny.

The two of then walked down the corridor towards the sign on the wall which said 'Way Out' that was accompanied by a bold painted pointing finger. Harryboy felt a tingle of excitement. How he loved those words: 'Way Out'. Soon, he thought, soon I'll be at the hideout and free. Inside his coat pocket, his hand caressed the open penknife.

Once outside in the bright October sunshine, Harryboy felt exhilarated. He had managed to escape from the goodies. He'd walked out of their fortress, right under their noses and they'd not noticed a thing. Nothing could stop him now. He would be at his hideout soon.

Clasping Peter's hand tightly and dragging him along, he rushed to the kerb and hailed a taxi. Bundling the boy in the back he gave instructions to the driver.

'I want to go to Pimlico,' he said.

THIRTY-FOUR

I had hardly shut my eyes when the telephone rang. I'd decided to take a nap on the couch rather than go to bed. However much I was tempted, I couldn't spare the time to spend the whole day under the eiderdown. I had too much to do. I reckoned a couple of hours' shut eye would revive me and then I could set about the business of the day.

I was just surrendering myself to the tendrils of sleep when the telephone's shrill call dragged me back. It was like a dentist's drill boring into my consciousness. I tried to ignore the blasted thing, but it was nagging and insistent. Reluctantly, Lazarus-like, I raised myself up and went to answer it.

The voice at the other end was familiar and unusually excited. It was Susan McAndrew. 'Johnny, great news,' she said, almost shouting down the phone. 'Peter's turned up. He's been found.'

Some inexplicable emotion took hold of me and my body trembled. I was filled with a strange mixture of relief, happiness and what I can only describe as melancholy.

'Tell me more,' I said simply, my voice hoarse with suppressed emotion.

'He's in hospital here at Charing Cross. He was brought in yesterday suffering from a fever.'

'Hospital!'

'But he's going to be all right, Johnny. I had a word with his doctor. He was in a bad way when they brought him in, but he's rallied very quickly.'

'What was wrong with him? Has he been hurt?'

'No, no, nothing like that. It was a fever but it's coming down now. I saw him last night and he is gradually improving. I didn't want to ring you until I'd had a word with the doc to find out the full situation. He is still a little delirious but that's to be expected. They think he should make a full recovery. It's just such a relief to get him back.' Suddenly her excited joy turned tearful.

'I'm coming to the hospital. I want to see him.'

'That's why I rang. Can you come now?'

'Try and stop me.'

She gave a sad little laugh. 'Come to reception and ask for me and I'll take you to see him.'

I had put the receiver down before I realized that I hadn't thanked her. Oh, well, there would be time for that, I supposed. Suddenly my weariness had dissolved and I felt reinvigorated at the news that my little Peter had been found.

I shaved in record time, nicking myself a couple of times in my haste, changed my shirt and was out on the street in less than ten minutes. I hailed a taxi: I wasn't going to walk this time. The occasion deserved such motorized luxury. As I sat back in the cab, I couldn't help smiling. It was a broad, unhindered smile, such a smile as I hadn't worn for many a long day.

It was probably my impatience, but the traffic seemed particularly heavy this morning. We moved forward sluggishly and then we had the misfortune to get stuck behind a lorry that had broken down. Gingerly, one by one the vehicles behind it had to mount the pavement and sidle by it. I was beginning to think it would have been quicker if I had walked after all, especially when we found ourselves in the herd of slow-moving vehicles trying to circle Trafalgar Square.

After what seemed an age, we eventually pulled up outside the portals of Charing Cross Hospital. I paid what I thought was an exorbitant fare and raced up the steps into the foyer. To my utter amazement the first person I saw was David Llewellyn. He was accompanied by Sergeant Sunderland and two uniformed officers. My surprise at seeing David was mirrored in his own features.

'Bloody hell!' he said. 'How did you find out or are you bloody clairvoyant?'

I hesitated. Surely this wasn't about Peter being found. That event would hardly require the presence of a detective inspector and a posse from Scotland Yard.

'Find out what?' I said with some apprehension.

David's face relaxed. 'Ah, so you don't know.'

'I don't know what?' I snapped, a sense of unease starting to grow within me.

David pulled me to one side. 'It's Harryboy Jenkins. He's done a runner.'

I closed my eyes in disbelief.

'And what's worse', David added, 'he's got your little lad, Peter, with him.'

Within minutes we had moved into the office of the hospital administrator, a small man with thinning grey hair and a goatee beard who stared at the world though wire-rimmed glasses. He sat glumly in a chair by the door and said nothing. Apart from myself, David and Sergeant Sunderland, we had been joined by a tearful Susan and the doctor and one of the nurses who had been ministering to Harryboy.

David was pacing up and down trying to contain his anger and frustration. 'How in heaven's name could this have happened? A bloody dangerous killer murders one of my constables and then walks out of here in broad daylight, taking another bloody patient with him. And no one notices. No one stops him. It beggars belief.'

No one offered up any kind of explanation. The administrator examined his fingernails.

'He is very cunning,' said the doctor. 'He had us all fooled as to the state of his health and strength. But it is clear that he is mentally deranged and you cannot expect him to act logically.'

'Great!' David slapped his forehead in exasperation.

'Look,' I said, 'the milk has been spilt. Let's concentrate on what we do now.'

David nodded. 'You're right. Where could this bastard have gone, taking the lad with him?'

Susan uttered a sob and the other nurse put her arm around her shoulder in comfort.

'If ... if it's any help ...' the doctor began hesitantly.

'Anything. Let me have it,' snapped David, his angry mood having been replaced by grim desperation.

'Well, when Jenkins first came in and was delirious he kept muttering in his sleep, "I must get back to the hideout". Something like that. He kept on repeating it.'

'Yes,' said the nurse. 'I heard him say that ... something about a hideout.'

'Wait a minute,' said David reaching into his inside pocket and bringing out several sheets of paper which had obviously been taken from a notebook. He scanned them for a few moments. 'Yes, yes!' he exclaimed at last. 'Here we are. These were some observations of Cartwright, one of the constables assigned to watch over Jenkins. He makes reference to his delirious mumblings. Listen to this: "Must get to the hideout. The hideout is where they won't get me".'

'Where the hell could that be?' asked Sergeant Sunderland.

David shrugged. 'God knows. It could be anywhere.'

'Maybe Rachel can help,' I said. 'She was his girlfriend for a time. She might know.'

'A girlfriend to that goon?' said David. 'OK, where can we find her?'

Benny looked totally bemused when David, Sergeant Sunderland and I walked into his café.

'A table for three maybe?' he said hopefully.

I shook my head, frowning. 'Where's Rachel?'

Benny returned my frown and threw in a reprimanding frosty look. I could tell that he thought I'd ratted on Rachel and got her into trouble.

'We just need to talk to her. We need her help.'

'She's in the kitchen,' he said reluctantly. 'What's this all about?'

'Inspector Llewellyn will explain, Benny,' I said, as I passed him and made my way to the kitchen. It had been agreed that I would talk to Rachel on her own. It was more likely she would be more relaxed with me without the intimidating presence of two burly Scotland Yarders standing over her.

Rachel was by the gas stove stirring a pan of what looked like soup when I entered. She turned and gave me a broad smile.

'Hello, Johnny. This is a nice surprise,' she said, moving the pan off the heat.

I went over and gave her a hug. She responded warmly but she could tell from my demeanour that something was wrong and her smile dimmed.

'What is it?'

As simply and economically as I could I told her what had happened at the hospital. At the news that Harryboy had escaped, her hand flew to her mouth in horror.

'He'll be looking for me,' she cried. 'He'll be coming to kill me.'

She began to shake with fear. I hugged her tighter. 'No, no, I don't think so. The doctor seems to think that he's not thinking straight any more. It's escape rather than revenge that's on his mind. While he was sleeping at the hospital he kept muttering something about getting to the hideout. He used that word "hideout" often. Does that mean anything to you? Did Harryboy ever mention anything like that to you?'

She thought for a moment. 'He never mentioned having a hideout in the city. I think we'd have gone there if ... wait a minute ...' Her eyes flashed brightly as a thought struck her. 'He did talk to me once about playing cowboys as a child. He boasted that he was always the chief baddie and had a great hideout. Yes ... those were his words, "a great hideout".'

Could it be that this is what Harryboy had meant? In his delirium, had he sort of regressed to a childhood state? Was this the ultimate escape for him. To return to the days of his youth and to the safest place he knew. His old hideout. Well, improbable as it might seem, it was the only straw in the wind we had managed to clutch.

'Where was this hideout? Did he say?'

Rachel shook her head. 'No. But I suppose it must have been somewhere near to where he lived when he was a boy.'

Within fifteen minutes David, Sergeant Sunderland and I were speeding in the police car to Pimlico. Also in the vehicle was Rachel. She had insisted in coming along as she wanted to help as much as she could. David had phoned the Yard for information regarding Harryboy Jenkins' old home address and had arranged for two armed policemen to come along to Benny's café just in case our friend turned up there. On our journey David filled us in on the Jenkins family background. There was no father, just the mother and Harryboy's elder brother who had lost his legs in a railway yard accident when he was a teenager. The family were poor but respectable. Harryboy was the demon cuckoo in the nest.

It was late afternoon when we drew up outside a shabby terraced house in Pimlico. A careworn woman dressed in a dull wraparound pinafore opened the door and peered at us with gentle curiosity. Her dry skin was stretched tightly over her high cheekbones, emphasizing her large watery blue eyes. Her fine wispy hair was tied up in a bun but several strands were loose hanging like errant spiders' webs about her face. I reckoned she would only be about fifty years of age but she looked much older. Worry, penury and hard work had taken their toll on this little woman. I felt very sorry for her. She seemed bemused to find us on her doorstep as though she never had any visitors, let alone four strangers.

David introduced himself and asked if we could come in. The woman nodded and without a word led us into the harshly lighted parlour. The curtains were already drawn in readiness for the night which still hadn't manifested itself fully. Sitting by the fire, in a wheelchair, was a youngish man, a discarded library book on his lap. I took him to be Harryboy's brother, Jack.

'What's all this, then?' he asked with the same kind of bemused gentleness.

'It's the police, Jack,' said the woman.

'Then it's Harryboy again. He's like a damned curse on this family.'

The woman perched on the edge of an armchair and began rubbing her hands together as though she was washing them with an invisible piece of soap.

'We need your help,' said David, simply.

Jack Jenkins shook his head. 'Look we haven't seen Harryboy in years. Nor do we want to see him. I told that to the police when they came round a few days ago after he'd absconded from the army. We know nothing about where he is or what he's done. He is no longer any part of this family.'

'I understand … and sympathize,' said David. 'But you see that's not the kind of help we need.' And then he explained. When he mentioned that Harryboy had kidnapped a young boy in his escape from the hospital, Mrs Jenkins gasped and cried out, 'Oh, my God. Whatever next?'

'So … can you help us? Have you any idea where this hideout might be?'

Jack Jenkins stared at the flames of the fire for some moments before answering. 'It's on the rec. That's a patch of waste ground not far from here. There's an old water pipe that sticks up above ground. Harryboy used to go down there and hide when we were playing cowboys. He loved it because very few lads would dare go down it as far as he did. He never saw the danger … he never does. He has no fear of consequences.'

'Can you show us where this place is?' I said.

Jack glanced at his mother but she averted her gaze.

'Yes,' he said. 'Mother, if you could fetch us a couple of torches, we'll need those.'

Mrs Jenkins rose without a word and went into the room beyond which I assumed was the kitchen.

'I'll take you there,' said Jack. 'It's not far, but we'll have to go on foot. I doubt if you could get all of us and my wheelchair into your police car, eh?'

Mrs Jenkins returned carrying two hefty torches. She passed one to David and one to me.

'Right,' said David. 'Let's make a move.'

THIRTY-FIVE

Peter was puzzled by the fact that while his skin seemed to be on fire, he was shivering so much he could not keep still. Shuddering and twitching in his fever, he wrapped his coat as tightly as he could around him while the man who had taken him from the hospital struggled to light a small fire in the depths of this dark cavern.

After the ride in the taxi when he had fallen asleep for a while, the two of them had made their way through a series of deserted streets to a large patch of waste ground, just stopping once on the way at a small shop for the man to buy some food – some tins of sardines – and other stuff like candles and matches.

Then they had scrambled down into the big cave which opened up out of the rough earth like a great gaping mouth.

'This is my hideout,' said the man, as pulled back the wire netting, ignoring the DANGER KEEP OUT sign. Holding Peter's hand in a tight grip, he dragged him down into the echoing darkness. 'We'll be safe here.'

'Where's Johnny?' asked Peter.

'Who?' Harryboy had no recollection of the name.

'Johnny. You said you'd come from Johnny.'

'Did I? Nah. There's just the two us now. But don't be scared. We'll be safe here.'

Peter fought against his emotions. He had been lied to. Lied to again! He wasn't going to see Johnny. He was going to see no one. So who was this man? Why had he taken him? What was he going to do to him? These thoughts troubled his mind as he was taken deeper and deeper into this echoing tunnel, with only a single candle to guide the way. Great shadows swam about the walls, shifting wildly as the candle flame danced erratically. The air was cool and smelt awful.

Peter felt as though he was living through some kind of nightmare. Maybe, he pondered, it was a nightmare. Perhaps he actually was asleep having a nasty dream. He would wake up anytime now and be safe and well. But this thought only stayed with him for a moment. As his body trembled with the fever, to his despair, he knew full well that he was awake and that things were going to get worse.

Deep, deep down in the cavern, they travelled, the candle providing only a feeble bubble of yellow light in the ebony nothingness. Eventually, Harryboy stopped. 'This is it,' he said with great satisfaction. 'This is as far as we need to go. No one will ever come this far. They get too frightened. But not me.' He laughed loudly, taking childish pleasure in hearing his voice echo away into the distance. 'This,' he announced to the darkness around him, 'is my hideout.'

He pushed the boy to the ground and lit another candle, placing both of them down on two of the many large stones which littered the floor of the cavern; and then he set about the task of scavenging for bits of wood and errant twigs. Soon he had enough to build his camp-fire as he had done in the days when he was king of the baddies, the days that he was reliving now. Within minutes the fire struggled into crackling life, the flickering flames gradually growing in intensity and along with two candles they illuminated the chamber like some surreal cathedral.

Harryboy grinned broadly. Now he was happy and he was safe. No one in the whole world could get him here. He squatted on his haunches and opened one of the tins of sardines he'd bought. He deserved some grub after all his efforts. He turned back the lid with the key and then dug his fingers into the tin, scooping up the cold greasy contents into his mouth.

He glanced over at the boy, slumped on the ground, huddled into his coat at the far end of the rim of illumination.

'Want some grub?' he called, but the boy did not respond. Harryboy shrugged. 'Please yourself,' he grunted, before bringing the tin to his lips and sucking out the remaining portions of sardines. He wiped his mouth on his sleeve as he had done when he was a kid, his eyes alive with pleasure.

Peter knew he had to escape. He just had to get away. The man was mad. He was like a frenzied crazy character from one of his comics;

like someone who had drunk a strange potion created by an evil scientist which had turned him into a kind of zombie. Who knows what he might do next? Perhaps he was a cannibal and intended to eat him. Peter's mouth went dry at the thought.

If he could creep back the way they had come, creep off into the darkness, he might be able to get away. Once he got beyond the circle of light provided by the fire and the candles, the man would not be able to see him. This thought gave him hope and he held it firmly in the forefront of his mind.

With patience he watched the man who, after finishing the sardines, threw the tin into the distance and then sat close to the fire staring at the flames. He looked as though he was hypnotized by the darting fingers of yellow light as they rose and fell, struggling to survive. Slowly, gently and silently Peter uncurled himself and gradually raised himself off the ground into a crouching position. Then he froze waiting to see if his actions had been observed by the man. Apparently they had not. He had remained gazing at the fire, as still as a statue, lost in his mad zombie thoughts.

Peter began to move. He knew that he had to get past the man before he could start to make his way towards the entrance of the tunnel. Holding his breath, he edged his way into the shadows behind his captor and began to circle the fire and the crazy man. His progress was slow because every few feet he stopped and waited to see if his actions had been noticed. Remarkably they had not; the man remained still and pensive, gazing into the flames.

In about five minutes Peter had reached the far side of the fire and was on the edge of the expanse of blackness which would eventually lead him to the entrance of the tunnel. He reckoned that if he kept to the side of the tunnel he could feel his way out of it. With a little smile, he rose to his feet in readiness to set forth into the inky dark.

Just as he did so an arm clamped around his neck and he felt a sharp object prod into his cheek. He tried to scream but there was no air in his compressed windpipe. With a sudden violent movement he was dragged backwards into the circle of light by the crazy man, his heels scraping and bumping along the uneven ground.

'Where do you think you're going, eh? Trying to leave me?' he growled, with suppressed ferocity into Peter's ear, his arm still tight around him. Peter could smell the strong stale, salty fish vapours on the man's breath. He opened his mouth to reply but no sound came out. This seemed to amuse the man and he giggled like a little girl.

Peter, his eyes wide with terror, glanced downwards and could see the shiny blade of a knife against his left cheek. Already bright red blood was seeping from the wound it had made. Peter wet himself with fear. The waking nightmare had grown more terrifying. There was no doubt about it now. This man intended to kill him.

THIRTY-SIX

A vibrant moon had made an early appearance in the still darkening sky, illuminating the stretch of waste ground where Jack Jenkins had led us. This strange half-light gave the area a surreal appearance like the landscape of the planet Mongo from those Flash Gordon serials.

With great agility, Jack manoeuvred his wheelchair down from the pavement, across the stretch of rough open ground, through the rubble towards the large concrete pipe which reared up out of the ground like a giant mouth ready to swallow the unwary. A feeble trickle of water emanated from the aperture which was covered by decrepit wire netting, an ineffective barrier to prevent anyone trespassing. The rest of us followed Jack towards the entrance like rats after the Pied Piper.

'It's a disused drainage pipe. God knows how far it goes down,' he said, pointing at the cavern. 'The council have been meaning to block it up for years. Now I think they're hoping the Luftwaffe will do their job for them. This was always where Harryboy went when he was playing cowboys ... or when he was in trouble. He was the only one who dared go beyond a hundred yards of the entrance.' He rolled his wheelchair forward a little and pointed down into the impenetrable darkness. 'That's his hideout.'

David and I exchanged worried glances. 'What do we do now?' he said, verbalizing both our thoughts.

'Go in after him, I guess.' I said at length. 'But not all of us. We'd make too much noise. And the last thing we want to do is panic him. Let me go. If he's got Peter in there, I want to get to him first.'

'Is that wise, sir? There's safety in numbers,' said Sergeant Sunderland.

David pulled a face and chewed on his lip for a moment. 'Actually, I think my one-eyed friend is right for once. If we all stumble down there we could make matters worse than they are. He's not exactly a rational fellow. Yes, I think that for our first shot, it should be just one of us goes in.' He turned to me. 'Are you sure you want it to be you?'

I nodded. 'Very sure.'

'OK, boyo. Give it a go … but you'd better take this with you.' He pulled a revolver out of his raincoat pocket and held it out to me.

I hesitated a moment and then common sense overrode my dislike of guns and I took it from him with a nod of thanks and slipped it into my own pocket.

'We'll give you fifteen minutes. If we've not heard anything by then, Sunderland and I will come in after you,' said David.

I was just about to pull back the rusted wire netting when Rachel rushed forward and gave me a tight hug. 'Take care,' she said softly and I felt the caress of her warm lips on my cheek.

'You bet,' I said, returning the kiss. And then I slipped behind the rusty wire netting and ventured into the mouth of the tunnel.

For a moment I was halted by the powerful smell of decay and drains which assailed my nostrils and challenged my stomach. I grimaced but pressed on. I was surprised how quickly I became used to the stench. It seemed a natural element of this strange underground world.

For a while the tunnel descended gently and then levelled out. Within a couple of minutes I had lost sight of the entrance and now I was using my torch, pointing downwards at my feet, to guide me forward, slowly but not always surely. The thought struck me of how ridiculous and melodramatic the situation was: here was I edging my way forward down a disused drainage pipe in Stygian darkness in the search for a crazed murderer and a little boy. There was no certainty whatsoever that Harryboy Jenkins was actually anywhere near this Godforsaken place. For all I knew this could be the wildest and darkest of all wild goose chases. Well, I told myself, I was here now so I had to go through with it.

After a while I stopped and strained my ears to catch any noise that might indicate another presence – a human presence – in the tunnel. I was certainly conscious that there were other non-human presences about. I had seen several of them in the beam of the torch scurry by: mice, rats and various unpleasant insects. But as I listened, apart from the gentle moaning of the wind as it passed along the tunnel, I could hear nothing of significance.

I pushed on further into the void. And then I heard it. A cry. An inarticulate, high-pitched cry. It wafted on the invisible air around me like the wail of a long dead spirit. But I recognized it as the cry of a living child.

Peter.

My God, we had been right. Harryboy was here – down here in this man-made Hades and he did have Peter with him. I hurried on, stumbling frequently in my haste, but I didn't care. I just had to reach the boy before it was too late. I prayed I would not face the bleakest of ironies that, after all our efforts, I would get there just in time to see Peter die.

The passage seemed to curve slightly and as it did so I saw a pin prick of light ahead. I was almost running now, the beam of my torch swinging violently on the ground. Then the cries ceased suddenly and once again the air was filled with that eerie almost-silence, just strange indistinct rustles and the hum of the wind. Then I saw them: two figures in the distance, illuminated by a small fire. It was like a nightmare scene from some Brueghel canvas. As I moved closer, I could see that Harryboy had one arm around Peter's neck and in the other hand he held a knife close to his face. The bastard seemed to be cutting the boy's cheek which was stained with blood. I could not tell whether Peter was still conscious or not: his body was limp and his eyes were closed. My heart thudded in my breast. Don't tell me he's dead!

My gut instinct was to cry out in rage and race forward, leap upon Harryboy and let him have it, a round of bullets in the heart. Thank heavens that for once I ignored my gut instinct. This reaction would have been disastrous. If Peter were still alive, my sudden appearance racing towards him out of the gloom would simply prompt Harryboy to stick the knife in.

I switched my torch off and, as I approached the feeble circle of light, I crouched low to the ground. However it was clear that Harryboy had sensed that there was someone out there in the tunnel. Maybe he had heard me running or glimpsed the beam of my torch. Whatever the reason, he knew. Dragging Peter's inert body with him, he took a step forward past the fire.

'Who's there?' he shouted, the cry reverberating down the labyrinth. 'I know you're there. I heard you. Come for Harryboy, have you?'

Now if this were a Hollywood gangster movie and I was Edward G. or James Cagney, I'd holler, 'Give yourself up Harryboy. The game is over. We got the place surrounded.' But it wasn't in a movie. This was for real and real lives were at stake. One in particular. And I reckoned I would spook the bastard more if I didn't respond at all to his cry. He couldn't be absolutely sure that there was anyone there out in the pitch black. That uncertainty would grow if I made no answer. That would unnerve him. And the more he peered into the dark and strained his ears to catch any sound to confirm his suspicions, the more likely it would be that he would leave Peter alone. At the moment he had the boy clasped in front of him like a shield. Peter's head had drooped down and I could no longer see his face. I still had no idea whether he was dead or alive.

I quelled all the strong mixed emotions that boiled up within me at the thought that Harryboy might have killed the boy and concentrated my efforts and thoughts on the task in hand: nailing the swine. I wasn't near enough to shoot him with any certainty yet. I dare not risk firing in case I hit Peter.

I shifted, slowly and softly to the left until I felt the wall of the tunnel. I picked up a small stone and threw it at the far wall. As I'd hoped, the noise caught Harryboy's attention. My plan was to draw him nearer to that side of the cavern while I circled behind him and grabbed him from the back. He took a few steps forward, moving towards the sound of the stone, dragging his limp charge with him. He thrust his head forward as he peered into the inky void.

My plan seemed to be working at first, but then suddenly the situation changed.

'Come out!' Harryboy cried. 'Come out where I can see you. Or else I'll have to cut the boy some more.'

At these words my blood ran cold. In my cleverness, I had actually increased the danger that Peter was in.

'I'll count to five,' he called again, addressing the dark. 'If I don't see you by then, the knife goes in again.' With glee he brandished the knife, its bloodstained blade caught by the flames of the fire.

What the hell could I do? The options were rather restricted, to say the least. If I wanted to prevent Peter from being wounded again, there were no options at all. Slipping the gun in my overcoat pocket, I called out. 'OK, I'm coming. Just don't hurt the boy.'

Slowly I moved into the circle of light created by the camp-fire.

Harryboy, who had been gazing in the wrong direction, expecting to see someone emerge from the right side of the cavern where I had thrown the stone, turned sharply as he heard my voice. Then he saw me.

'You,' he snarled in anger. 'You again. I should have killed you when I had a chance.'

'Let the boy go,' I said quietly. 'You can deal with me. You and your knife. Just let the boy go.'

His eyes flickered wildly and his features formed themselves into a chilling leer. 'Don't think I will. He obviously means a lot to you. That's good, that is. You see I can amuse myself by causing him some pain and at the same time hurt you. Double the fun, eh? I can deal with you later when the boy is dead.'

I took another step forward.

'Stay right there. Do not move again ... or else the boy dies straight away.'

I froze. It seemed that Harryboy held all the prime cards in the game at the moment. If Peter had not been there I would have launched myself on him with my bare hands, risking the peril of his knife. But as it was I couldn't do anything like that without endangering the boy.

He hauled Peter's inert figure up higher until his little face was on a level with Harryboy's shoulders and then he took the knife to his face. 'Another cut,' he grinned, 'just to make sure you know I mean business.'

He drew the blade of the knife across Peter's cheek producing another thin red line along the pale flesh. Suddenly Peter's body jerked violently and his eyes shot open. The pain had propelled him from his comatose state into full consciousness and he yelled out in agony. My heart leapt as I saw that Peter was still alive but I also felt sick to the stomach to see such torture. And I was helpless. I knew full well if I so much as made one move towards Harryboy, he would stick the knife right in and I'd lose Peter altogether. However self-controlled I was because of this terrible knowledge, I couldn't stop myself calling out the boy's name.

'Peter,' I cried, my voice almost breaking as I did so.

His eyes widened in surprise at the sound of his name echoing around him in the shadowy chamber. He turned his head in my direction and saw me for the first time. All at once his eyes widened and his sad, frightened face became animated with excitement.

'Johnny,' he bellowed in recognition. Without a thought of the knife which hovered inches away from his face, his little body wriggled, twisted and gyrated, like someone experiencing the fiercest of fits, desperate to be free of its restraints. It was as though his body had received a massive electrical charge: his small form was convulsed with energy and it was all focused on reaching me. In one frantic movement, he seemed to physically shrink his body while thrusting forward, propelling himself out of Harryboy's clutches. He fell to the floor and began squirming along the ground like a furious snake towards me. His violent actions had shaken Harryboy's stability. He tottered clumsily like a drunken man and for a moment it looked as though he was about to fall over but instead he stepped sideways in an attempt to steady himself. In doing so, his foot landed in the fire. It was his turn to cry out in alarm. I intended to add to his distress. I had already snatched the gun from out of my pocket and stepped forward. Now that he had no shield to protect him, he was mine.

THIRTY-SEVEN

Sitting at a desk, smoking a cigar in a large well-furnished office in an anonymous building in Whitehall, his face in shadow, the important man addressed the other occupant of the room who was sitting opposite him.

'You've made a bloody mess of things, haven't you?' he said, leaning back in the padded leather chair. The important man was at home here and in total control of the situation, relaxed and confident. He was not only in possession of all the facts concerning this unsavoury little affair, but, more importantly, he was cognisant of the bigger picture also. And in the end, that is what mattered. There were going to be rough patches along the road to victory. Innocent people would be hurt, killed even, but the government, the country must trundle on, overcoming any such unpleasantness along the way. His tone was easy, matter of fact. He could have been passing comment on the weather. He saw no need to express his dismay and anger in words. That was a futile exercise.

'I suppose I have,' said Sir Robert Gervais.

'You and your bloody lap dog, France,' said the important man, puffing heartily on his cigar. 'Well, he's paid the price for his overzealous diligence. But it leaves rather a nasty mess on the carpet for us to clean up.'

'I never thought it would get out of hand the way it did.'

'You turned a blind eye, my dear sir, when you should have been censorious.'

'I am sorry.'

'Let us hope so. The whole business has been most unsavoury. You have caused problems where none should have existed. To be frank, we've put up with your little peccadilloes for long enough because of

215

your importance to us – to the war effort. It is now time for restraint.'

'I understand.'

The man exhaled a gentle cloud of pungent smoke. 'I wonder if you do.'

'What is going to happen?' asked Sir Robert after an uneasy pause.

'We're going to take you away for a while. There's a safe house in Scotland ... you can carry on your work there for a few months while the air clears down here. You've left some bloody big cracks for us to smooth over.'

'Scotland.'

'You leave tonight. And, sir, no more dresses for the time being. Is that understood?'

'I understand.'

'Good. I think that's all,' said the important man, a tight smile easing his features. 'Leave the rest to me.'

THIRTY-EIGHT

I really didn't intend to kill Harryboy Jenkins. I am not a murderer. Despite my hatred and contempt for this despicable lump of inhumanity, I did not regard myself as his great judge and executioner. My hands are soiled enough without taking on that role also. I just meant to wound him, to incapacitate him sufficiently so that I could take him prisoner. But as I raised the gun, he leapt forward with a manic roar and before I had time to aim carefully, he was almost upon me and so I fired. I fired twice. For a split second, the great ox was stopped in his tracks by the gunshots and then as two great badges of blood flourished on his chest, his whole body shuddered and flew backwards with the force of the bullets. He fell dead on the ground, his face frozen in a terrible grimace.

Slowly Peter clambered to his feet, and like me stared down at the monster, not quite believing it was all over. We stood for what must have been a minute like this before he turned and looked up at me, a smile quivering on his lips. 'I told you I could help you catch criminals,' he said.

I grinned back at him, but as I moved forward to give him a hug, he fell into my arms in a dead faint. I felt his brow: it was on fire. The fever had taken over again. Scooping him up in my arms and with the aid of the torch, I hurriedly began the trek back to the opening of the cavern. I had to get this boy to hospital pronto.

Behind me lay the twisted body of Harryboy Jenkins, the dying flames of the little fire still illuminating his twisted features.

Later that night, I shared a pint of beer in the Guardsman with David. It certainly had been a fun-packed evening for me. Once emerging from the tunnel and hurriedly recounting my adventures, we set about getting Peter to the hospital. Sergeant Sunderland raced back to the police car and radioed for an ambulance and for more men to help recover Harryboy's body.

While we waited for the ambulance, I observed Jack Jenkins as he sat in his wheelchair peering into the dark of the cavern, his face immobile, his expression enigmatic. I could only wonder what tangled thoughts were going through his mind. No matter how evil Harryboy was, he was still his brother and now he was dead. Could he accept that situation with equanimity, or would that filial cord be wrenching his heart out? No doubt he was also aware that he would have the burden of telling his mother that her youngest son, her demon son, had been killed. Whatever his feelings, he kept them securely to himself.

Accompanied by Rachel, I travelled in the ambulance to the hospital with Peter, while David and his sergeant organized the retrieval of Harryboy Jenkins's body.

That hospital part of the evening is like just a vague dream in my memory now. Peter was returned to his old ward. I remember I was told by the doctor who examined him that the next twenty-four hours would be critical, but he was hopeful. I had to resign myself to that and left the medics to their ministrations. I managed to find Susan McAndrew, who was on duty on another ward, and gave her a brief résumé of events. She reacted to the account as though it was a horror story, which I suppose it was.

I felt weary and empty as Rachel and I stepped out of Charing Cross Hospital into the bitter cold night air.

'You look done in, Johnny,' she said softly. 'I think you should go home and get some rest. Come back to the hospital tomorrow.'

I nodded. 'I'll see you home first,' I said.

'Nonsense. I don't need you to do that. I'm not frightened now. There's no Harryboy Jenkins waiting in the shadows for me any more. I'll be fine.'

'If you're sure,' I said, not really having the energy to argue.

'I'm sure. You get a good night's rest.'

I hugged her tightly and we kissed.

On arriving back at Hawke Towers I realized that a good night's rest was an unlikely prospect. My body was tired but my mind was awhirl with images and thoughts. I was sure that even if did I lay my head on my pillow old Morpheus would refuse to wrap his arms around me. So, on the off chance, I rang David's office at Scotland Yard. He was still there.

'Fancy a last pint at the Guardsman?' I said.

'Do I,' he said.

'How is the boy?' David asked after he'd downed a good quarter of his pint in one gulp.

I shrugged. 'He looked pretty poorly, but the doctor was hopeful. It's a waiting game.'

'Ah, these young 'uns. They have great resilience, y'know. I'm sure things will be OK.'

I nodded wearily.

'And you can congratulate yourself that you've saved the taxpayer a spot of money and the hangman an unpleasant task by getting rid of Mr Harryboy Jenkins for us.'

I winced. 'I didn't really mean to kill him—'

'Don't you worry about it, boyo. You did us all a favour. You have nothing to reproach yourself about. He was the lowest of the low. He killed two of our fellows and a man of the cloth. That's what we know for sure and there will probably be more. I reckon you deserve a medal. That's two killers you've brought to justice in one week.'

'My God, yes,' I said. 'I'd forgotten about the White Rabbit for a moment.'

'White Rabbit?'

'Oh, my little nickname for Bernard France. How are things progressing with your enquiries in that matter?'

Suddenly David's face darkened and his whole demeanour changed. 'I'm glad you asked me about that.' He gave a little embarrassed cough. 'We're closing the case.'

'What!' I almost spilt my beer in surprise.

'Well, we have the actual murderer – he's lying in the police morgue as I speak – so that's the end of the matter.'

'But he wasn't acting completely alone. We know the other fellow was aware of France's actions – if he didn't sanction them, he obviously approved of them.'

'By the other fellow you mean Sir Robert Gervais.'

'Of course I do.'

'We'd never get enough evidence to implicate him – so, as I've said, we're closing the case.'

This was errant nonsense. I knew it and David knew it. I was about to protest but he held up his hand to silence me. 'We are closing the case,' he repeated softly but emphatically, adding, 'on orders from above.'

'Orders? What orders?'

'I was called upstairs today. To the commissioner's office. I was instructed to close the file on the investigation.'

'But why?'

'Because our friend Sir Robert is involved in vital work for the War Office. I was told he may have behaved foolishly, recklessly even, but he was not directly involved in the killings, and so we must … leave him alone.'

'But he held me up at gun point!'

'You are still here to tell the tale, so no harm done, eh?'

'This isn't you talking, David.'

'Oh, yes it is. It's me talking … under orders. It doesn't mean I believe or accept what I'm saying, but I'm saying it because I've been instructed to do so. I'm no happier than you are about the situation but I have been told that it is the best for the country and for both of us.'

'Both of us.'

'Oh, yes. Don't have any ideas of following this up on your own. You must drop it too. Those are my instructions to you.'

I shook my head in disbelief. 'Or else?'

'Bull's eye.'

I could not believe what I was hearing. 'So he's going to get away with it. He's an accessory to murder at least. Because of him two people have been killed.'

'We have no proof. And if you found it, someone would make sure you'd lose it again. The matter is out of our hands now. Just forget all about the case.'

'Because the case is closed,' I snapped sarcastically.

David gave me a non-committal glance before draining his pint. 'I think we have time for another. I reckon we both need one.'

While David made his way to the bar, I gazed around the smoke-filled room at the faces of the late night boozers, mainly men now, with their slack smiles and expressions eased with drink. Looking at them, one would hardly think there was a war on or, in fact, any evil in the world. They seemed to wear life so lightly. I envied them, but

I knew that tonight for once alcohol was not going to make me feel any better. My body ached, my brain ached and I just wanted my bed. I went to the bar where David was still waiting to be served and tapped him on the shoulder.

'I think I'll skip on this pint,' I said, unable to keep the weariness out of my voice. 'I'm heading home for some kip.'

My friend turned and gave me an understanding smile and a sympathetic nod. 'OK, boyo. Sleep tight. Don't let the bed bugs bite.'

I gave him a friendly pat on the shoulder and made my way out into the cold evening air.

The telephone woke me early the next morning. It was Susan. She told me that Peter's condition had improved slightly overnight. This cheered me a little and I told her that I'd visit the hospital that morning.

An hour later I was in Benny's café passing on the good news to him and Rachel.

'That boy has got guts,' said Benny. 'I knew he'd pull through.'

'He's not out of the woods yet,' I observed with caution.

'It's only a matter of time. Mark my words, Benny knows. Now take a seat, I reckon the hero deserves a free breakfast this morning.'

'Free breakfast. Now I'm beginning to worry about your health too.'

Benny rolled his eyes and then pointed to an empty table. 'Sit!' he ordered.

Strangely, I hadn't really felt hungry that morning, but when the food arrived with its seductive aroma, I tucked in with gusto. By the time I'd finished and lit up a cigarette, I had a warm glow in my stomach and I was beginning to feel like my old self again. I sat back and idly watched the smoke spiral to the ceiling and tried not to think about the case that was closed. And then I found Rachel pulling up a chair and sitting by me.

'How are you today?' she said with a smile, squeezing my hand.

'I'm fine,' I replied, utilizing one of my pack of white lies.

Her expression darkened. 'I have some news, Johnny.'

With a strange kind of intuition, I knew immediately what her news was going to be. 'You're going back home,' I said.

She nodded. 'Yes. I know it sounds a little crazy, but suddenly I've realized London isn't really what I wanted after all. The glamour and gloss are paper thin, aren't they? Besides, it's not the place, or the people is it? It's yourself that makes life worth living. I think I was trying to escape from myself – but that's impossible. Anyway, I've learned my lesson. Strangely it was Harryboy who taught me that lesson. I intend to go back and live a better life down there, down where I belong.' Her eyes shone brightly and her pretty face was more animated than I had ever seen before.

'I'm pleased for you. I reckon you're doing the right thing.'

'Thanks, Johnny. I will miss you. I think I was falling a little bit in love with you, you know …'

I did know. The feeling was mutual. 'That would never do. My life is complicated enough.'

Her smile faded and she looked at me seriously for a moment before leaning over and kissing me hard on the lips. Then without a word she left me and returned to the kitchen. I glanced over at Benny standing at the counter. He twisted his fist into a thumbs up sign. That, I mused, makes two disappointed men.

When I went in to see Peter he was propped up in bed half asleep, but, as I neared the bed his eyes flickered open lazily and he saw me.

'Johnny,' he croaked, his dry flaky lips stretching into a smile.

'Hello there, soldier. In the wars again, eh?'

He nodded. 'But we caught that bad man, didn't we? I was like your detective assistant, wasn't I?'

'I suppose so.'

The smile broadened. 'We'll make a good team when I get better … When I get … You wait and …' His eyes closed again and he slipped back into sleep, but the smile remained on his face.

When I left the room, I found Susan McAndrew waiting for me.

'You still here?' I said.

'I slept in one of the nurse's rooms last night.'

'How is he?'

'The doctor said he thought he was over the worst, but it'll take a while before he's strong enough to leave'.

'Poor devil. He's been through a lot.'

'What are we going to do with him, Johnny? We can't send him back to Devon. You can't have him and neither can I.'

I knew she was right. We both had jobs which were unpredictable and involved working all kinds of strange hours. And mine involved crazed murderers breaking into my office and threatening me at gun point. This was not the ideal domestic situation in which to bring up a ten-year-old boy. However, I was also determined not to let the little blighter too far out of my sight this time. Knowing Peter, if I did, he'd only run away again.

'We've got to keep him in London,' I said.

'Where? You're not suggesting an orphanage?'

'I am not. That's the last place ... It's just that I know two spinster sisters who are about to lose a lodger and they may very well take kindly to looking after a well-behaved little boy. And I'm sure we'd have visiting rights.'

Susan beamed and her tired face lit up. 'Tell me more.'

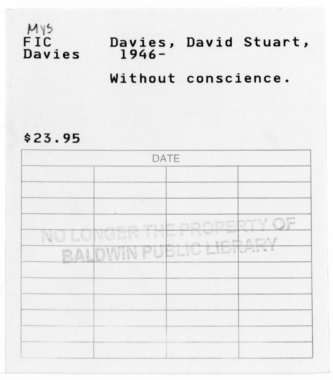